The Flat on Malabar Hill

The Flat on
Malabar Hill

Chitra Kallay

iUniverse, Inc.
New York   Bloomington

The Flat on Malabar Hill

iUniverse books may be ordered through booksellers or by contacting:

iUniverse
1663 Liberty Drive
Bloomington, IN 47403
www.iuniverse.com
1-800-Authors (1-800-288-4677)

ISBN: 978-1-4401-4642-8 (sc)
ISBN: 978-1-4401-4641-1 (ebk)

Printed in the United States of America

iUniverse rev. date: 07/17/2009

Acknowledgements

The seed of this book was a tiny filler-story in a Mumbai newspaper. I used some basic facts from the article and built a fictitious family around them. I have a number of people to thank for helping bring my dream of writing to fruition.

My children Maya and Tom had unwavering faith that I could write a novel. They encouraged me, read the several drafts and helped keep me on the right track when I wrote of medical or health matters. Thank you both for your love and trust.

When I lived in India, my cousin Vijaya Gupchup and I always spent holidays together: either she came to Bangalore or I went to Bombay/Mumbai. She too read my book in its early form and advised me. She and her husband Vijay Gupchup are always warm in welcoming me to their flat on Malabar Hill. Thanks to them, I love Mumbai and could make it the background of my book.

My friend and colleague Dr. Alan Buster read through the book in all its different stages. He was generous not only with his time but also with his gently-voiced, excellent suggestions. I owe Alan a debt of gratitude.

My friend and travel companion Hope Boyd was also one of the first to see the early shape of the book. As she is such a superb teacher of English, I knew I could trust her critiques. Thank you—Aren't you glad we traveled to Mumbai together?

My very creative, talented friend Matt Arnold offered to design the cover for my book. Needless to say, I jumped at the chance. I love his cover and owe him a sea of gratitude for his work and generosity.

Jim and Pat Whiting helped me with the technical aspects of formatting: thank you! I certainly couldn't have done it without you.

Srila Singh read the manuscript and continually urged me to push it to publication. If it hadn't been for Srila, *The Flat on Malabar Hill* would still be just another file on my computer. Thank you!

My parents Dr Anant Rao and Yamuna Rao nurtured me and permitted me to adventure into a foreign country. Alone. For their faith and trust and for their ability to let me fly free, I owe infinite gratitude. They are my Shanti and Vinod. They did not live to see this book, and it is to their memory I dedicate *The Flat on Malabar Hill.*

My sister Kusum Loganadan and her husband Sukumar Loganadan resemble the fictitious Kishore and Anjali in only one way. They moved in with my mother after my father's death and cared for her with devotion and love for forty years, especially through her many years of debilitating Alzheimer's. To their memory as well, I dedicate this book with love and admiration.

Shanti

I T HAD RAINED ALL NIGHT, big bulbous drops which merged into punishing sheets. By morning the rain had diminished, but the streets were flowing rivers. Looking through the car window, Shanti saw men and women struggling, sloshing to work, with their pants and saris hiked up over their knees. Some of the younger men had tied knots at the four corners of their kerchiefs and placed them on their heads in a futile defiance against the tempest. Their efforts only brought the water dripping along their necks in a steady stream. The traffic lights had quit, and the cacophonous horns and bicycle bells made driving in Mumbai a worse than usual nightmare.

This chaos did not deter Shanti from driving the waterlogged miles from Malabar Hill to the suburb of Colaba. She was on her way to see her first grandson; a mere monsoon could not stop her. Of course, Anjali's mother had stayed with them for the first month after the baby was born—that was custom—and had left yesterday to return to New Delhi. During that month, Shanti had not interfered. Now she was eager to help with the baby's oil bath and to let her daughter-in-law Anjali get some rest. They finally reached the building, and Shanti stepped out of the car, right into a puddle. She looked down at her sodden slippers—the border of her sari, too, was soaked at the bottom. None of it mattered. She smiled as she rang the doorbell.

1

A wide-eyed Anjali opened the door. Dressed in black tights and a loose Boston College T-shirt, she was wiping her sweating face on her sleeve.

"Amma? I wasn't expecting you. Why didn't you phone? Come in, come in. Baby's sleeping and two of my friends are here; we're doing aerobics. I must lose some of this weight. Shall I have Shiva make you some tea, some snacks?"

"No, no, don't bother. You go back to your friends, and I'll sit in the baby's room with that sweet boy. If he wakes up, I'll take care of him. You finish your exercise."

"Are you sure? I'm sorry—I wish you had phoned. Anu, Reeta—I'll be right there. Amma, are you sure you'll be all right?" Anjali had already joined her friends, and Shanti heard the rhythmic music, the voices counting in unison one-two-three-four.

She gazed with soft eyes at her grandson. Just like Kishore. So much black hair and a rose petal of a mouth. Kishore and Anjali had combined their names and the baby was Kisan. She sat in the rocking chair with a hand on the cradle remembering how helpless she had felt as a mother at twenty.

Thank goodness she had gone, as tradition dictated, to her mother's. Her Amma had taught her how to feed the baby, rock the little one to sleep—everything; when she had returned to Mumbai, (it had been called Bombay then) her mother-in-law had been her guide. Now, Shanti relished the idea of helping Anjali with Kisan and his oil bath. She was sure Anjali had not dared to try it on her own—nor had her mother guided her.

Frankly, that woman had seemed rather helpless and ignorant, though Shanti would never say so.

Oh, it would be so sweet to hold the naked little boy and massage him from head to toe with coconut oil! To then hold his glistening slippery body and pour warm water over him, wrap him in a big towel. He would be so ready for his feed and a nice sleep. Kishore had crowed with pleasure during his oil baths when he was about four months. While she was gently rocking the cradle, a woman entered smiling, hands together in a respectful "*namaste.*" She spoke in English, "I am the baby's ayah, Ma. Anjalima calls me nanny." Shanti smiled at her, silently appraising this woman who would be entrusted with her grandson. She saw a slender woman in her late thirties or forties, probably experienced. She wore several colored glass bangles and a gold cross on a thin gold chain around her neck.

"*Achcha.* You've looked after little babies? Know how to feed them, give them baths, everything?" Shanti inquired.

"Yes, Amma. After my husband died, I have done this kind of work only. I am ayah to many babies in Colaba."

"Will you stay day and night with Kisan-*baba* or only day time?"

"Daytime, nighttime, all the time, Amma. I will look after Kisan Raja very well."

Shanti smiled at the "Kisan Raja" and looked at the nanny more indulgently.

"Do you have any children, huh?"

"I have two girls, Amma. They are staying with my sister and going to convent school. On Sundays, Anjalima will let me go to Church, and I will see my Grace and Miriam. Both are studying to become nuns, Ma," she said with pride shining in her eyes.

The music stopped, and Shanti heard goodbyes being said. Soon Anjali entered, speaking over her shoulder to the maid Radha, asking her to get a bath ready.

"I wish I had known you were coming, Amma. Kishore asked me to meet him for lunch at the club today—it's the first time I'll be going out since Kisan was born. If you like, I can send Shiva to the market to buy some vegetables and prepare lunch for you here," Anjali said.

Shanti swallowed. Was Anjali going out even now, now that Shanti was here? Maybe she didn't understand that her mother-in-law had not dropped in just casually but with a purpose. But she smiled and said, "No, no. I don't need Shiva to make anything special for me. I came today because I wanted to only help you with Kisan's oil bath. I'm sure you are nervous about trying it by yourself, *nai*? How Kishore and Dev loved their oil baths!"

Anjali was biting her lower lip. In the bathroom, Radha was adjusting the water temperature in the filling buckets, readying them for the bath. Shanti turned to her sleeping grandson. Slowly her smile faded even as Anjali started talking.

"Oil bath? What is that? It sounds lovely. Maybe when you come next time, you can teach me about it. Now I must get ready. I don't want to be late for lunch. You must come again soon, Amma, but phone first, okay?"

"Oh, I see you're busy. What about the baby when you've gone to the club? Who will look after him? What about his feed? I can stay with him."

"No, no, no need, the new nanny is well trained. I see you met her. She came to us highly recommended. She'll give Kisan a bottle at two o'clock. I'm sure I'll be back for his evening feed. You must come another day to teach me this oil bath. Radha, is the water ready? I'm sorry, Amma; I have to go." And before Shanti could protest, Anjali headed to the bathroom. Embarrassed and ashamed, Shanti drove back through the rain to Malabar Hill.

By the time she reached her flat in Kalpana Apartments, humiliation rose bitter in her throat. She had driven so far in the pelting rain to spend *half an hour* with her grandson. She hadn't even held him nor talked about him to Anjali. In her relationship with her own mother-in-law, Shanti had always been deferential. Never, never would she have gone out when her mother-in-law came to visit. She would have sacrificed any pleasure or program to show her deep respect. After all, parents and elders were there to help and guide.

After she and Vinod were married, they had lived for twelve years with his parents. Her in-laws were an integral part of their every day lives. But of course that was more than twenty-five years ago. Had times changed so much? She would have to ask her friends if their daughters-in-law treated them so perfunctorily, so dismissively.

But Kishore and Anjali were different…maybe because Anjali had spent so many years in America. When Kishore finished his college at St. Xavier's, he had won a fellowship to MIT to work on a Ph.D. in computer engineering. Imagine their joy when he wrote and told them that he had fallen in love with a girl attending Boston College. Thank God she was Indian, Shanti had thought, and from a wealthy family. He had brought Anjali to Mumbai for a lavish wedding and reception for 600 at the Taj Mahal Hotel where the waves of the Arabian Sea almost lapped the front entry. The young couple had flown back to America after a short honeymoon in Goa down the coast—Kishore had three more years to finish at MIT. Shanti's happiness was complete when, after his graduate work, Kishore accepted a job with Sun Micro Systems in Mumbai and returned with a pregnant Anjali.

Now Kisan was a month old, and today Shanti had eagerly anticipated being the guiding hand. Instead, she felt unwelcome in her own son's house. Why didn't she phone indeed! Whoever heard of relations—a mother-in-law—phoning to drop in on their children? Eyes stinging with tears, she went into her bedroom to change her sari, which was dripping as she had struggled through more deep puddles coming into the flat. Thank goodness the rain seemed to be letting up. Vinod should have an easier time driving home from work. Although he had retired last year, he continued as a consultant at Novartis. It seemed that his hours had not shrunk at all.

Shanti emerged from her bedroom in a freshly ironed pink cotton sari, her short black hair still damp, curling around her face. The silence in the house mocked the despair in her heart. She didn't need to talk to anyone. She had already given the cook his instructions on what to prepare for lunch and dinner. The maid Malika had been with them so long, she needed no instructions. They were in the servants' quarters, busy with the cooking, ironing, and whatever. Only her little Lhasa Apso Bhim followed Shanti from room to room, wagging his tail. Bhim had been an impulsive buy when Dev, her second son, was about fifteen and she could not stand the loneliness of the flat. Both the boys were busy with their school work, their music, and their friends. Kishore and Dev had loved the idea of calling the little dog after the warrior Bhima from the *Mahabharata* and had derived endless pleasure playing with him, yelling, "Bhim, Bam, Boom!" She absent-mindedly stroked his silky fur while he rolled over for a tummy scratch. Thank goodness he was always here.

She almost called out to Malika, just to chat about how sweet Kisan looked. But the sting of having to leave her grandson so soon still hurt. This is why she had let herself into the flat with her key instead of ringing the doorbell for the maid. She didn't want to face anybody yet.

She sought solace in her sanctuary, her puja room, where she could pray and meditate without disturbance. This little room, set apart from the others in the house, held her brass idols—Rama, Shiva, Ganesha, Saraswati. Malika had brought in fresh jasmine, tuberoses and tulsi leaves and arranged them on a silver platter. Shanti lit the wicks in the small oil lamps, held the match to the incense sticks and gently rang the prayer bell. Then holding the brass aarti with the small flame in both hands, Shanti circled it three times around the idols. Finally, she offered the flowers to the gods and put a small red *kum-kum* dot on her forehead. Much calmer after her prayers, she walked over to sit in the drawing room by the window.

She decided to call her good friend Ganga; she had to talk about her little Kisan to somebody. And Shanti spoke glowingly about what a beautiful baby he was. So much black hair and his complexion was very fair. Ganga delighted in Shanti's news and then began her complaints about her own daughter-in-law. The girl liked only to shop and go out. Listening to Ganga, Shanti opened her mouth wordlessly to speak of her morning's experience. But she couldn't—wouldn't—speak ill of Anjali. After all, she was Kishore's wife. She was still new to Mumbai and the family. Poor girl, she didn't know how things were done in India. Agreeing to meet Ganga the next day at the club, she hung up the phone.

After a while, she called Malika and asked for a cup of tea. The maid was eager to hear about Kisan. As Shanti drank her tea, the maid squatted nearby listening with her large black eyes shining and a big smile on her face.

"Yes," said Shanti in Maharati, "Kisan has grown. He has so much black hair, just like Kishoresa'ab." She hoped that the new nanny would be as loyal to Kisan as Malika had been to their family. How many years had passed since the day this distraught woman had come begging for work and a place to live? Malika had thrown herself at Shanti's feet, weeping; she said her husband beat her mercilessly and had thrown her out of the house. She had no place to go. She'd lived on the streets, but men thought she was a whore and harassed her. Shanti looked at her carefully and saw underneath all that grime, Malika was a young and attractive woman. She listened to her heart, brought Malika in, gave her food and a room. It proved to be one of the best decisions Shanti made. Yes, Malika missed her two sons, but her husband had poisoned them against her. They vilified her and spat on her just as he did. She became part of Shanti's family, and when she finally accepted that her husband would not hunt her down for the money she was now earning, she gradually shed her fears and jumpiness.

Although Malika was often her confidante, Shanti couldn't confess why she was home for lunch instead of spending the day with Kisan and Anjali. How could she speak about the pain in her heart to anyone? It eroded the woman-essence of her. But Malika felt Shanti's pain and brought more tea and turned on some favorite music.

Shanti and Vinod had moved to this flat twenty years ago from his parents' house after Dev was born. Two children and four adults had made that house too crowded, so using Vinod's inheritance they bought an apartment in a then new building, Kalpana Apartments, on Malabar Hill—the Beverly Hills of Mumbai. Their drawing room windows had a fine view of the ocean and the twinkling lights along Marine Drive which the British had named "The Queen's Necklace."

Kishore and Dev had gone to Cathedral School and St. Xavier's College—the best in Mumbai. How they had filled the house with their friends, their projects, their parties. Always the noise of voices, cheerful, or despairing—boisterous, alive. Not this deadening silence. Although Shanti had not gone to college, she learned German at the Max Mueller Institute and French at Alliance Francaise. Thus by becoming fluent in two European languages as well as English, she subtly helped Vinod with his career which brought him increasingly international contacts.

When the children were growing up, she'd exposed them to classical Indian and western music. She knew that they would find the popular Bollywood movie songs and the Madonnas and Bruce Springsteens on their own, as of course they did. When Kishore had renounced his violin lessons to teach himself guitar, she protested only slightly. Dev was studying tabla and switched back and forth easily between the Indian drums and the western drum set he desperately begged for and received. She had also taken them to every art exhibit available in Mumbai, from ancient Egyptian to modern American. And of course travel—what would any of this mean without context? Vinod's job took him to Europe and America, and whenever they could afford it, the whole family tagged along. What adventures they had!

When they were in Paris many years ago, she had gathered her courage, gone to a salon and had her long hair cut into a chic style. Poor Vinod had almost had a heart attack. She could still hear him, "Oh, my God, Shanti. What have you done?" Eventually he came around and admired how the soft frame of her hair made her look younger and more beautiful.

Anajli did not know that her "orthodox, conservative" mother-in-law had many different sides to her. Perhaps she was unaware that Shanti was not old, but only in her fifties. To Anjali, maybe she was mired in the rut of tradition, afraid of change. While there may be time to win Anjali over, *this* was the time for Kisan. This time was primal—unwritten, unspoken, passed on to each generation of mothers in every language and every culture. And she had learned it from her mother.

She had held Kishore and Dev with their little heads close, close to her heart, passing the love she bore for them through the rhythm, through the cadence, through the skin into their souls. She had learned from her mother the sibilantic nonsense rhymes that could lull a baby to sleep. The clapping poems, the rocking poems, the hand twirling poems—each one could evoke a smile or a chortle from that little face. She ached to do all these with her first grandchild, to teach them to Anjali so she too could enjoy these irretrievable moments. And so Shanti sat at her window wondering how to reach and touch her grandson. And how to teach—no, show—Anjali the heart-hidden secrets that were essential to Kishore's roots and his heritage.

But Shanti was not one to be disheartened too long. She knew she would win Anjali over and would have her time with Kisan. She looked at her watch—almost lunch time.

She thought about her good fortune. She had a devoted husband who understood and indulged her. Kishore was back in Mumbai with a beautiful wife and a baby boy. Only Dev—well, Dev was happy playing the drums for a band at some nightclub in Mumbai. Just as she was thinking about him, Dev emerged from his bedroom. Freshly shaved and showered, dressed in blue jeans and a crisp cotton shirt, he looked debonair and suave. He gave her his lopsided smile, said he was going to the club for lunch and headed out the door.

Yes, Dev still lived at home, but she rarely saw him. He hardly ever ate meals with them; it seemed he used his room just to sleep. She worried about him; when would he get married and settle down? And she knew Vinod worried about when Dev would get a 'real' job. Vinod did not think that playing drums at night clubs constituted a career for a man. She secretly agreed, though she always defended Dev from Vinod's diatribes.

Shanti sighed. She had everything God could give; why did she feel so profoundly sad? She sat in her favorite chair and looked out the window. The rain had paused—it never stopped during the monsoon—and a weak sun was struggling to break through the dark clouds. A few brave sparrows and pigeons were foraging for food, as were the stray dogs on the street. Cars honked angry warnings at mopeds which had ventured out in the brief respite. Garbage and paper caught in the flow and strength of the rain clogged the drains and deepened the water in the streets. However, leaves on the trees were washed clean of grime and pollution inevitable in a city of fifteen million.

She gazed out at the Arabian Sea wishing the waves could bring her some answers as she sat in her large empty silent flat, alone.

Anjali

ANJALI HATED THE SHOWERS IN India—they were so drippy, just a drizzle coming out of the shower head with no pressure. She preferred having two buckets of hot water which she could cool to her liking and pour over herself with a large brass cup. Now, while Anjali soaped herself in the bathroom, she felt twinges of guilt. Should she stay home and entertain her mother-in-law? No, dammit. She hadn't been out for so long. But, she could go out tomorrow with Kishore; she really should stay home with Shanti who had come over in the torrential rain. She dried herself, slipped on a caftan, and went to the bedroom to say she wasn't going to the club after all, but Shanti had already left. Anjali was relieved—and virtuous because she had been willing to stay home. She felt light-headed—she could dress up and go out! How long it had been.

Her mother, Subadra, had descended on them when Kisan was born and stayed a whole month; Anjali had almost gone mad. She did not respect her mother, nor did she expect to get worthwhile maternal advice from her. The woman was tentative, trembling, and foolish. Anjali's attitude toward her mother was perfectly understood by her peers when she lived in Boston. Now that she was in India, however, everyone, old and young, expected her to respect and revere Subadra. Since she could do neither, she'd kept her feelings to herself.

Kishore had serenely accepted Subadra's presence in their flat. He kept assuring Anjali that this was the way it was done, that she should take advantage of it and rest. What he did not understand was she was fearful that Kisan would be dropped on his head every time Subadra lifted or carried him. Well, she had finally left last night—to everyone's relief.

Anjali stood in front of a mirror, removed her caftan and appraised her body. Still a roundness in the tummy…well, she would aerobicise that off in a few weeks. She wriggled into her slimming black Guess jeans. Uh-oh. She couldn't button them at the waist. She lay on the bed, sucked in her stomach and pulled on the zipper. She was working up a sweat, and the zipper wasn't moving. The jeans were not worth it. She threw them carelessly on the bed and reached for a forgiving salwar kameez, with the drawstring pants and the loose flowing top. She flipped through several, finally settling on an ethnic white print on a celadon background. It would keep her cool in this heat and humidity.

She put her guilt about Shanti aside and entered Kisan's room to give the nanny instructions on caring for the baby. She looked at him sleeping peacefully; she caressed his tousled head, surprised by her feeling—she didn't want to leave him. She, Anjali, the Boston sophisticate, the party lover, was feeling qualms about leaving her baby with a nanny. Who would believe it? Giving the infant one last look, she told herself she would be back in two or three hours—tops.

The driver had driven slowly on the Mumbai roads and turned into the entrance of the Willingdon Club. The long driveway was smooth and lined with perfectly manicured beds of red zinnias and saffron marigolds. At the entrance, he got out and held an umbrella over Anjali even though they were in a car port. She smiled at the red turbaned Sikh doorman who smartly opened the front door. In the foyer were several talking, laughing club members, shaking out their umbrellas and signing in for lunch.

Anjali loved the Willingdon for its exclusivity and beauty. The entrance alone bespoke wealth: white marble floors inlaid with crimson squares. The stairway with the glistening Burma rosewood banister split in two at the second floor dining room and gently curved into the foyer. A sparkling crystal chandelier hung in the entry hall where the members signed in. Anjali chose not to go up to the dining room but went onto the verandah which looked out on the lush green lawn and garden. Here she was sure to find some friends having a drink.

She had deliberately arrived at the club early. She wanted to be seen, admired. She was tall, for an Indian woman, and quite striking. She wore her dark brown hair shoulder length, soft around her oval face, and the celadon kameez emphasized her kajal-lined hazel eyes. Everyone could see that she had almost regained her pre-baby figure.

"Anjali, is that you? My God, you look fab!" Sure enough, rising from a table, her new friends were rushing to surround her, as glad to see her as she was to see them. Secretly pleased, she waved away their compliments: "No, no. I still have so much more to lose. I can barely fit into my clothes. Thank God for the salwar kameez; you can be as plump as you want under it." She hoped they would notice how slim she already was.

Anjali had grown up intermittently in New Delhi. Her dad was in the diplomatic corps, and when he got a posting in Washington D.C., he took his family with him. Anjali, fifteen at the time, went to high school in D.C. and then on to Boston College. These women at the club she'd known for only the short six months that she and Kishore had lived in Mumbai. And she had no compunction about judging them. These girls comprised "the idle rich." She could see them playing bridge or gin rummy at the club in a few years, the card room becoming the highlight of their lives. Conversation with them was light, shallow and effortless.

"How is it being a mother? Have you found a good nanny?" They were eager to know about her baby and how she was adjusting.

"Oh, Kisan is an angel. You all must come and see him soon. He sleeps most of the time, and thank God he doesn't have that colic some of you scared me about."

"So now you can go out? Listen, do you want to go with us next

Wednesday? Sheeraz is having a private showing of her new designer clothes. It's going to be marvelous. I hear that she has gossamer like chiffon kurtis embroidered with the tiniest beads. She only has the best colors and styles."

"Anjali, if you buy a salwar kameez from her, you'd have something new to wear to the D'Souzas' big bash next week. You are coming, no?"

Soon, Anjali was buoyed by their infectious spirits. After being cooped up in the house for so long, she was living again. Clothes! Parties! Shopping!

When the white uniformed waiter came for her drink order, she automatically said, "Gin and lime—oops. I forgot. Make that a plain lime and soda, no ice. I shouldn't drink." Looking around at her new friends, the smiling faces that included her in all they did and would do, she suddenly blurted out, "Guess who came by today? Unannounced and uninvited. Right in the middle of my aerobics routine." They all looked blank. "My mother-in-law. She wanted to teach me how to give Kisan an oil bath, if you please. Now what's so special about an oil bath for a four-week old?"

There were some sympathetic murmurs. "If you live in India, that's what happens. In-laws, cousins, cousins of cousins, they all feel they can drop in any time. And everyone expects you to give up your plans to entertain them."

"My mother-in-law was a godsend when Mirai was born, I tell you. I came back from my parents' home—there my mother had done everything; here I was helpless with the new baby. Thank God my mother-in-law came every day. I tell you it would have been hell without her. I could just hand over the baby when she was crying and go take a nap. I don't know what I'd have done."

"Sometimes they like to interfere too much. They have to tell you how to do everything, how to look after the baby, what to eat, how to dress, how to cook for their precious sons. But, really, they are the ones with experience—we should listen to them. But, Anjali, your mother-in-law seems so modern—you are so lucky, no? But tell me, what did you do?"

"Well, I told her that I had plans with Kishore for lunch."

Eyes widened at her response. Suddenly, their voices were hushed.

"You sent your mother-in-law away? Your own mother-in-law? I wouldn't have the courage." And they lowered their eyes and shook their heads.

"I told her I'd phone her and she could come and teach me the stupid oil bath routine another time. What's the big deal?"

Sonali, the most outspoken of the group, looked at Anjali with reproach. "So Anjali, have you been away for so long that you don't even understand some basic rituals, eh? All over India, even the poorest women, spend time with their babies to massage them with oil. It removes the flaky dead skin that so many babies have; more than that it makes a baby feel soothed and loved. In the west they would probably include this ritual under their idea of bonding." She paused, then with a sly smile, "Hell, I say, in America, don't people pay a hundred dollars or more for a massage? Here, I pay a woman a hundred rupees—that's *two* dollars—to give me ayurvedic oil massages twice a week. Ayurveda has been around for centuries, and ayurvedic oils have healing qualities, not just scents and aromas, like in your spas. Maybe the west is just catching up with us, no?" Sonali was pudgy and plain, but what she lacked in looks she made up for in brains. Anjali, to her own surprise, found herself respecting Sonali's opinions and ideas over all others. If she would ever make a true friend, it would probably be Sonali.

Now, Anjali sat speechless; she never expected such a reaction. Nor had she ever heard about oil baths and ayurvedic massages. Something to check out. The practice of yoga was omnipresent in America, but ayurvedic massages? No, in Boston, it had been aromatherapy everywhere. Why had no one told her about these massages before? She could use a soothing massage two or three times a week. Maybe even Kishore would like one.

"Well, I'll phone her soon and apologize and ask her to come over and teach me about oil baths. I wonder if she has an ayur—what do you call it? Sonali, could you give me your person's name? I could certainly use someone like that—and for just one hundred rupees. That's bloody cheap, isn't it?"

"Ooh, looks like a handsome man is looking for you."

Anjali looked towards the door. Even after three years of marriage, her first unbidden thought when she saw Kishore was "Mmm! I'd like to get you in bed, gorgeous."

Kishore was tall and slender, dark-haired. His crooked smile gave him a quizzical look. His eyes were so light brown, they appeared tawny, sitting against his olive skin. Now those eyes were riveted on Anjali alone as he walked toward her while saying casual hellos to all the other ladies.

"Ready for lunch, Anju?" His voice had a hypnotic timbre.

"See you all later. Call me about the Sheeraz showing and Sonali, I want to get your ayur—whatever person's number. Bye."

All eyes followed the handsome couple as they floated upstairs to the dining room. Anjali had not felt so—well, beautiful and admired—in months. Kishore was delighted to see his wife looking cheerful. Talking to her friends had been good for her. After they ordered their lunch, Kishore asked, "So, what were you and the girls gabbing about?"

"Oh, nothing special—you know, shopping, parties, the usual."

"Well, I'm glad you are having a good time with them. They're good company for you, no?"

"Sure, they're fun. I'll get to know them better once I start going out more." Kishore was eager that Anjali make her own friends so that she would feel more comfortable in her new surroundings.

As lunch progressed, Anjali thought she had not enjoyed herself so much in ages. She had the total attention of Kishore, the admiring glances of every man in the dining room and the envious looks of most women. All too soon, she felt her breasts get heavy and swollen and knew she had to return home. She glanced at her watch—3:30 already—it would take at least an hour to reach home. Getting into the car in the rain which seemed to be pelting sideways got her thoroughly soaked. The drive home was a death crawl.

She could hear Kisan's hungry screams as she entered the flat. The sound of his voice caused her milk to spurt and soak through the nursing pads and through her kameez. She ran into his room, tearing off her clothes and unhooking her sopping bra as she went. Settled with him in the rocker, she gazed at her son whose cries had quieted to whimpers. Then a satisfied snuffling sound told her that he was drinking. He had such strong suction—and it felt so wonderful. She looked at his fist lying against her breast, gently stroked the fingers and marveled at the dimples that were beginning at the knuckles. He was tiny and perfect. Placing him against her shoulder to burp him, she sniffed the new baby smell of his head. Intoxicating! She never thought she could love another creature as much as she loved this little one.

After his feed, Kisan went to sleep, and she had nothing to do. Already the euphoria of the lunch was wearing off. She tried to read, she listened to music, she lay down for a nap—nothing worked. The only constant was the unending splash and roar of the rain. The weather exacerbated the noise: the cars honked incessantly, people yelled more loudly—everything was magnified.

She could hear her neighbor Gita shrieking at her servants about some small infraction. Dogs in the adjoining flats barked and whined—they were bored too. Anjali wandered listlessly around the flat, wondering what on earth she was doing here. She had no friends and nothing to do. In Boston, she could go to the mall, the library, a movie…here every outing was a major undertaking. She finally screamed out loud, not caring that the servants were the ubiquitous ears in the flat, "When will this fucking rain stop? God! I hate it." She wanted nothing more at that moment than to return to Boston. She wished she'd never agreed to come and live in this frightful city, but Kishore had made it sound so wonderful. Why had she ever listened to him?

It was almost seven when Kishore called on his cell phone to tell her he was on his way home. He walked in half an hour later, shaking droplets of rain from his hair. He left his dripping umbrella outside, and once in the flat, sensed a palpable distress. What could have happened? He checked the baby's room—all was well. Anjali seemed fine too, if a bit subdued. Her cheerful lunch mood had faded.

When they were getting ready for bed, he stood close behind her, pressing his body to hers, cupping her breasts. "What's wrong, Anju darling?" he murmured.

"I don't know. I felt fine all afternoon, now I feel so cooped up and…and it's so damn humid."

"Cooped up? You have a car and driver to take you anywhere you wish, anytime you wish. That nanny is here to look after Kisan…"

"It's this fucking rain. When is it ever going to stop? It's driving me crazy."

"Come on, sweetheart—it's no worse than a Boston winter."

"Oh, yeah? At least in Boston the roads work and cars can function. But you're right. I'm being a brat. But Kish, I have no friends here…"

"What about the girls I saw you with at the club?"

"They're all so shallow. They talk in such superficialities. If you sent them an idea by registered post, they wouldn't know what to do with it."

"Come on. I went to school with most of them—and they're all smart. Any one of them could have won a scholarship like I did. Do you know that Sonali scored the same as me on the SAT? She is very clever. But she and all the others have just chosen to stay home to raise a family. You know, the famous feminist choice—career or family. These girls have made theirs—and in a few years, once their children are grown, they may choose careers and be successful."

She nuzzled into his neck, leaning back sensually. Then she whispered, "Kish, darling, I feel so tense, so depressed sometimes. Do you think you could get me some pot? I'm sure you could get it from Dev. Please?"

He stopped his languorous swaying and stiffened. He whipped her around to face him, his eyes cold as two amber pebbles.

"Are you crazy? You may as well put an I.V. drip into Kisan's little arm and blow the marijuana directly into it. What's wrong with you, Anju? Tense and depressed? Your American friends would envy you—a large flat in an upscale area, a cook, a maid, a nanny, a driver and a car. What more could you possibly want?" He angrily huffed off and lay down in the bed. No love making tonight.

Of course, he was right—yes, she did have all those things. But when she was home all day, listening to the eternal rain, the cacophonous traffic, people in the neighboring flats arguing loudly, she wanted—what the hell did she want? She didn't know. Company, someone to whom she could confide these ambivalent and confused emotions?

She lay down next to Kishore, saying "I don't know what got into me, darling. You know I would never do anything that might hurt Kisan. You know how much I adore him. I'm sorry." He turned and cradled her. He began crooning a sweet soothing wordless tune.

"What song is that, Kish? It's very lovely."

"Hmph. I don't know what part of my brain I dragged that out of. It's a song that my mother sang to us when we were babies. I must have picked it up when she sang to Dev. Haven't thought of it for years."

As he continued his humming, she made herself stop talking. He didn't understand. He thought she should be satisfied with all that he provided—and, of course, she was. It was an inner ache, that yearning for an unnamable something that he didn't get. For the first time, she felt a hint of apprehension about this man who had swept her into a tumultuous courtship and marriage. Was he going to be insensitive to her feelings? Some of her American friends constantly talked about the thoughtlessness of their boyfriends or husbands. She'd been sure Kishore wasn't like that.

Now she listened to his gentle snores. She untwined herself from his encircling arms, turned on her side with her back to him and tried to quell the amorphous fear that was suffusing her. Tomorrow things would look different—out of the murk of night.

Kishore

Kishore woke up later than usual the next morning with Kisan between him and Anjali on the bed. She had fallen asleep nursing him again. His heart swelled with tenderness as he gazed at the two of them, until his eye fell on his watch. *Shit!* He must have slept through the alarm. He went into the hall and yelled for Shiva to have breakfast ready in ten minutes. Damn! He was going to be late for work. Thank God one of the servants had crept in earlier and turned on the geyser so the water would be hot for his shower.

He looked out the window. How foolish to think it might have quit raining. It would go on like this for the next three damn months. Anjali was right—a Boston winter was a piece of cake compared to a monsoon which punished streets that were ill-prepared for the mountains of garbage, the crush of humanity, the clangor of traffic. When the British had built the roads of Mumbai, they had not anticipated eight lanes of cars, mopeds, bicycles, motorbikes, pedestrians, cows, and dogs on the streets.

He dressed in a hurry. On the bed, Anjali stirred and stretched, one breast exposed. He felt himself aroused, wished he had the time to make love to her before work. When he rushed into the dining room, she followed him. With her rumpled hair, pouty lips and sleep-filled eyes, she looked adorable.

"When will you be home, Kish?" she yawned.

"I'll try to be home by 7:30, but I'll call you," he said, stuffing toast in his mouth and gulping his chai. "What will you do today?"

"Maybe I'll call Amma. She came by yesterday."

He stopped chomping and stared. "She came yesterday? Why didn't you tell me? What did she say about Kisan? How long was she here?"

"Stop! She came when I was doing aerobics, so she spent some time in Kisan's room. Then I told her we had a lunch date, so she went home."

Kishore's jaw tightened. "You sent her home? Anju, you could have called me and we could have had lunch today…"

"Kish, I haven't been out of the house for weeks. I was looking forward to the club."

"I have to go now, I'm late. But we will discuss this tonight. Call and invite her today or tomorrow, when it's convenient for *her*. Promise me." With a quick kiss, he was gone.

In the car, Kishore phoned his secretary to say he'd be late, then leaned back to read the paper. The driver could not make any headway, and fifteen minutes later they seemed to be permanently parked in front of St. Xavier's College. Kishore recalled the happy days he had spent there. Because academics had come so easily to him, he had become a player among the girls. He was handsome, charming, and smart—powerful aphrodisiacs to help with his seductions. Much of the time, the surreptitious groping had to be done in parked cars since he lived with his family as did the girls. They eagerly waited for parents to go on holiday so that various friends' houses could become the playground for booze, drugs and sex. He had entered college at seventeen and lost his virginity that same year, an achievement in India on a par with his perfect grades. When Kishore scored 1560 out of a possible 1600 on the SAT, scholarships from top schools in the U.S. poured in. He chose MIT.

In Boston, he found a whole new world open to him. He could take classes at Harvard and MIT simultaneously and work on an MBA in addition to his Ph.D. in computer engineering. But much more stimulating was the world of women. He loved their bodies and their minds. Although his girl friends in India were smart, a touch of ancestral heredity made them subservient to men. In Boston, he loved the physical and mental wrestling with women where they won as often as he did. But he sorely missed home and his family. Kishore venerated his mother, although like most Indian boys he would never tell her so. He missed her cooking, her gentle touch—the way she guided the household with reins of silk. When he saw Anjali at a foreign students' gathering, he was ripe to fall.

Here was a girl who was beautiful, smart—and Indian. She would have little trouble adjusting to Mumbai and to the culture. He was blind to the fact that she had spent her high school and college years in Boston. All he recognized was that she was Indian. Their courtship was tempestuous, their engagement swift, and their marriage splendid. Kishore was only twenty-four—but then he had always done things ahead of the class. Now at twenty-seven, he was back in Mumbai, a father, and on the fast track to the top spot at Sun Micro, India.

When he finally reached the headquarters in the Fort area, he went into the small room he called his office. The furniture was old and faded, the machines were well-used and often repaired. If he'd stayed in the States, he could have had a plush room with plants and carpets. Here, he was glad to have a reasonably comfortable chair and an efficient secretary. And best of all, he could send any one of a number of teenage boys to run errands delivering memos and mail all over the city. How they maneuvered through the traffic on their bicycles was a miracle!

During his workday, he called Anjali often to see how she was doing. Underneath her bright chatter, he sensed an undercurrent of restlessness. He promised to be home early.

When he arrived at 8:30, he bounded in, removing his wet shoes and giving his umbrella to the maid who had opened the door to him. Where was Anjali? Curled up in the living room watching some mindless Hindi soap opera she couldn't even understand. She was cool to his kiss and told him that Kisan had cried more than usual, and she was exhausted. Okay, then. Never mind his harrowing ten hour day of meetings with the top American directors of the company.

He poured himself a gin and lime and thoughtlessly asked, "Can I fix you one, darling?" She withered him with a look, then called for Shiva to bring her a lime and soda. Idiot. How could I be so stupid? he thought.

"So, did anyone come over today, any of your friends?"

"No, didn't you notice that the Great Flood has started? I'm sure no one ventured out today who didn't have to."

"Did you call Amma? When is she coming to see Kisan and you?"

"Yes, I spoke to her." Anjali cut the TV and turned to face him looking bereft. Poor girl. She was so lonely. "Kish, tell me what is this deal with the oil bath? She wants me to learn how to give Kisan one." The tension visibly left Kishore's body as his eyes lightened. He sat on the couch, grew animated and leaned forward, gesturing as he spoke.

"I used to watch Amma when she gave Dev oil baths. She would massage oil all over the baby, even into the little knee and elbow creases and the belly button. In the bathroom, she would hike her sari or salwar to her knees, you know, sit on a low bathing stool and hold little Dev balanced between her knees and feet. The ayah would pour the warm water, but Amma never let go of the baby for an instant. How Dev loved his oil baths! He would gurgle and crow. I'd forgotten all about that." Eagerly putting a hand on her thigh, Kishore said, "This is one of the reasons I want us to live in India, Anju. You can learn these things from my mother, and Kisan can have as happy a childhood as I did."

Anjali's face clouded. "Yes, I know how happy you are here. You have all your school and college friends, your job that keeps you busy, your golf and tennis…and I don't begrudge you any of it. Heaven knows you deserve it, darling…but where does that leave me?"

"Anju, you are my wife—you share in it all."

"Kish, is it possible that a position in Sun Micro may open up for you in, say, California? Would you take it?

Kishore could not conceal his shock, his dismay, his bewilderment. "What are you saying, Anju? You want to leave Mumbai? Don't you have everything—what else can I give you?"

"Oh, Kish, it's not you. And yes, you have given me everything. But something is missing for me."

Kish rose, his lips tightening. "I'm going to shower and change into something more comfortable. Tell Shiva to get dinner ready. While I am showering, you think about what is missing for you," he said.

As he let the tepid water drizzle over his body (damn low pressure again) he felt his anger rise. How could she want to return to the States? They'd been in Mumbai only six months—how could she already be unhappy? She even had the most beautiful baby to keep her busy. What was bugging her? She had known going into the marriage that he wanted to live in India. Damn it, she had everything she could want. He did not need this after his day at work.

He emerged from the bathroom vigorously wiping the water off his hair. He turned on the overhead fan immediately so the humidity wouldn't have him sweating in a few seconds. Of course there was air conditioning in their bedroom, but they used it only at night and in the afternoon to conserve electricity. It was horrendously expensive. He changed into a light cotton kurta and drawstring pajamas. With his hair still wet, he returned to the dining room.

At the dinner table, as Shiva brought out piping hot rotis, he tempered his voice and asked, "So, what's all this about going to California?"

"Well, Kish, as I told you, I feel so lonely. I have no friends here. *(You don't have friends in California either, he thought, but he bit his tongue. He didn't want to upset her even more.)* Remember the job I had in Boston, research in the library? I know it wasn't much, but it gave me validation—I had somewhere to go, I was someone in that office."

"Sweetheart, you are more than someone here. I adore you, my parents do too. Once Kisan is a little older, once you stop breast feeding him, you can move around more easily with friends from the club and others. There's all sorts of things to take advantage of in Mumbai. You could start a book club. Did you know Amma learned French and German here? Come on, Anju. You don't need a job to validate you."

"It's just that I feel like such a stranger here. I'm not used to someone picking up after me—doing everything. Radha is all the time dusting, sweeping, swabbing, mopping, washing, ironing. It drives me crazy. I have nothing to do. I don't even do our laundry, for Christ's sake. And I sometimes hate having someone around all the time, you know? I have no privacy. I don't know. I just feel so depressed. I never felt like this in the States." As he listened to her, he wondered how she could be so ungrateful…surely she wasn't suggesting that she would like to do any of those chores? No, of course not. What the hell did she want?

Suddenly, he comprehended. He had heard of this phenomenon in the U.S., never in India. Post-partum depression—was this ailing Anjali? Maybe that was it. In India, women always went to their parents' homes to have their babies and had the constant company of a mentoring mother. Poor Anjali didn't have that, so she was lonely and depressed. What should he do? He must call his mother later; she would advise him.

Anjali was speaking again. "Could you negotiate with Sun Micro to split your year—six months in Mumbai and six months in the U.S.?"

Oh my God. I may as well immolate my career. I must stop her thinking like this, he thought. And right there, with their dinner only half eaten, he took her hand and kissed the palm. Looking into her eyes seductively, he continued, "You've had a rotten few days and the rain doesn't help. Come, let's go to bed and we'll see what we can do to make you feel better."

He led her into the bedroom and undressed her slowly. Keeping his eyes fixed on hers, he walked backward to turn on the air conditioning unit removing his kurta slowly and tossing it on the floor. As the cool air swept into the room, he moved toward her again, untying his pajama, letting it fall, stepping out of it. Her eyes widened with desire, and she licked her lips. He approached her, his arms almost lazily engulfing her. He knew she liked it slow.

He pulled her on to the bed, tumbling her on top of him. He caressed her back, then her breasts with whispering fingers, as she arched her back and closed her eyes. He stroked her thighs sensually, just brushing against her until she was begging for him. He continued to massage her back, kiss her neck, and swirl his fingers around her erect nipples. She purred with desire, reaching for him, guiding him until he entered her. As he came he panted, "Does this validate you, darling?"

He fell asleep very quickly, so he didn't see her rise from the bed, slip on her caftan and sit in the chair in the room. He didn't hear her cry. Kishore just slept while Anjali rocked and sobbed. He slept deeply, dreamlessly and happily.

Vinod

VINOD WAS A MAN DEEPLY content with most of his life. It was his sixtieth birthday, and he knew Shanti was planning a surprise party for him. He would not disappoint her—he would be surprised. He knew her joy was multiplied because she had little Kisan, now a curious, energetic five-year old, to help her.

When Kisan had been a baby, Vinod had sensed some friction between Shanti and Anjali. However, Shanti with her gentle, intuitive ways had taught her daughter-in-law the joy of caring for Kisan, feeding him, bathing him and crooning him to sleep. Now Anjali was pregnant with a second baby, so Kisan spent more and more time with his grandparents, and they were happy to have him.

Kishore was glad to be back in Mumbai and doing well. Because Anjali had at first been so unhappy in Mumbai and yearned to return to America, Kishore had transferred to California when Kisan was one year old. When Anjali became pregnant again, they realized that looking after two children would be easier in Mumbai. He hoped that they had got that wanderlust out of their systems. Kishore was making a brilliant career for himself. He made Vinod proud.

He wished he could say the same about Dev. Dev had yet to find a purpose in life; he could not—should not—make a career playing drums at night clubs. The boy had no ambition. He drank too much and probably took drugs. He was approaching thirty and laughed disdainfully if Shanti suggested a girl for him to meet. An arranged marriage? He would give Shanti a big hug and say with a smile, "How could I find a woman to compare with you? You have spoiled me for other women, Amma."

Vinod leaned back in his desk chair and stroked his head. He was a trim man of medium height. He was losing most of his graying hair, and it didn't bother him one bit. His face didn't bear wrinkles, just some around his wise dark brown eyes. He considered himself lucky if, at sixty, he had worries about only one son.

Vinod determined to ask Kishore about the drugs—Kishore would know. Vinod was sure that Dev was smoking ganja again—a year ago Malika had found a chillum pipe in his room when she was cleaning. With innocent curiosity, she had asked Shanti what it was. With equal innocence, Shanti had asked him. Eventually, they had asked Dev who said one of his friends had probably left it in the room. In a private conversation, he had insisted Dev tell him what the pipe was used for, and reluctantly Dev had told him it was for marijuana. Now he probably hid his habit and its accouterments more carefully.

When Dev was in his early twenties, hadn't he made life miserable for the whole family? He would come home staggering in the early hours, speech slurred, lurching into the furniture. Then there was that dreadful time when he started stealing. Oh, it was never much—Shanti would find a few hundred rupee notes missing from her purse. She would always pretend that she must have forgotten where she spent them. When Vinod 'lost' his watch, it broke his heart to know that his son had become a thief. Both Rama and Malika had been with the family for so long, it never occurred to Vinod and Shanti to question their honesty. More than once they had sat down with their son—*their son*—and accused him of taking money and valuables. Dev would weep and promise he would never do it again. He would give up his wastrel ways. And he would—sometimes for a week at a time.

Now, Vinod had reason to suspect that Dev was on something

again. What if he was taking that dangerous "brown sugar"? What was it? Adulterated cocaine? Or that "ecstasy" Vinod had recently heard about that was being brought in from America? To Vinod, the whole idea of drugs and what they did to the body and mind was so repulsive that it pained him immeasurably to think his son was succumbing to their lure.

Vinod remembered a time when he was in college someone had mixed bhang into a glass of milk and coaxed him to drink it. He had felt like he was floating above the scene watching himself play the fool. The next morning he vowed he would never go near such stuff—he hated being so out of control.

He wished that Dev would settle down, get married, find a real job. He was handsome in a rakish way, with his too-long hair and his eyes like deep chocolate pools. He wore a diamond on his right ear lobe and a thick gold chain around his neck. Girls found the dark aura of wickedness around him irresistible. He lived with his parents, sleeping past noon, eating when he felt like it and going out with his unsavory friends. Vinod sighed, continuing to stroke his balding head. Every family had a black sheep—and Dev was theirs. He wondered if Dev would be at the party tonight; he hadn't seen him for days.

Kishore never gave him cause to worry—he excelled in school, went to MIT, found a lovely girl. At first, he had wondered if Anjali would ever fit into their family, she was so westernized. There had been that rough patch when Kisan was born. He remembered the call Shanti had received from Kishore when the baby was two or three months old. He'd said Anjali was depressed and lonely, even talking about wanting to return to America. Poor Kishore. He didn't know what to do—spoke about something called "post-partum depression" that women suffered after giving birth. The things they had in America! Here, women went to their mothers' homes to give birth, learning how to care for the baby from their Ammas. They did not suffer from depression—not that he had heard, anyway. Families looked after their own—in America, women prized their independence so much, they hardly asked for help. No wonder they found looking after a tiny infant overwhelming. Anjali's depression, if it was that, was handled it with Shanti's usual calm delicacy. Vinod himself had no idea what magic she had worked, nor had he asked.

All in all, his whole family was healthy and successful—well, except for Dev. He thanked God for their good health; it was the biggest blessing. One thing nagged at him—for the past months, he found himself breathless even after a short walk, especially if he was walking uphill. And he felt a tightening in the throat. Once he reached home, the feeling went away. *Chalo!* It was nothing. He wasn't going to mention it to anyone, not even Shanti. After all, he was sixty today; surely feeling a little tired during exercise was his right. He waited contentedly for the evening.

That night, he was touched to see so many of his friends at the party. He and Shanti had lived so long in Mumbai, they had a large circle of acquaintances most of whom loved to gather for dinner and drinks. He'd entered a dark house and been appropriately surprised when a loud welcome greeted him. Shanti, with Kisan's help, had decorated the flat with bright orange, yellow and green streamers. Flowers in vases were placed everywhere. Kishore, an efficient bartender, plied everyone with drinks. Yes, even Dev was there at his roguish best. He passed around the chips and chilli pistachios, chatting easily with his father's friends. He had brought a good-looking Anglo-Indian woman whom he introduced as the singer in his group. Shanti looked over to Vinod conveying the unspoken message, "This is a beautiful girl, but not the one for Dev to marry."

At 10:30, smiling widely, Rama and Malika brought the food to the table, and Vinod saw that Shanti had demonstrated yet again how effortlessly she arranged parties. Rama had made a splendid mutton biriani, fragrant with cinnamon, cloves and ginger, delicately tinged with saffron and sprinkled on top with deep-fried crispy onions. Of course, there was plain pulau rice with dal, and dhai vadai swimming in yogurt spiced with green chillies and coriander for the vegetarians.

The purple skins of the eggplant glistened through the sauce of the baingan bharta; the bhindi was perfect with the okra spicy and crisp, not slimy. These were Vinod's favorite dishes. He looked at Shanti with love and a thank you in his eyes.

Everyone ate fast, as they were wont to do. Malika brought in the rose scented gulab jamun and Rama proudly carried in a huge cake alight with candles. There was the obligatory singing of the Happy Birthday, Kisan singing the loudest. Finally, it was over. After the guests had gone and Dev had left with his singer for a performance, Kishore and Vinod sat in the living room sated with food and drink.

Shanti and Anjali were making sure that Kisan was sleeping and that the servants had enough to eat. As they returned to the drawing room, Anjali was giving Shanti the latest gossip.

"Amma, do you know what Rekha told me? She heard that Leela and Vikram are having problems—Vikram has even moved out. Can you believe that? I thought they were such a happy couple."

"So that's why she said they couldn't come. Poor Leela. That Vikram has a hot temper and an eye for women. Sometimes I've even seen her with bruises on her arms. I suppose she couldn't bear it any longer," said Shanti. She and Anjali joined their husbands in the living room, and Shanti changed the subject to something more immediate.

"How surprised you looked," Shanti said happily. "I was so afraid that Kisan would spill the beans."

"When I came into the dark house, I thought the current had failed because of this bloody rain. I wondered why Malika was giggling when she let me in," Vinod lied.

"Poor thing. She was so excited and nervous. Anyway, what do you both think of Dev's latest, Anita? She is certainly gorgeous," Anjali asked, gloating in her heart that Shanti and Vinod would not approve of Anita, because of both her career and her caste.

Vinod said emphatically, "I wish Dev would find someone suitable. That boy needs to settle down. That Anglo-Indian is not the right one for him."

"How long has Kisan been asleep? I don't know how he could sleep through all the noise we were making," said Kishore, uncomfortably.

"He went to sleep in your old room right after he sang Happy Birthday to his Papa. I think you should carry him to the car pretty soon so we can go home," said Anjali.

"Why not you let him sleep peacefully here? He can go to school from here only in the morning," said Vinod, sitting relaxed and drowsy. "I just want to tell you how happy you have all made me this evening. Shanti, it was a lovely party. To have you all and Dev was..."He never finished his sentence. He clutched his throat, eyes closed, his face a pain-filled grimace. Slowly he slid off his chair

"Oh my God. What is it, Vinod? What's happening?" Shanti was at his side, holding his hand.

Kishore began shouting, "He's having a heart attack. Get some aspirin, Amma."

Shanti looked up at Kishore, not comprehending, tears spilling over. "Amma, *now*. Get some aspirin. Anju, do you know where they keep their medicines? Find some aspirin, somebody. Rama! Malika!"

When the two wide-eyed servants ran in, Kishore asked, "Papa's tablets *kidar hai?* Where are his medicines?" Rama shook his head, but Malika went cowering to the bedroom to look.

"Anju, call downstairs and tell the watchman to have Ibrahim bring the car around. We must get him to Breach Candy Hospital immediately." Kishore watched his mother run to the bedroom to get the aspirin. He crouched next to his father and took his hand. It was icy. Kishore took out his handkerchief and dabbed the perspiration from Vinod's upper lip and forehead. "Papa, how are you feeling? Where does it hurt?" he asked softly. Vinod looked ashen.

"I'm all right. Only this arm is paining..."Vinod murmured, massaging his upper left arm near the shoulder.

"Here's Amma with the aspirin. Take two tablets. Now, can you tell me the name of your doctor?"

"No, No. I'll be all right in a little while. Don't bother the doctor in the middle of the night…" said Vinod, his voice fading as his pallor increased.

"Anju, you should stay here and try to get some sleep. Amma and I need to get him to Breach Candy."

"How can I sleep? But I should stay with Kisan."

"Amma, what is the number of his doctor? He must meet us at the hospital. Amma, what's his name? His number?"

Shanti got up from Vinod's side and went to her small phone book. "Dr Rajan and his number is 537-2956."

"Do you want to call him? You know him. If not, I can talk to him," Kishore said. "No, better we phone him from the car. *Chalo*—let's go."

Gently, he helped his father stand with Rama supporting him on the other side. "Papa, can you walk? We can phone for an ambulance, but it'll take longer, especially at this time," said Kishore.

Vinod whispered, "Yes, yes. I can walk. Just take me to the bed and let me sleep."

"No, Papa. Dr Rajan will meet us at the hospital and make sure you're all right. Malika, bring a blanket. Amma, are you ready?" Rama and Kishore helped Vinod walk to the lift and then to the waiting car. In the car, Kishore wrapped the blanket around his father, and stood aside for his mother to get in. He noticed that the grayness of his father's face was giving way to a healthier color and his hand felt less clammy. Kishore sat in front, telling the driver where to go, calling Dr. Rajan and stressing the urgency of the situation. Shanti murmured endearments to Vinod. Then she turned to the front seat, and clutching Kishore's shoulder, said, "What would I have done without you, *beta*? Thank God you were with us."

By the time they reached Breach Candy Hospital, Vinod was no longer sweating and his color was almost normal. In the hospital, Vinod was quickly wheeled away with Shanti at his side; Kishore waited for the doctor who arrived within a few minutes. Kishore once again described what had happened and felt gratified when the doctor patted him on the shoulder and said, "You did the right thing. Now I'll go and examine him. *Chalo,* take your mother to the waiting room, and you can sit with her there."

There, in an uncomfortable chair Shanti sat praying while Kishore paced, talking on his mobile to update Anjali and trying to reach Dev. Damn him. Dev's phone was turned off. Probably gone somewhere with Anita. In the tense half-hour that followed, Kishore stayed busy, trying to reach Dev and reassuring his mother. Finally, the doctor came out with news. "Yes, he might have had a mild heart attack, but I can't be sure until I run some tests. Now he's resting comfortably. We'll keep him here for observation, *achcha*? Shanti, don't worry," he said.

Looking at Kishore, he said. "There's nothing more to be done tonight. You should both go home and get some rest. Yes, yes, you can see him before you go. I'll know more about his condition tomorrow. He'll be perfectly fine."

"Can I stay with him tonight?" Shanti quavered.

Dr Rajan took her hands in his. "Shanti, look at you in your beautiful sari. You must have been at a party." Her eyes filled and she whispered, "Vinod's sixtieth…"

Dr Rajan looked at her, gauging her emotions and fatigue. "If you had the party at your house, you must be tired. Go home, get some rest and come in the morning. Vinod is sleeping peacefully. *Chalo*, Kishore, take her home now."

Kishore took a quietly weeping Shanti home, still trying in vain to call Dev. He phoned Anjali and told her that they should spend the night with Amma so she wouldn't be alone. Thank God, Kisan's school was close to the Malabar Hill flat, and the boy had his clothes and a set of books there. Kishore and Anjali too kept a few changes of clothes at Kalpana for convenience.

The next morning, after Kisan was sent to school, Kishore went into Dev's room and found him sleeping deeply. He shook him roughly to wake him up.

"Idiot. Where were you last night? Papa had a heart attack, and you were nowhere to be found."

Dev opened his eyes, sat up sluggishly and shook his head, trying to clear the fog. "What? What are you saying? A heart attack? When?" Dev's speech was slurred, and he was incoherent.

Kishore filled him in, watching him sober up fast. Dev dressed hurriedly so he could rush to his mother's side. As soon they were all ready, Kishore dropped them at the hospital and drove on to work, promising to be back as soon as he could.

It was three in the afternoon when Dr Rajan came out to assure them that the stress test they had run on Vinod showed no damage to his heart.

"The old pump is in good shape. I want to keep him in the hospital for a few days, so we can make sure there is no recurrence of last night's episode," said Dr. Rajan. Kishore and Dev squeezed Dr Rajan's hand, saying over and over, "Very good news, Doc. Thank you, thank you." Shanti closed her eyes in a silent prayer of thanks while Anjali hugged her and cried with relief. Before Dr Rajan left, he told them they could see Vinod in his room at any time.

Dev

WHILE THEY WERE WAITING FOR word about Vinod's transfer to his private room, Dev sat in the rickety metal chair, head leaned against the wall, eyes closed. His impossibly long lashes fanned his cheeks, almost covering the puffiness under his eyes. His head throbbed and even four cups of strong coffee had not cleared the cotton in his mouth. Pounding in his head with the rhythm of the drums he played was the familiar refrain, "Screw up. Fuck up." He had heard it all his life.

He'd enjoyed his father's party last night, although, to tell the truth, he had gone only to please his mother. During the evening, thank goodness, he had not sensed the usual tinge of disapproval from his father. And he had a trophy—Anita—to show off. Actually, he couldn't wait for dinner to be served and the obligatory "Happy Birthday" sung so he could whisk her away, tear her clothes off, and get her into bed. She was gorgeous and willing.

So instead of being spending the evening with the family, especially on his father's special day, he had lied about having to play at a club, turned off his mobile phone, taken a hotel room and enjoyed the pleasures of Anita's flesh while his father might have died.

Such a screw up! Even on his Papa's birthday he had been helpless, unable to deny the hot fire which flared in his groin whenever he looked at Anita. He knew that he could never marry her under any circumstances. Being the progressive man he was, he didn't condone the antiquated caste system. However, he understood that his parents, very liberal in most things, would never countenance his marriage to an Anglo-Indian, and a low class one at that. And frankly, Anita and he had nothing in common besides sex. So this was just an intoxicating fling with a predictable end. He knew he would never have any deep feelings for her.

He slit his eyes open and looked at his mother's tension-riddled face. Her lips were moving in silent prayer. He squirmed with guilt; he should have been with his Amma. He adored Shanti and would do anything she asked—except marry a girl she chose. She had always been a buffer between Vinod and him.

Dev knew that Vinod preferred Kishore, the golden boy, to Dev. Who wouldn't? Kishore enjoyed all the privileges of the first born son; in addition he was handsome, brilliant and popular. Poor Dev, whose talents lay in music not academia, found it excruciating to follow his brother at Cathedral School and at St. Xavier's College, to listen to daily exhortations from the teachers, "Your brother did so well in (name any subject); why can't you put in a little more effort?" It was in high school he stopped trying. In fact, he could mark the day—the day Kishore got his SAT scores, that rarefied 1560 out of a possible 1600—he knew he could never compete; why he'd be lucky to crack 1000. It wasn't that he lacked the brains; he just wasn't interested in book learning. So he turned his full attention to his drums and instinctively knew he had found his niche.

He began to desert his academic friends and found himself drifting more and more to the very wealthy—the indulged sons and daughters who were given everything by their parents, who would never have to work a day in their lives. Dev's use of alcohol and drugs increased, since these new friends had ample supply. Groups would meet weekly at faraway beach houses and drink and smoke until they got giggly and high, then careen home with screeching brakes and weaving cars. The danger itself gave them an additional high.

He knew he could never rely on them as true friends in case of a crisis; he could surely depend on them for a bottle of rum or a packet of ganja. It was one night, in a smoke-filled beach hut at Juhu Beach that the plump and very rich Shloka told him about a band in need of a drummer. This band played at hotel dining rooms and was really on the way up she said. Dev sobered up enough to ask her more, but she snaked her arm around his neck and drew him down to her. No more conversation that night. However, the next morning, he phoned her, got the information, and at the end of the week he had his first job—as drummer for Fred D'Cunha's band.

His parents never understood. Shanti indulged him, believing he would grow out of it. Vinod was implacable. It was as if his son had descended to the level of nautch girls—beautiful nubile young women brought in to dance for and service wealthy rajahs, when rajahs ruled. But Dev continued on his chosen career path—playing first at the smaller hotels, then at the larger ones where people liked Sinatraesque music in the background while they dined. He was hoping to move to the Oberoi and the Taj—the best in Mumbai which catered to westerners. He had invited his parents to come to hear him play, but his father always refused abruptly. Dev discerned shame lurking in Vinod's loving eyes.

And Dev wanted nothing more than that shame to be erased; he wanted his father to be proud of him too. But the two of them just couldn't get along. Put them in the same room, and immediately the air crackled with tension. They tried to have an ordinary conversation, to express their ideas, but instead circled like two growling dogs taking each other's measure. And now Vinod was having his heart mended while Dev sat nursing a hangover. Screw up! Dev vowed, as he had many times before, that he would stop drinking, never touch another drug—he would be clean.

After Dr Rajan left them, the family went in to Vinod's room, anxious to see for themselves how he had fared. He smiled at them weakly, saying, "You are all here? I gave you all a fright, didn't I? Dr. Rajan says I am fine, so don't worry."

"Papa, how are you feeling?" asked Kishore.

"I'll be as good as new, you'll see. That Dr. Rajan is quite a magic-wallah. He made me walk on a treadmill, and my heart began to pump like a twenty year old's. That Raju! He mended my heart and didn't make a single cut in the skin. Don't look so worried, all of you—I am only joking. Shanti, you look so tired. You should go home and sleep. Even Dev is here. Come here, *beta,*" said Vinod, giving Dev's hand an especially hard squeeze.

"I've already made arrangements for another bed in this room, so I can stay with you at night. You never know how slowly these nurses may come when you need them," Shanti smiled.

After some more minutes of chatter and reassuring themselves that indeed Vinod would be fine, they all went to the Kalpana flat. They found a scared Kisan at home; Malika and Rama had told him that his grandfather had gone to the hospital. Kishore and Anjali assured him that his Papa was fine and would be back in just two or three days. Soon Kishore hoisted the little boy to his shoulder, and they went down to the garage and drove home. Meanwhile, Shanti packed a small suitcase and left for her overnight stay at the hospital.

Dev was alone in the big flat. Of course he had been alone before, but this time he felt vulnerable. His father was in the hospital—that had never happened before. Dev sat in the cavernous drawing room and thought, "Papa might have died. He might have died last night." This larger than life figure was powerless in the face of aging and death. And Dev felt diminished because he could not fight off this threat—or any threat—to his father. Tears swelled his throat and he closed his eyes. As he had innumerable times before, Dev vowed he would become the son Vinod would be proud of.

Soon a routine was born: for the next two days, Shanti came home for a bath, a change of clothes and her puja. After instructing Rama on what to cook for Dev and what food to send with the driver to the hospital, she returned to spend day and night with Vinod. And each day and night, Dev was alone resisting the temptation to drink or use drugs. After three days Vinod finally came home with dietary instructions and an admonition to exercise every day. Each evening, Kishore, Anjali and Kisan stayed for dinner; Dev too, unusually, was at the table at his charming best. Rama had the hardest time learning how to cook without fat, oil or ghee. Within a month, everything slipped back to a normal routine.

Dev made a monumental effort to stay away from drugs and alcohol and was clean for a whole week. But by the second week, he was sipping rum and smoking ganja—in moderation. Never, never would he revert to the user he had been. His clashes with Vinod had all but ceased.

Then, after two months of serenely monotonous living, Dev became the epicenter of yet another shock to their world. When Vinod, Shanti, Kishore and Anjali were quietly watching television one night, Dev staggered in.

"Deepak's dead," he could barely utter the words. Deepak had been his best friend through school and college.

"What? What are you saying?"

Shanti closed her eyes, saying "Hari Ram. Ram. Poor Pratiba and Ravi."

Dev sank into a chair, eyes unseeing, blankly staring into space. He clasped his upper arms and rocked.

"What happened? Was it a car accident?" Kishore and Vinod both asked.

"No, no." Dev covered his eyes with his hands, trying to erase the picture in his head. "He overdosed and…" with a swelling sob, "I found him."

"Oh, my God. Oh, Dev, I'm so sorry. How absolutely terrible for you," Anjali went to sit near him and stroke his back.

Vinod was still incredulous. "Just last week I met Ravi at the club, and he said that Deepak was doing well. You know, for a long time Pratiba and Ravi kept his drinking and drugs a secret. They took him to temples for a cure, but that didn't work. Then they finally took him to a psychiatrist who put him in a rehabilitation center."

Kishore nodded and added, "I heard that after he left rehab, he had to attend N.A. two or three times a week."

Shanti asked, "What is this N.A.?"

"Narcotics Anonymous. You meet other addicts and talk about your problems," Kishore explained.

"Why?" Shanti wondered.

"Sshh. I'll explain it to you later," Kishore said.

Anjali was soothing Dev, "It'll be all right. Remember, it's not your fault."

Dev shook his head roughly, clasped his arms again, his drowning eyes large with horror. "Oh God. We were supposed to go clubbing together tonight. I went to pick him up. Pratiba aunty and Ravi uncle were watching T.V. so I…"

Both Vinod and Shanti blanched and looked sick. "You mean they were at home, and they didn't know what was happening? Oh my God!" exclaimed Vinod.

"*Yes*, they were home. I went to say hello to them first, and then went to Deepak's room." He gave a long shuddering sob. "I heard water running in the bathroom, so I yelled at him for always making us late. He didn't answer, so I yelled louder." Dev dug the heels of his hands into his eyes, as if trying to blind himself to what lay ahead. "I turned up the volume on his stereo. You know he hated anyone touching his precious stereo. No reaction from him. I got a bit concerned. Then I opened the door to the bathroom—oh God, oh God!"

Shanti's tears were flowing and Vinod's eyes glistened

Kishore joined Anjali to comfort Dev. They kept murmuring, "It'll be all right."

Dev went on; he couldn't stop. "He was slumped against the toilet, head against the wall, bleeding. He must have fallen down. I shook him by the shoulder saying, 'Deepak, stand up, man. Don't play the fool so much. We're going to be late.'"

"Then I saw a half full bottle of rum on the sink, and next to it, a small square of paper. He'd drunk half a bottle of rum and on top of that, he had snorted some brown sugar. He *knew* how dangerous that was. *Why did he do it?"* he asked, clutching Kishore's hands.

Only silence met that question.

Dev looked at his hands and continued as if he were hypnotized.

"I kept shaking him, getting annoyed. I was actually angry with him. I shook and shook him. He was limp. Oh God. Can you imagine, his body was still warm? If I had gone a little earlier, I might have saved him. I might have saved him! I shouted for Pratiba aunty and Ravi uncle and after they came up and all the *galata* started, I left. Why did he do it? Tell me, *tell me!"*

Finally Vinod said, "*Beta,* before you ask why, you must ask who he was and how he died. Only then may we ask why. We may find an answer or we may find nothing."

"What do you mean?" asked Dev, listening intently.

"Who was this young man?"

"He was my friend," Dev said, shaking his head.

"Yes, but look at his family, *beta.* He was the only son born into a very wealthy family. Did his parents deny him anything? No. Did he work and use his mind after college? No."

"That's true," Kishore agreed; "he was a dilettante."

Dev looked down at his hands as if they were bloody. He rubbed them to wipe off the scent of Deepak.

Vinod gently continued, "Now ask how he died. He died in a bathroom, near the toilet, alone—no family, no friends near him. He did not have the will to stop drinking and taking drugs. He had been given all help by his parents and his friends. Alcohol and drugs became more important to him than his family, his friends—and life itself. So he died with his alcohol and drugs—they had become his family and his friends. Is this not true, Dev?" Vinod shook his head with deep sadness. "Imagine, being so alone, so young, and to die with no one to hold your hand." Vinod sighed under the weight of that infinite loneliness. "When I die, I want to be holding your hand, Shanti."

"Don't talk such nonsense, Vinod." Shanti's tears began afresh.

Dev protested, "But he wanted to give up the alcohol and the drugs…" just like I do, he thought.

"Now, *beta,* now you can ask yourself why he did it. And you must answer that question for yourself. Each one of us in this room probably has a different answer." Vinod imparted his wisdom thoughtfully.

Dev's sobs had calmed down to throat-catching breaths.

"Your friend knew that he had friends and family who loved him. But he was too weak and let his desire for drugs overcome his knowledge. One should always let reason rule desire, *beta.*" Vinod got out of his chair, walked over and laid a hand on Dev's shoulder. "*Chalo,* that's enough lecturing tonight." Slowly, Vinod went to bed.

Shanti came and put her soft hands on Dev's wet cheeks. "This has been a terrible thing for you. It is no comfort to you now, but what happened tonight was Deepak's karma. Try to get some peace from that."

Soon after, Kishore and family left with Anjali saying, "Take care, Dev. We'll call you in the morning. And remember, it was not your fault. Don't blame yourself."

In his room, Dev threw himself on his bed, his pillow muffling his sobs. Again he dug the heels of his hands into his eyes; nothing would ever erase the pictures of Deepak now branded in his brain. Just as he could never block out the sound of Deepak's desperate voice in the telephone call last week, "Dev, I'm in agony. Please, please get me something, anything. Man, I feel like I'm jumping out of my skin. It's never been so bad. You've got to help me, *yaar.*"

Dev had tried to resist. "Come on, man. You're supposed to be clean, *yaar.* I don't want to set you on that path again."

"I thought you were my friend. Fine friend you are, *yaar.* Okay, I'll just have to get it somewhere else. Who knows if it'll be contaminated… well, if it is, it'll be on your head. Goodbye, *friend,*" Deepak had said belligerently.

And Dev had said, "Wait, wait. Don't be like that, man. I'll drive right over…"

Anjali's words, "It was not your fault. Don't blame yourself," twisted like a sharp knife in his heart. His pain, his guilt were unbearable. He had to do something, take something to get through the night. He'd feel better in the morning, stronger. Slowly, he opened the drawer of his nightstand and examined the pills hidden there. Surely two Valium could not harm him; they would help him to blot out all the pictures and voices in his head. Yes, he needed darkness. Tomorrow he would throw out all the drugs. He would be clean. He would be clean. Tomorrow. Tomorrow.

Anjali

S HE WOKE TO THE SOUND of the baby crying. Five-thirty. Kishore groaned beside her and turned over. Anjali sat up, then padded over to the cradle, whispering shushing sounds. She changed the wet diaper while little one's hungry screams intensified. Finally, she settled in the rocking chair, put a pillow on her lap to support Priya, and offered her breast. Priya's voice softened to contented whimpers as she drank. Anjali gazed at the translucent bluish eyelids covering light brown eyes; she played with the tiny fingers and toes—so perfectly formed, the soft nails like miniature nacreous shells. She kissed the damp forehead and inhaled the baby smell. There was nothing like the smell of a newborn's head—indescribable. She was so lucky to have two perfect babies—and one of each sex. Everyone was happy to have a little girl in the family.

Anjali gazed over at the sleeping Kishore—the man she thought she'd never marry. Sushila, her friend at Boston College, had told her about this handsome, brilliant guy from MIT whom she *must* meet— they'd be perfect for each other. Anjali was not interested in any guy from India—they all seemed to be such nerds. But she went to the party to please Sushila. And when they did meet, all Mr. MIT did was sit speechless with his mouth agape. Anjali knew she had been right about him—a nerd—albeit a handsome one.

Anjali had long determined never to get involved with an Indian, certainly never marry one. Her parents' marriage was an example she did not want to follow. Of course, that marriage had been arranged and was a catastrophe. Her father, Ranjit, had trained to be a top diplomat and became a skilful one, moving from the less desirable posts in Africa and South Asia to the plum positions in Europe and finally to the United States. Her mother Subadra was happiest gossiping with her Indian friends and relatives. Her knowledge of world affairs was perfunctory; she was intellectually incapable of grasping the nuances of Ranjit's life and career. Because of their diametrically opposed characters, the tension between Ranjit and Subadra was palpable and permanent.

When they had to attend a function, Ranjit would impatiently coach Subadra on what she could and couldn't say. If she did not pick up ideas swiftly—how could she?—he would berate her for being stupid and impeding his career. For most major events, Ranjit would go alone saying his wife was suffering from some mysterious ailment, much to her relief.

Many a night Anjali cowered in bed, her head under a pillow to block out her father's tirade.

"Why can't you get it through your head? You're a bigger idiot than I thought. I told you this only last week," Ranjit hissed.

"I'm sorry, Ranjit, I'm sorry. Don't be angry please. Anjali will hear you. I'll try and remember next time. Now, tell me please, what you want me to say to the Egyptian ambassador's wife?" Subadra whispered.

"You are so stupid, even a donkey has more brains than you. Why should I tell you? You'll forget by the time we get there. Just say nothing. Just smile. But, for heaven's sake, don't go and sit in a corner with your shoulders hunched and your head down like a broken bird. That's what you did at the Belgian party, and you completely embarrassed me."

"Maybe it's best if I don't come." Subadra now had tears in her voice.

"Unfortunately, you have to. Look, try not to say anything stupid—talk about shopping or some nonsense like that," Ranjit would growl and stomp off.

Anjali feared and despised her father for his oppressive personality and for the way he treated Subadra. He certainly had little time for Anjali, until she entered Boston College. When she came home for occasional weekends, he noticed that she had matured. For the first time, he saw she was beautiful and she could hold her own in society. Abandoning Subadra without a thought, he commanded, "Anjali, from now on you will go with me to the embassy parties."

"But Papa, I don't know anything about politics, I wouldn't know what to say…"

"You'll do much better than your mother, I'm sure."

So, whenever there was an important diplomatic event, he summoned her from Boston to Washington, gave her money to buy new clothes and demanded that she accompany him. After overcoming her shyness and reticence, Anjali enjoyed her new role, especially as no one expected her to be too cognizant of world affairs. Ranjit basked in the glow of Anjali's aura at these events; she was young, beautiful and men and women admired her. But after the party was over and they were driving home, he sat cold and stone-faced, never speaking a word to her. He remained aloof and tyrannical in her eyes.

Subadra also did not win Anjali's love. She was awkward and ill-at-ease in the different countries where they were stationed, each with its own customs. She never helped Anjali with her efforts to fit into schools and societies alien to them both. When Anjali was a young girl in her teens, she gave up all hope of guidance from her mother. She pitied Subadra for the way she was treated, but she wished her mother would show some spine, some guts. Surely she didn't have to cringe like a whipped puppy. The only times Anjali saw her mother happy were when the two of them went to India for summer vacations. Anjali enjoyed meeting her cousins, but she didn't enjoy New Delhi very much; it was miserably hot and humid. Subadra, on the other hand, blossomed with her family and their attention and understanding.

Thus, Anjali brought herself up virtually parentless but with a picture of marriage before her that she knew she wished to avoid. She would never marry an Indian man who would treat his wife abusively and with so little respect. And she would never live in a country where women were subservient to men, the way her mother was to Ranjit.

Anyone who met Anjali saw a confident and lovely young woman. She was the envy of all her friends in high school.

"You've lived in Tashkent and Dubai? Where is that? What was it like?"

"You went to school in Casablanca and Abu Dhabi? Do they speak English there? Was it hard to be in school? Did you have to wear that robe which covers your face?" Her new classmates in America had never heard of some of these cities and showed their ignorance with bubbly questions.

When Anjali was in college, she went to glamorous parties that were written up in magazines and newspapers. She was *so lucky*. Only she knew it was just a façade. Inside, she was a child who had never won praise or love from her parents. Anjali carried her secret shame deep in her heart. She felt she was unlovable when she met Kishore.

Kishore overcame his speechlessness and pursued Anjali relentlessly. He fell hopelessly in love and adored her unconditionally. She resisted, but finally succumbed to his passion. He told her stories of his childhood and his ideal family. She wanted desperately to believe that such a family could exist, but secretly felt he was exaggerating because he was homesick. He insisted that he wanted to return to India when he had his degree.

"It's the best place to live and raise a family. You should see our flat—the drawing room has a huge window from which you can look out at the sea. I want you to meet my parents—I know they would love you," he said. But she did not take him seriously. She was sure he would get a job offer in the States and be happy to take it. Why would anyone want to go and live in India where it was so chaotic, so hot, so volatile?

When Kishore asked her to marry him, she was stunned. Not by his proposal, but by her profound desire and need to say yes. She wanted to live the rest of her life having him love her, having him believe she was worth loving. And, to her further surprise, she discovered that the emotions that fluttered inside her when she thought of him, saw him or was with him showed her that she loved him. All her life she had defended herself against loving anyone and being hurt. She knew Kishore would never hurt her.

Anjali told Kishore, "I'm a bit afraid to tell my parents about our engagement. I don't know how my father will react."

Kishore was surprised, "Surely, they won't object to me, darling, you think? But, if you're nervous about it, let's tell them together. Okay?" And so they did.

Ranjit was hearty with his congratulations and questions about Kishore's future plans. Subadra smiled and smiled, but Anjali could see her dithering inwardly as she wondered how she could manage the wedding. Kishore finally broached the sticky subject of where the wedding should be.

"Sir, would you grant permission to have the wedding in Mumbai?"

Panic reached Subadra's eyes. Ranjit raised his brows, "Well now, I can't—and Subadra too, of course,—we can't take much time to go to India to make all the arrangements." Kishore then haltingly offered, "Sir, my parents will make all the arrangements at the best hotel in Mumbai. They are familiar with the place and know people."

The relief in the room was swift and visceral. Ranjit blustered, "That would be a huge favor, especially since we don't know Mumbai too well. We have lived the lives of gypsies, my boy, never settling long enough in any place to call it home. We are unfamiliar with Mumbai, so your parents doing this will be a huge burden off our shoulders. Please thank them for me, for us, my boy. Also please tell them that, of course, I will pay for the entire cost of my daughter's wedding." And so it was settled, and Anjali was spared her parents' involvement.

Kishore's parents made the arrangements, phoning and consulting Anjali at every turn. She was delighted by the traditions (which she didn't know), the glorious colors (which she didn't expect) and the fun it turned out to be. The room in the Taj Mahal Hotel twinkled with lights. Anjali was resplendent in a gold embroidered red sari with the traditional ruby necklace coming down her center part ending in the diamond and ruby pendant on her forehead. The sari and jewelry were presents from Shanti and Vinod.

Kishore, wearing a high-collared cream sherwani, rode in on a white horse. The Taj provided an exquisite buffet that mixed western and Indian fare for the five hundred guests. Anjali had never been so happy. Even her parents seemed relaxed. After all, they had done nothing except pay for the wedding. Their gift to the young couple also bespoke their lack of imagination—at the reception, they gave Kishore a large check. Anjali did not let her parents ruin her memory of that perfect day—how many of her friends in the U.S. had had such a stress-free wedding?

Just as Priya was finishing her feed, Kisan burst into the room. "Can I hold her? Can I hold her, please?" he yelled waking up Kishore. Shanti followed him in saying, "I tried to keep him in his room, but he wanted to see his sister. How is the little pet this morning?"

Anjali settled Kisan on the rocker and gently placed Priya on his lap. Looking at the way he gazed at her, no one would believe he had wanted a brother so badly. When Priya was born, he had just learned the Christmas story in school about how the Virgin Mary laid her babe in the manger. So when Kishore brought him to visit Anjali and Priya in the hospital, he had sidled up to his mother and whispered, "Mummy, will you lay a little brother for me now?" Of course, this story was now part of Kisan's history. He laughed uproariously whenever it was retold, though he didn't know why it was so funny.

Everything was so much easier with Priya's birth. When Kisan had been born, Subadra had come to help and had proved to be more nervous and inept than the new mother. She was clumsy and awkward, and it was a relief to all when she left after a month.

Anjali felt alone and abandoned then engulfed in a sadness which Kishore secretly thought was post-partum depression. And perhaps it was. He appealed to his mother for help and cajoled Anjali to welcome

50

that help. Anjali was resistant—why would Kishore's mother be any different than her own? She put Kishore off, saying "Yes, yes I'll call her tomorrow." Inwardly, she was terrified that Shanti would wrest Kisan's love from her. And she wanted to be first in Kisan's life. She was also afraid to spend much time with her mother-in-law; what if Shanti saw that Anajli was unworthy of Kishore? However, soon the mothering chores overwhelmed Anjali, and she called Shanti, saying, "Amma, can you come tomorrow to show me the oil bath?" But Anjali had her defenses built up strongly against hurt.

Shanti came to help Anjali with Kisan every other day, gently guiding her on how to rock the baby with soft soothing songs, "Here, Anjali, learn this song. It helps the baby sleep. And rock the baby on your lap while you sing it, like this," she would demonstrate.

And when Anjali heard the lovely melody which Kishore had hummed to her one night, she began to melt. She learned the oil bath routine and saw how Kisan loved it. One day when Kisan was about six months old, after his bath, they had swaddled him in a large towel, laid him on the bed gurgling with delight. Anjali looked at Shanti to share a pleased smile.

"Look at him. How much he loves his bath. Just like Kishore," Shanti said proudly, looking back at her.

The love Anjali saw brimming in Shanti's eyes both for Kisan and herself made her breath catch. Anjali's defenses crumbled and from that time, Shanti became the mother she'd never had. And it became easier for Shanti to teach her songs and rituals from Kishore's childhood, to help Anjali revel in the joy of motherhood rather than the weariness. Thus by keeping her busy, Shanti delicately drew her out of her post-partum depression.

Even though Anjali consulted Shanti about everything to do with Kisan, never could she speak about her loveless childhood and her fear of being unlovable. And despite the warmth that developed between them, Anjali continued to subtly work on her campaign to have Kishore transfer to the States. When Kisan had been about a year old, she'd succeeded, and they moved to Santa Clara. Anjali was at first dismayed by the void left by Shanti's absence, but she soon adjusted and made friends. After four years, when Anjali was expecting again, Kishore transferred back to Mumbai.

Early in Anjali's second pregnancy, Subadra had called, "I am sorry, Anju. I can't come for your confinement. My arthritis has become so bad, and my legs and hands are paining so much, I wouldn't be any help to you." Anjali felt twin emotions of pain and relief—and then insecurity. How would she manage on her own? She couldn't even tell Kishore her fears. She didn't have to. When Shanti heard that Subadra wasn't coming, she insisted that Anjali and Kishore move in to the Kalpana flat before the birth and stay until Anjali felt strong enough to go home. They could bring Lakshmi, the old ayah, to look after Kisan and the new baby. And, of course, Rama and Malika would be so happy to have the little ones there. Rama and Kisan had over the years formed a special bond, and Rama shamelessly spoiled the boy with specially cooked treats.

"We have two extra bedrooms lying empty. One would be for you and Kishore and one for Kisan. It would give us so much pleasure to have you both, Kisan and the baby with us," Shanti said. "You can get some rest. When you are ready, you can go home."

Anjali began to appreciate the Indian customs where a young mother always had her mother (or, in Anjali's case, her mother-in-law) to help her through the first few months after childbirth. Her friends in America got occasional baby sitting if their family were in the same city; if not, they hired help. Her friends with new babies, while elated with the infant, were tired and often depressed with the overwhelming tasks of motherhood. At Kalpana, she didn't even have to feel guilty about leaving the children with her mother-in-law; after all, Lakshmi and Malika were always there. No one was burdened, overworked or tired of babies with all these extra pairs of loving arms. Here in Mumbai, Anjali had time to take naps, have massages three times a week, go out occasionally without a "nanny cam" set up in her flat..

As the days slipped into weeks, she appreciated the care and attention she was getting from Shanti and Vinod. Shanti invited all her friends as usual to lunch and tea, but mostly to admire her little granddaughter. Anjali thought she would be annoyed by the constant barrage of visitors, but when all they did was praise her little baby, how could she resist? Anjali began to know Shanti's friends. They were a wonderful tight circle of intelligent women who'd known each other for decades. They gathered for bridge or rummy, for book club meetings, for just socializing at least once a week. More and more, she joined them in their card games and enjoyed their raucous humor. And Anjali saw for the first time the web that formed this stratum of Mumbai.

Kishore was now at the crux of his career and working late hours more and more often. If she had been living alone in her own home, she'd have been excruciatingly lonely. Imagine, if she had been in an apartment in Santa Clara, she'd have gone crazy with no adult conversation daily. True, she would have been more independent in California, but where could she have gone without worrying about baby sitters? Kishore was right—Mumbai was a good place to raise children, and strong family support was critical. Clearly, Kisan was doing wonderfully with his many friends at school, and she had no doubt that Priya would do equally well.

Kishore's working hours—the only thorn in this otherwise happy life. When Kishore came home at night, he had barely enough time to look in on Kisan and Priya before saying, "God, I am so exhausted," and falling into bed. They hardly made love any more—and he didn't even seem to miss it or mention it. So, surrounded by people, Anjali felt lonely.

When Priya was about four months old and her feeding schedule became reasonable, Anjali began to go more often to the Willingdon or Gymkhana club or to restaurants for lunch with her friends. Shanti encouraged her to leave the baby and enjoy herself. However, the evenings were still deadly dull. Shanti and Vinod and she had dinner together every night, chatted about the day's events, watched some television and went to bed. Occasionally, in the evenings, Shanti and Vinod's friends would drop in, but while she enjoyed playing cards with them, Anjali found just talking politics or sports or cooking very boring. One evening when Kishore actually came home early, Anjali complained about his late hours.

"Really, Kish, I hardly see you any more. If I didn't have your parents for company, I'd go crazy. And don't tell me to go to the club. I do go to meet the girls during the day, but I can't go by myself in the evenings."

"Anju, I'll try. But I'm telling you that this is the busiest time at the office, it's crazy. I have to be there, it means a lot to my career."

"Being with me means a lot to our marriage. And what about Kisan? Shouldn't he know his father?"

"Anju, I know, I know. Don't you think I miss seeing you and Kisan and Priya? They are both growing up so fast—and I am missing it all. God, I don't know what to do—look, I don't think these crazy hours will go on much longer. What the hell? *Achcha*, come to the Willngdon tomorrow at nine, and we'll have dinner. How's that?" said Kishore.

"Oh, that'll be great, Kish," she smiled, already planning what she could wear.

The next night, she dressed with care in a shimmering turquoise salwar kameez and wore her sapphire earrings and necklace. She hadn't been to the Willingdon at night in ages. So many people were there—strangers to her. She sat on the terrace and ordered a fresh lime and soda, feeling awkward without a companion. Not for long.

A voice called, "Anjali, is that you? Why are you by yourself?" Rustum Maneckwalla, one of Kishore's oldest friends, was walking toward her. Rustum was Parsee, a sect that comprised the most progressive and westernized of Indians. Originally from Persia, they worshipped Zoroaster, and had their own customs. All this Anjali learned after living in India. Rustum, like Kishore, had also grown up in Mumbai, where the largest population of Parsees lived. Like Kishore, he had won a scholarship to study at the University of Pennsylvania, but he'd turned it down. He was an only child, and he chose to stay home to care for his elderly mother. Rustum was brilliant, a very witty raconteur. However, he was short, already balding and wore thick glasses. He had no success with young Parsee women, or any women. Anjali liked him enormously.

She turned to him with relief. "Hello, Rustum. Kishore is coming to meet me for dinner."

Just then her cell phone rang. It was Kishore—he was tied up, couldn't get away, so sorry, so terribly sorry. To hide her hurt, she said with a lilt in her voice, "That's okay, Kish. Guess what? I have Rustum here for company; we'll have a fine time." Was she trying to make Kishore jealous? What got into her? And to use Rustum so shamelessly.

She turned to Rustum with an apologetic smile. Oh, God. Maybe he was meeting someone else. She'd just assumed that he'd be alone.

"Kishore is tied up. He can't make it for dinner," she said, as she snapped her cell phone shut violently. She turned and saw a look of pure happiness on Rustum's face. "Well," he said, "you'll just have to put up with me." She relaxed—he wasn't upset, and soon her anger with Kishore also dissipated.

She was amazed how easy it was to talk to Rustum. She had never been alone with him before. Even though some people at the club looked at them askance, Anjali didn't notice or care—certainly Kishore had seemed relieved that Anjali had some company. About nine-thirty, just when she thought about going home, Rustum asked, "Anjali, have you ever eaten at Indigo? It's the new trendy place in town. It's a little distance from here in Colaba, right near that Cotton World shop, which I'm sure you know. I hear the food is great and the place has a nice ambience. Would you like to try it?"

Anjali hesitated. Go out alone with Rustum? The other option was to go home and have dinner yet again with Shanti and Vinod. But she was all dressed up—she deserved an evening out. This was, after all, Kishore's fault.

"Why not? Yes, sure," she said softly and smiled at Rustum.

As they left the club and waited outside for her car, Rustum said, "Why don't you send your car back to Kalpana? I'll take you home after dinner." It seemed like a good idea to Anjali. After dismissing Ibrahim, her driver, they drove to Indigo, and Anjali was enchanted to find it was an old house that had been converted to a restaurant—the bar was in the living room furnished with comfortable sofas, the dining room had originally been three bedrooms. Upstairs were more dining rooms—all packed with people talking and laughing. Fortunately, they did not have to wait long to be seated.

As always happened in Mumbai, friends stopped by their table.

"Hello, Anjali. How is little Priya? Where is Kishore? Nice to see you out and about again." Anjali relaxed as they enjoyed a wonderful meal. She knew that Rustum was a professor at Mumbai University, so she asked him about his work. As she had learned from her diplomat days, always ask a man questions about his field of interest.

"Do you know, you are the first woman who has asked me what I do, Anjali? Here, so often, people are identified by their family, whom they are related to. In America, they are identified by their jobs, nai? Isn't that a curious thing? Well, anyway, to answer your question, I teach biophysics at the university. I've been fortunate to have some articles published and have been invited to present them in different cities, so I traveled quite a bit after my mother died. Rio de Janeiro is my favorite city. It is really beautiful, especially at night. I know you've been all around the world too, Anjali. What's your favorite city?" he asked. And they chatted easily, comparing their travel adventures.

After he'd had a couple of whiskies, he confided to her about the lack of romance in his life.

Anjali reassured him, "I'm sure the right girl will come along, Rustum. You are a wonderful guy; any girl would be lucky to have you."

He shook his head dolefully. "Look at me, Anjali. I'm short, bald and overweight. No woman wants to be seen with me. They judge me by my appearance, never give me a second chance. Kishore is so lucky to have found you. You are not only beautiful, you are smart.

I wish I could find someone like you that I could sit and talk to. You are really wonderful."

Anjali became uncomfortable, so she looked at her watch—eleven-thirty. Where had the time gone?

"Heavens, it's so late. I must go home. Shall we leave, Rustum?" she asked.

He drove her to Kalpana, both agreeing they'd had a lovely evening. Of course, everyone was asleep when Anjali came in. She crept to her room and crawled in beside the sleeping Kishore. Why was she feeling these twinges of guilt? She had enjoyed being with Rustum—what she had enjoyed more was his unabashed happiness in being with her. Feeling Kishore's increasing absence, she had relished Rustum's obvious pleasure.

As she lay in bed next to the sleeping Kishore, she thought, "I could so easily make Rustum fall in love with me." Oh, God. Where had that come from? No, she didn't want that. She loved Kishore, she loved Kishore. But, she had enjoyed the blatant adoration that she had seen in Rustum's eyes. How long had it been since Kishore had looked at her like that? She wished that Kishore would at least half-wake up and put his arms around her. She wondered what it would like to kiss Rustum. Oh God, No! Why was she thinking this way? She didn't want to hurt Kishore or his friend.

The next morning, after the baby's early morning feed, she gave Priya to Lakshmi and went back to sleep. She missed the ringing of several phone calls. When she appeared for breakfast, she sensed an uneasiness from Shanti.

She asked, "Is something wrong, Amma?"

Shanti answered, "No, *beti*. I'm sure it's nothing. But tell me about last night. We were fast asleep when you got home."

Buttering her toast, Anjali told Shanti about reaching the club, getting Kishore's phone call and Rustum saving her.

"Really, Amma, if Rustum hadn't showed up, I'd have been home by nine-fifteen. It's no fun sitting alone at the club. Anyway, then Rustum suggested we go to this new restaurant called Indigo for dinner—have you been there? It's near Cotton World? We met some of Kishore's friends who were probably scandalized to see me with Rustum. I must have got home about eleven-thirty or so. I hope Priya didn't give you any trouble?"

Shanti's face began to clear with each of Anjali's sentences. She smiled, "No, no, the little devi woke up for a small snack about ten and then slept again. *Beti,* I know Kishore's long hours are hard for you. Every woman goes through that time when her husband is just reaching success. I suffered the same thing with Vinod. I stayed at home with the children and counted the minutes in the evenings."

"What did you do, Amma?"

"I relied on Vinod's parents for company. Even now, women don't go out on their own at night. And Anjali, I should warn you that though Mumbai has millions of people, it's a small town where people of our level of society know everyone and they talk."

"What do you mean?" Anjali asked, puzzled.

"You haven't lived in India for very long, so you don't know the malice and pettiness that feeds the gossip. Do you know this morning I got five phone calls from people who mentioned that they saw you with Rustum last night? I knew you were planning to meet Kishore at the Willingdon—I didn't know what to say. I just said, Rustum was Kishore's good friend and had probably joined you both for dinner."

"Oh, my God. I can't believe they would call you and report me. They're probably calling Kishore too. I should phone him right now and tell him about Indigo. He knew I was with Rustum at the club and was glad I had company because he couldn't come." Anjali got up from the table, her stomach churning with guilt. Why did she feel guilty? She had done nothing.

Shanti was saying, "In India, *beti,* you must be very careful of your name and reputation. It can be ruined with just a few vicious rumors and poisonous gossip. I don't know how different it is in America, but here women especially are noticed."

Now Anjali's guilt began to blend with resentment. What the hell! She had gone out to dinner with her husband's good friend when her husband had stood her up. Did she have to type an explanation and nail it to her chest?

She reached for the phone to call Kishore when it rang.

"Hello, Anjali? This is Rustum. I just wanted to tell you again what a marvelous time I had last night. You are a wonderful person to be with. Really, I never had such a good time talking to anyone. Listen, I can get tickets to a new play called "Fire and Rain." It's going to be playing at the National Center at Nariman Point next month. I was wondering if you'd like to see it."

Anjali's throat closed up. What was this? She didn't need it now. Was Rustum becoming infatuated with her—the only woman to notice him and spend some time with him? She managed to say, "Thank you. Let me talk to Kishore and I'll call you back. Bye." Shit. She didn't mean to be so rude. Shit, shit, shit. Now she had hurt him.

Shanti asked, "Who was that?"

Anjali turned her flaming face away. She cast her eyes down in shame. She whispered, "That was Rustum." Why didn't she lie and say it was a wrong number?

Shanti looked stricken as she murmured, "Oh." Then she turned and went to the drawing room to sit in her special chair from which she could gaze at the Arabian Sea. She knew that a difficult period was coming to the family. She knew that her friends, the same friends who played cards with her, would be whispering half-truths and spreading rumors. She wondered how long it would be before she would have to distance herself from them.

Anjali heard Priya crying and rushed in to her. She couldn't face Shanti. Why, why, why had Rustum called her? As she nursed her baby, she felt flattered and angry at the same time. Rustum had lavished her with attention, and after the current aridity between Kishore and herself, she relished being the center of someone's thoughts. After Priya finished, Anjali called Kishore.

"Hi, Kish. This morning you left before I was even up. I wanted to tell you about last night. I went to Indigo with Rustum; it is such a lovely place. We must go there some…"

"Yes, yes, I already heard about you and Rusi at Indigo. Listen, I can't talk now—I'm late for a meeting. I'll call you if I can, or I'll see you tonight."

"Kish, Rustum called and asked…"

"Sorry, got to go." And he hung up.

Anjali stood with the dead phone in her hand. He'd never hung up on her before. No one had hung up on her—ever. And she felt the resentment rise thick in her and fill her mind with red, deepening red. He couldn't even spare a minute to talk to the wife he hadn't seen in more than twenty-four hours. He wasn't even curious about how she and Rustum came to be at Indigo. Damn him. To calm down, she thought about Rustum and the "you can do no wrong" admiration oozing from him. This was the elixir she needed. She picked up the phone and dialed Rustum. She would ask him to get three tickets to "Fire and Rain" and hope that Kishore could go, or else she would go alone with Rustum.

"Hello, Rustum. I'm sorry I couldn't talk earlier, but the baby was crying. Anyway, why don't you get three tickets to the show, and Kishore and I will go with you. It will be fun."

"Oh, Anjali, that will be wonderful. I'll call and let you know the date, and I'll make it a Saturday when Kishore is not working. Again, I have to tell you how much I enjoyed being with you. Kishore doesn't know how lucky he is."

"You mustn't say such things. I had a good time with you too. Phone me when you get the tickets." And she hung up in a much better mood.

At dinner that night—without Kishore, of course—Vinod remarked that his friends had mentioned seeing Anjali either at the club or at Indigo. So, she thought, I will hear about Vinod's friends' opinions of me as well. But Vinod seemed more interested in the new restaurant and asked, "So, how is this Indigo that everyone is talking about?"

Anjali murmured, "The food was excellent, and it's a charming place." Again, for no reason, she felt her cheeks flush. Guilt without sin. When she stole a look at Shanti, she saw worry written across her face.

When Kishore finally came home that night, Anjali had worked through her feelings and forgotten her resentment. She kept him company at dinner and told him all about the club and Indigo. Kishore seemed unconcerned. He was delighted that Anjali had had a good evening out. "Rusi's a fine chap. People are put off by his looks, but he's smart, funny and a good friend. I'm glad you ran into him, and he took you to Indigo. I wish I'd been there." Not a breath of jealousy, nor did he refer to the people who'd told him at work about seeing Anjali and Rusi together.

"Rustum wants us to go to a play called "Fire and Rain" with him in about three weeks. Will that be all right with you? You can make it on a Saturday, no?"

"I think that this bloody schedule will have eased off by then. Tell him sure. Even if I can't go, you should, Anjali."

"Kish, Amma warned me about people talking, gossiping. Do you know this morning she already had five phone calls about me being at the club and Indigo with Rustum and without you?"

"These people have too much bloody time on their hands. What nonsense. It's not as if you are doing it behind my back—and Rusi's my best friend. He'd never try to steal you from me. If he did, would you let yourself be stolen, huh?"

"What rubbish you speak, Kish. Of course not." She couldn't tell him that Rusi seemed to be infatuated with her. Nor could she tell him how much she had enjoyed the admiring light in Rusi's eyes, a light missing in Kishore's.

The calls coming to Shanti dwindled, and so did the card parties and lunches. After a couple of weeks with no social events, Anjali asked Shanti about the next rummy game at Kalpana. Shanti said she was getting tired of the ladies and their chatter and would much rather spend time with her grandchildren. Anjali never suspected that Shanti was deliberately withdrawing from her friends because she was really tired of the gossip that was swirling around Anjali.

Rustum phoned often, just to say hello, and Anjali gave him her mobile number so that his calls would not disturb Shanti. Really, if she was honest with herself, it was so Shanti would not know how often Rusi did call.

The day for the theater came, and everything was fine until Kishore got a desperate call at 3:00 needing him in the office for an emergency. Kishore swore he would be at the theater by 8:00, and he called Rustum to ask him to pick up Anjali.

Anjali again dressed with care in an emerald green silk sari and her rubies. When Shanti saw her, she smiled approvingly, "You look so lovely. Now have a good time. And don't worry about the babies."

It was just before curtain call that Kishore phoned Anjali to say he'd try to get there by the intermission. At 9:00, he called again to ask Rusi where they should meet for dinner. After the show, when Rustum and Anjali went to China Garden as agreed, he wasn't there but phoned to say he was so exhausted he was going home to bed. Anjali was furious, but smiled through gritted teeth. Rustum glowed because once more fortuitously he was alone with Anjali.

The religious symbolism of the play had eluded Anjali. Although Rustum was a Parsee, he was very familiar with Hindu scriptures and explained the deeper meaning of "Fire and Rain." Their Chinese dinner was wonderful, thanks to Rusi's careful ordering. They had garlic fried pomfret, chili chicken, fried rice and crispy fried spinach. Rusi was obviously a gourmet as well—but not too careful about watching the fat. When he dropped her off at about midnight, he took her hand and raised it to his lips. Anjali flushed with the thought, "Oh, my God. The watchman must be looking. Now all the servants will be in on the gossip."

Gossip, gossip, gossip. It spread its tentacles, reaching into corners gathering and swelling with venom. A big city with fifteen million—but Anjali couldn't get lost in it. Her every move was in the spotlight, it seemed. What did it matter to anyone that, once again, it was Kishore's fault that she was out with his friend? Did anyone know or care that Kishore stood her up for the second time? The insidious spread of rumors was nothing she could defend herself against.

Once again, Shanti heard the whispering among the servants about The Kiss. Yes, Rustum sahib had kissed her hand, just like in the American cinemas. And from the servants, through their friends, it spread into the houses on Malabar Hill and beyond.

Shanti bore the brunt of the friendly attack. Ladies from her card playing group, her lunch group and book club group felt the urgent need to warn her and her daughter-in-law that people were talking. This was not America where men and women kissed publicly and casually. The funny thing about gossip was that no one really wanted to hear or believe the truth. So, Shanti tried to explain Kishore's busyness, his plan on being with Anjali and Rustum at the play and dinner knowing full well that her explanation would somehow be twisted. The well-meaning callers always advised her to tell Anjali "be careful. A girl's reputation, you know…I know Anjali, but she has lived in America for so long, she doesn't understand…"And those same well meaning callers probably phoned each other to dissect Shanti's explanation and conclude, "You know, I think that marriage is in trouble. I'm telling you, Shanti can try to hide it, but really…And the new baby is only a few months old. What a shame. Poor Shanti. Do you think it'll lead to divorce? Poor Shanti and Vinod. One son a drug addict and now this. Tsk, tsk, tsk."

Anjali felt the tension in the flat. Although Shanti continued her loving care of the children, Anjali sensed a faint tinge of disapproval toward her. How could she not? She knew that Kishore had told Shanti the whole story—about the dinner, the show, everything. But could she blame Shanti for wanting no hint of scandal to touch their family? And Anjali again felt the guilt rise in her. Poor Shanti, she suffered enough with Dev and his ignominious career. Now Anjali was bringing shame to the family. It was hard to believe that a stupid misunderstanding could lead to dishonor.

Now with Shanti withdrawing more and more from her friends, Anjali and she were left alone for long hours in the flat. Their carefully built up camaraderie began to slowly unravel. Anjali felt she was the wedge between Shanti and her friends. She became hypersensitive to any inflections in Shanti's voice and more and more uncomfortable in Kalpana.

Anjali began to persuade Kishore that they should move back into their own flat. They had been at Kalpana for almost five months. Their flat was closer to Kishore's office. Their own servants needed to be put back to full time work. Shiva was basically keeping up the flat, and they had given the new maid Shamala these months to go visit her family. Who knew if she would return? They still had Lakshmi of course; she would be happy to stay with Kisan and Priya and she was familiar with the flat.

Shanti and Vinod protested, "Aren't you comfortable here? We will miss the chatter of Kisan and little Priya."

Anjali suggested, "Kisan can come here from school, since it's so close. He can play with his friends, do his homework and be sent home for dinner. And, of course, Amma, you and Papa must come daily to see Priya, or I will bring Priya here."

Before they left, Shanti again warned Anjali about the toxicity of gossip and how it could hurt or ruin a person. Anjali's eyes filled, "Amma, you know both times I was alone with Rustum, it was because Kishore cancelled at the last minute. What could I do? I hear you explaining on the phone and I see what this is doing to you. I feel as if I am coming between you and your friends. I feel so guilty although I have done nothing."

Shanti kissed Anjali on the forehead, blessed her and sent her to live in her own flat with the words, "I know, *beti*. I will miss you all very much."

Anjali settled down quickly into a routine in her flat. Shiva was happy to be cooking again. Shamala returned swiftly as well; apparently her family had not welcomed her considering her an expensive burden.

She gladly settled into the routine of cleaning, washing and all the other chores. Lakshmi was happy to be back where she did not have to be subservient to the long-serving Rama and Malika. Anjali was again living the carefree life of a young, upper middle class woman in an Indian city.

She went on shopping trips and to restaurants. She went to openings of art shows and plays. When Yanni, the tempestuous Greek musician, came to town, she got one of the first tickets. Though she couldn't quite understand it, she was swept along with the excitement when Zubin Mehta, one of Mumbai's own, visited as a guest conductor for a week. So she quickly filled her social life, and Kishore came when he could. If not, she called some of her friends and went with them. She talked often to Rustum, but never went out with him alone.

One time when she was having lunch with Sonali at the Willlingdon, Anjali went to the ladies' room. When she was in the toilet, two women, strangers, came in giggling.

"I hear she has been seen with him, three or four times alone. What can she see in him? He's so short and fat…"

"And she has the handsomest man in Mumbai in her bed each night. How can she even look at that Rustum when she can be doing it with Kishore every night?" More tittering.

"Really, you are so naughty."

"She spent so much time in America, she thinks she can be loose with her morals. Someone should tell her it's not like that in India. Anyway, do you think they'll end up with a divorce?"

"Don't be so hopeful, I say. You think he'll bother to look at you or me?" The voices faded.

Anjali slowly emerged pale and shaken. Everyone *was still talking* about her, and it had been months since the Fire and Rain episode. They thought she was ready for divorce. What could she do? She had no defenses; this was worse than she imagined. No wonder Shanti looked worried—she, Anjali, was dragging Kishore's name through the mud. Doing nothing. She was so ashamed she couldn't bring herself to speak of the incident to anyone, not even Kishore. She just stopped going to the club. She had her friends and Shanti over more often.

Kishore's hours eased and he was home in the evenings. It was on one such evening that Rustum dropped in. After they had had some drinks and snacks, it was time for dinner.

"Hey, man. Why don't you stay and have dinner with us, if you don't have other plans?" Kishore said heartily. Of course, Rusi had no plans.

Soon he was visiting two or three times a week and staying for dinner. One night after he left, Kishore remarked, "Poor Rusi. It's no fun being alone in the evenings. His mother died, oh, about six years ago, I think. He spent his time looking after her and now he has no family in town, and not too many friends. I can understand why he comes here. I think we have become his family."

One evening Rustum appeared on a day that Kishore was working late. Anjali naturally invited him for dinner, not thinking that the servants' eyes were watching her. It was Ibrahim, Anjali's driver, who self-importantly carried the word to Rama and Malika at Kalpana about Anjali and Rustum having dinner without Kishore. By now all the servants knew that Rustum had been out alone with Anjali twice, and had kissed her hand when he brought her home. They knew that once Kishore and family moved back to their own flat, Rustum had been a frequent guest for dinner with them. Last night was the first time he had dinner alone with Anjali—it was news to be discussed, dissected and decried.

The servants had their own underground; gossip about the families they worked for was their sustenance. The loyal Malika told Shanti. Again, Anjali was unaware that she had done anything worthy of disapproval.

When Kishore came home early that night, he was grim. Anjali feared that things had gone awry at his work. Before she could ask, he said, "I got a call at the office today from Amma. She was very distressed because she heard that Rusi comes over often and stays for dinner, sometimes alone with you."

"Why does that upset her? Oh God, not that Rusi thing again. Really, don't people have something better to do? Look, didn't you yourself say that he is lonely with no family and he sees our family as his own—didn't you? When he came over yesterday, and even though you weren't home, naturally I invited him for dinner. What's the problem?"

"Anju, you have to be a little more circumspect. People are talking, and your reputation and the family's name is being tarnished…"

"I don't believe this. I was out alone with him because *you* cancelled both times, and I invited him for dinner because *you* suggested he was lonely and needed company. What should I do, Kish? You tell me what the hell I should do."

"Anju, I've seen the way he looks at you. I think he is falling in love with you. But he is my best friend, and I'm sure he wouldn't betray me." His voice seemed to echo as she heard his last sentence reverberate in her ears. She felt her hand itch and rise. God, she would love to smack that self-righteous smirk off his face. She willed her hand back to her side.

"*What?* What are you saying? God, you are so dense sometimes. I could just smack you. Do you even know what you just said to me—he is your best friend and wouldn't betray yo? Do you mean that *I might*? Is that what you are saying, Kish? Is it? Is that what you think of me?"

"No, no. I never meant that…"

"Tell me what you meant, Kish, tell me what the bloody hell you meant." She was so angry, but she didn't want to cry. She swallowed back her tears and her voice rose. "Tell me what you want me to do, to keep the family honor untainted." She couldn't hold back her sobs. "Why don't *you* tell your friend not to show up here any more, even though you trust him so much. Would you like to do that? Why don't you tell all the fine folks at the Willingdon to mind their own fucking business. I haven't *done anything* for God's sake. I feel like that woman in that stupid book I read in high school. *The Scarlet Letter,* that was it. Should I wear a red A on my chest, Kish? Maybe I should have an affair; may as well enjoy it since everyone thinks I'm already…"

Kishore came over and gripped her wrist tightly.

"Anju, calm down. The servants…"

She wrenched her wrist away and began rubbing it. "Why do you care about the servants, huh? How about *me?* You care about everyone else, how things look—how about caring about me? Calm down, hell. I don't give a shit about the servants. I am being accused by my husband, my in-laws, the Willingdon Club, all of Mumbai of having an affair with Rustum Maneckwalla. You know what, Kish, I thought you would never hurt me, but my God…this is too much. I …" She couldn't finish the sentence for her sobs.

"Shh. Shh. Anju, darling, I don't think you are having an affair, nor does Amma. We just want to protect you from the vicious gossip that could make you miserable. Come, sweetheart. Let me hold you. It'll be all right, I promise."

He went and put his arms around her. She stiffened and remained rigid, arms against his chest, fists clenched. She had never ever felt so alone.

Kishore

KISHORE LAY STIFFLY IN BED, wide awake. He stole a glance at Anjali—she hadn't moved. She lay still in a tightly curled fetal position, facing away from him. God, how had this happened? They were in a fight over—what? He didn't even know. Shit. He squirmed as he thought of the wounded look in her eyes as she accused him, "I thought you would never hurt me…"

How could he have been such an idiot? He heard his own voice resonate in his head, "He is my best friend, and I know he would never betray me." He didn't for a moment intend to imply that Anjali might. Bloody hell! How could she even think such a thing? On the other hand, she was the target of all the innuendo and gossip. No wonder she felt under attack from him too. He turned on his side and gently tried to mold his body to hers, spooning her. She lay motionless, unresponsive.

Kishore planned his strategy while he showered, cursing as again the shower had no pressure and the water drizzled out. He dried himself and dressed for work, stepping into his blue pants and tucking in his starched white shirt. As he brushed his dark hair, he leaned forward and stared into the mirror. Damn. Some grey hairs were sprouting near his temples. He appraised himself: would this silvering make him look distinguished or old? He wished he had a thick black mane like Dev's.

Then he could cover the grey. In these few minutes, the humidity plastered the shirt to his back, wet patches rapidly spreading. Another sticky day in Mumbai—was there any other kind?

Sometimes he wished he were still back in Santa Clara where everyone dressed casually in collared tee shirts. In Mumbai, businessmen still followed the stiff-upper-lip British formality and wore suits to work. Never mind that suits were totally inappropriate for the weather, besides being uncomfortable. How much better it would be to work in a loose cotton kurta. Ah well, he thought as he tightened the knot in his silk tie, he had more important things to think of right now.

He would send Anjali a huge bouquet of flowers—that should appease her. He looked over and saw that the bed was empty; Anjali was already up, uncharacteristically early. His heart caught when he gazed at the indentation left by her body on the sheets. How could he convince her that he would do anything to take back what he said?

He lingered over breakfast hoping for a truce. Anjali sat like a robot, her face a mask. Finally, Kishore said, "Anju, we must talk. Look, I'm sorry about what I said last night. I didn't mean what you thought I did. I trust you totally. Look, sweetheart, we cannot let all this gossip tear us apart. That's what gossip can do. If we even hint at coldness between us, these people will have us in divorce court in no time…"

Anjali looked up and whispered, "I've already heard that in the ladies' room at the club. Two bitches were snickering about who would snare you next and get you in bed. Can you imagine—they thought I'd give you up for Rustum." Suddenly, the absurdity of the situation struck her and she started laughing. Startled, Kishore joined in, muttering, "What nonsense these people talk, isn't it?" happy to have his Anjali back.

Hooking his jacket with his forefinger casually over his shoulder, he kissed her on his way out saying, "Why don't we have dinner at the Willingdon tonight? Let's show a strong united front and break down their forces."

She looked at him quizzically, "Are you sure you won't cancel on me? What if Rustum shows up here in the evening?"

"Bring him along. The three of us together should shut them up, no?" he said.

In the car being driven to work, he thanked God that he and Anjali had come through this reasonably easily. Even so, he would send the flowers. She must be reassured about his devotion. Poor innocent Anjali, caught in a web spun by idle people's idle minds. How different it was for men. Was anyone whispering about Rusi? Of course not. They were probably praising and envying him for being linked to such a lovely woman. They might laugh about his looks—his baldness, his weight, but when the young men thought of him with Anju, they surely felt jealous. Never mind that she was married to someone else.

He let his mind wander over how many girls and women he had been attracted to because of their beauty. It seemed so unfair that some really brilliant men and women were unattractive—and he felt complacent. If people approached him because of the way he presented himself, he was able to deliver the brain power to complement his good looks.

As he neared his office, he thought of his secretary, Jameela. Another case illustrating what he was thinking about. He had almost not hired her because although smart, she was rather plain, a bit overweight, almost dumpy. She was short, and her face was pocked. She had never cut her hair, and she wore it in an unflattering bun at the nape. Her eyes hid behind thick glasses with black plastic frames. She came from a family of Muslims who had struggled to put their daughter through college. Now she worked in a prestigious business and earned a good salary, all of which she gave her parents. She was fiercely loyal and devoted to Kishore. In fact, she was hopelessly infatuated with him, more so because he was forbidden fruit. And he knew it.

During the past year when the work load was inordinately heavy, Jameela worked in the office as late as he did. Soon, he began inviting her to dinner with him at nearby restaurants—after all, the girl had to eat, and these evenings were clearly a treat for her. As she became more comfortable with him and a little less awed by his position, she began telling him about her childhood.

"I come from a large family, sir—six brothers and three sisters. But you know, we Muslims tend to do that, no? Have many children? I am the only one to go to college. My sisters are all younger than me, and they are married." With a deprecating laugh, she continued, "My father always said that with my looks he'd never be able to marry me off, though he tried from the time I was fourteen."

"What nonsense, Jameela. You are smart and efficient…" Kishore stuttered.

"That's not what Muslim men want, sir. They want a woman who will produce sons. I must accept that I will live with my parents all my life, though I know I am a burden to them."

"How can you say that, Jameela? I know that you turn over your whole salary to your father. Tell me, you have brothers—why don't they help?"

"Two of them live at our home with their wives and children, sir, so they have their own families to provide for. And you know, they didn't go very far in their education because my father wanted them to work. They both don't earn much. With three families in one small house, it's quite noisy, let me tell you," she smiled joylessly.

Then, there had been one night a few months ago when he had taken her to the Oberoi Hotel for a late dinner. He was flattered as she praised him. "No one else, sir, does the kind of job you do. You get everything done on time, so clear, you have such beautiful writing. You know I took English literature in college before I did my business degree, my B. Com., so I enjoy reading your letters and memos."

She was dressed in an unflattering drab brown salwar kameez. Even through her thick glasses, her eyes shone bright as she gazed around the opulent room, clearly overwhelmed. Never had she seen anything like this before; never would she see anything like this again. Kishore was pleased, and he basked in her wonderment. The poor girl had so little joy in her life, but now she was smiling widely. She looked so childlike.

He began looking around the dining room of the Oberoi with new eyes. Damn—it was lovely. A band played the latest soft rock music in the background. Crystal chandeliers glistened overhead, reflected in the marble floor. The waiters were well-trained and well-mannered. And, Kishore thought, probably not one of them wants to be an actor, like the ones he'd met in California. He began to appreciate his surroundings and not take them so much for granted.

A little later, she said, "This is such a beautiful hotel. Have you ever stayed in one like this?"

"Sure. When I travel, I stay in hotels just like this."

"The rooms must be very nice. I would love to stay in one for even one hour," she removed her glasses and peered at him through her lashes. Kishore's heart lurched as he realized what she was suggesting. Oh, shit. No, she couldn't be thinking that. He looked at her, into her eyes. Yes, the poor girl was indeed thinking that. Here she was, a love-starved woman who had probably, no certainly, never had sex. She was trying to seduce him. And even though she was so awkward, so clumsy, almost endearingly inept, Kishore was tempted—he hadn't slept with another woman since marrying Anjali, and he certainly hadn't slept with a virgin since he was seventeen. He could teach her so much. To see her flush with pleasure, to hear her moan! He could get away with it too, since he knew the manager of the Oberoi. Arjun would gladly give Kishore a room for a couple of hours and never tell a soul. Could he really count on Arjun's discretion? Oh, hell. What was wrong with him? Why was he thinking this way? He could never betray Anjali and drive a wedge into his marriage. Damn, it was hard being a man with so many temptations.

Instead of saying, "Come, let's go; I'll show you one of the rooms," he said, "Let's get back to work, okay?"

She looked mortified. She grabbed her handbag, saying, "Of course, sir." In the car, she started to cry, speaking hesitantly. "What you must think of me. I'm sorry, sir. You know, I am twenty-eight years old and have never had a man look at me with desire, never felt a man's touch. When I was in school and college, I filled my head with romance books. What dreams I had. I was going to be swept off my feet by a handsome, mustached man on horseback. By the time I was twenty two, I had listened to my parents for eight years lament daily about how difficult it was to find a husband for me, and I was convinced they were right. And they were. I don't know what happened to me this evening; it must have been the music, the room, everything. I am very sorry."

Kishore naturally reached out a hand to pat hers, then quickly withdrew it and put it on his lap. He said, "It's all right, Jameela. Let's pretend this never happened."

She cried even more vehemently. "It wouldn't have, sir. But, you know, I thought your marriage was not happy because everyone is talking about your wife and Mr. Maneckwalla, so…"

Furiously, he turned on her. "So what? Did you think I needed comforting and that *you* should be the one to do it? Bloody hell. What nonsense, Jameela. There's no problem in my marriage. If there was, believe me I wouldn't ask you. If you hear anyone saying anything about my wife, you tell them to mind their own business, you understand? Is it clear? My private life is my own—don't bring it into the office. Now let's get back to work and forget this sorry incident, shall we?"

She wiped her eyes and straightened up; they had reached the office building. They rode up silently in the lift. Then Kishore went into his office and slammed the door.

How dare she bring up Anjali and Rusi? Bloody, fucking hell. Well, he clearly had to either fire Jameela or have her transferred within the company. Damn it. She was used to his ways, and a good secretary would be hard to find. As the days slipped by, he dropped the idea. Jameela got over her initial awkwardness and continued to work efficiently. As Kishore had suggested, they both forgot the sorry incident. And two months passed.

Now thinking of this latest flare-up with Anjali, he wondered how much longer the city was going to gossip about Anjali and Rusi. The incident with Jameela flitted through his mind and he thanked God he had not given in to temptation at the Oberoi. He did not need to have further complications. Last night, Anjali and he had almost had a terrible fight—over nothing.

When he entered his office, the truce with Anjali foremost in his mind, Jameela asked if she could see him about something important. Kishore started to tell her to send a huge bouquet to Anjali, when Jameela began to speak first. With downcast eyes, she said she had to give notice. Kishore was stunned. "But why?

Her voice held a tremor. "I am getting married."

"*What?* To whom? I thought you said..."

"Yes, sir. I believed my parents when they said they could never find a husband for me. Every night for so many years I heard my father curse the day I was born because he could never find me a husband. Now he has. His name is Anwar Khan. He is a widower with two daughters. He is a farmer outside Mumbai. He needs sons to help him with his farm. My parents will go into debt to give him a big dowry to marry me." Then she lifted her drowning eyes and looked at him, "He's fifty-nine years old."

"Oh, my God, Jameela. You are educated and smart. You are used to working in a nice office in a big city. How can you be a farmer's wife?"

"It is the will of Allah, sir. Is it all right if I just finish out the month? My wedding is to be in six weeks."

"Jameela, can I talk to your parents and tell them how wrong this is?"

"*No, sir.* My life is hell now. Every day I hear about the dowry they have to give for me. If you speak to them, it will only become worse. May I say, sir, that the time I spent working for you was the best time of my life? You taught me so much, and I will always remember you." As she headed out the door, she turned and, with ironic bitterness, said, "I don't think he even owns a horse," then she snapped her fingers, "Poof. My dream of a handsome man on horseback." And she waved her hands as if she were strewing confetti.

Kishore's heart went out to Jameela. Another smart educated woman among India's millions was to become a submissive, son bearing vessel. He knew what Anjali's opinion would be when he brought up the topic at dinner that night. He was so glad that Anjali was a free spirit, who was unafraid to voice her views. He silently blessed his parents for raising him as they had and for accepting his choice of Anjali as a wife. They were so broad-minded and liberal; they didn't look at caste, family, dowry or any other old-fashioned nonsense.

Just then, the door opened and Dev walked in, looking pale and shaken. Oh, God, thought Kishore. Another drug problem. He was supposed to be clean.

Dev sank into a chair and whispered, "You have to help me, man. You are the only one who can talk sense into them."

"What are you talking about, Dev?"

"Amma, but mostly Papa."

"What have you done now?"

"Come on, man, give me a break. I haven't done anything. God, they are so obstinate. Remember Anita I brought to Papa's sixtieth? Well, I want to marry her and they won't hear of it."

Dev

TWO YEARS AGO, DEV'S BAND had lost its singer, Renuka. Renu had been fabulous and built up a huge following. Mostly due to her, the band, called The Black Nuggets, had moved into the intimate night club of the Oberoi. Every night the room was packed with her young fans. Sure enough, when she was about 21, her parents arranged a marriage for her, and then she was gone. Some of the guys in the band took the mike, including Dev, but however well they sang, they were inadequate substitutes for Renu. The audience wanted another sexy woman at the mike. The crowds dwindled, the management of the Oberoi grumbled, and the Black Nuggets knew that their stint was in peril.

So they began auditioning singers. No one had the charisma of Renu. The Oberoi was losing money, and the Nuggets were losing confidence. Then one day, Anita walked in, and the Nuggets stopped whatever argument they were having and stared. She looked like one of their servants—poorly dressed, afraid to look up at anyone. Frankly, they thought she had wandered into the wrong place. Looking steadily at the floor, Anita asked, "You are looking for a singer, nai? I learned to sing in the convent, but I don't know what you want." She had a strong Maharashtrian accent, not something that would go over well at the very westernized club.

The leader of their group was about to send her away, when Dev impetuously said, "Let's give her a chance, I say. What can we lose, *yaar?*"

As they accompanied her, she sang a popular song from the latest Bollywood movie. The purity and sweetness of her voice stunned them all. However, she had no stage presence, no pretensions and no guile. When they asked her to sing a current American rock song, she shook her head.

"Sorry, sir, I don't know any, but I can learn if you teach me," she said. Dev took a CD and played a Carly Simon number. Anita was right. She could learn, and quickly too.

And so, Dev took her under his wing, teaching her not only the latest songs but how to stand at the mike, how to sway, how to flirt with her hands and how to be seductive with her body as well as her voice. The Nuggets were so sure that she would bring the crowds, they invested in a fashion consultant to help her buy clothes and teach her how to put on make-up. And Dev spent hours every day training her on the latest songs from both Hollywood and Bollywood. She was a fast learner. As he saw the work of the fashion consultant, he recognized her potential.

He excitedly told his band, "I tell you, *yaar*, we will not regret hiring this girl Anita. She's a real looker. Wow, you should see..." He shaped a voluptuous female body with his hands.

"When will we see her, Dev? You've been hiding her, keeping her all to yourself. When will she come and rehearse with us?"

"How about next Monday? You won't believe your eyes, I'm telling you."

He had her dress carefully in a plain blue silk sari and took her to rehearsal. He was gratified to see their eyes bulge with incredulous wonder. Was this the same waif who had wandered in some weeks ago? Now if she could only sing...

She could.

On the night of her debut, Dev paced and wiped his sweaty palms on his pants. He kept reassuring everyone who would listen, "she's going to be fine." People in Mumbai had heard of the new singer and had packed the club. The band played until 9:00—and then it was time for Anita.

She glided to the mike confidently with a smile. She wore a red sari with an almost backless choli, and every eye in the club was riveted on her. Dev had never seen her look so beautiful—he thought he had never seen anyone so beautiful. She looked back at him with a small nod, turned to the mike and began to sing. In a few minutes, she had everyone eating out of her hand, the hand she waved so gracefully like Dev had taught her. And Dev smiled and smiled and lost his heart.

Since he had to practice with her every day, it was easy for him to seduce her. At first he felt he was taking advantage of her, but she was willing, even eager. He could not take her to his room at Kalpana, his parents' home, so he began to 'borrow' flats from his rich friends—empty when their parents left town. He never for a moment considered marrying her; he understood she was not of his class, and his father would probably have another heart attack. He never even thought of introducing her to Kishore and Anjali; they would have nothing in common. For many months, Anita and he lived in their rainbow bubble.

Slowly, Anita began asking him, "Tell me about your brother and his wife. They have two children?"

Or, she would say, "Your mother must be very nice."

He would answer all her questions, never once dreaming that she wanted to meet his family. Finally, tired of his obtuseness, she asked, "I say, when I will meet your mother?" God, he was screwed. Then he remembered his father's birthday party that same week, and said, "You know, there's going to be a party to celebrate my father's sixtieth birthday. Why don't you come with me? Then you can meet everyone."

And things changed after the party. Now Anita said, "You live in a beautiful flat. Everything looks so expensive."

Or she said, "Your mother, father are very rich, no? Do your brother and family live in the same flat?"

Then one day she said, "You know, my mother and father want me to get married soon, but they have no money for a dowry."

Dev would try to laugh it away, "Yes, I know, parents are the worst about marriage. My mother has been trying for years to find a girl and arrange a marriage for me. Let's not talk about that anymore. Do you know how beautiful you looked when you sang today?"

Finally, one day, Anita said outright, "Dev, why you don't take me to meet your family again? Do they object to me? Because I am not the right caste? Because why? I am Anglo-Indian? I should listen to my mother. She tells me all the time 'that Dev will never marry you.'"

Dev blurted out thoughtlessly, "No, no. No such thing. We'll get married one day." And he actually thought for a fleeting moment that his parents would agree. What a stupid ass he had become. Now here he was begging Kishore's help.

"What rubbish, Dev. I can't imagine Amma and Papa objecting to your choice of Anita," Kishore said, glad that his brother was thinking of getting married and settling down.

"Apparently being a singer is the same as being a whore, a nautch girl. I asked if they thought of me as a gigolo, and *ha!* Papa just looked down and didn't say anything. I think I really love this girl, Kish, but they are objecting so strongly. Amma and Papa won't listen to me because she is Anglo-Indian."

Dev sat back in his chair and told Kishore about Anita's background. He began to speak about a British tea planter in Assam. Then to help Kishore understand, he leaned forward and asked, "Don't you remember that handsome guy from Coorg who went to college with us? The guy with a coffee estate in Coorg? When he was on the estate, he had nothing to do but get stinking drunk every night. He said it was a miserably lonely life—said once he inherited the estate, once he had to live there, he would drink non-stop, so they could just pickle him in rum and bury him."

"Look, I don't care about Coorg. Let's get back to you and Anita, okay?" Kishore said.

"Know what, Kish? I should have gone to America like you. I'd have been free to do what the hell I wanted." Dev's left leg began to jiggle up and down. "Christ, what's up with your a.c., man? Do you always work in such a hotbox?"

"They're repairing the bloody a.c. since last week. It broke down, and in this country, every little thing takes a damn year …anyway, the generator should come on pretty soon. Now tell me about Anita."

"Assam's the same as Coorg," Dev said. "Okay, here goes. This English teawallah, who probably had a wife and children in good old England, began to eye the lovely sixteen year old Shakuntala who plucked tea leaves on the plantation. Whether he raped her or she was willing, no one knows, but they had a long sordid affair. When you think about it—how could an uneducated sixteen-year old not succumb to the big boss English sahib? Anita was their child." Dev looked uncomfortable, mopping his forehead with a large handkerchief. But he pressed on, talking of a time and place that seemed foreign to two young men from Mumbai.

"Soon enough the Englishwallah finished his tour of duty and was to leave for jolly old home. Just before he left, he called Shakuntala into the big house and gave her one thousand rupees. I suppose that soothed his conscience about his Anglo-Indian daughter. Now the plantation fell to a new overseer, an Anglo-Indian himself, who clung to the tradition of excessive drinking and raping young helpless women. One night, after she had been dragged to the big house, beaten and raped, Shakuntala took baby Anita and the thousand rupees, went to the train station and found her way to Mumbai."

Dev's voice dropped and he lowered his eyes. He twisted his handkerchief in his hands. He did not want to continue. "She knew no one in Mumbai and had to earn some money. She probably became a prostitute to get by," he mumbled. "But she didn't want Anita to waste her life plucking tea leaves. So she earned money anyway she could and put Anita into some convent school. Anyway, she finally found a widower with a young son. The man was at a loss about how to bring up his son so he married Shakuntala to help with the boy."

"I hope he's good to them. What does he do?" asked Kishore

Dev hung his head, reluctant to speak. "I don't want to tell you. You're going to judge, just like Amma and Papa," he said finally.

"Come on, man. Tell me. How bad can it be?"

"He works in the post office," Dev whispered, shaking his head.

Oh shit—that bad, huh? Kish thought. "Well, he doesn't deliver letters, does he?" he said aloud, smiling at the ludicrous idea.

"No, no. He's a supervisor," Dev lied.

Suddenly, a loud banging and a jerky roar announced the starting of the generator.

"Well, there's the bloody generator—now we'll have to yell. Come on, man. I can't talk to Amma and Papa without some facts. Tell me about her family. What about Anita's mother? Does she work?"

Again, Dev avoided Kishore's eyes. He spoke into his chest. "She cooks for some families,"

"You mean she's an ayah?" Kishore blurted out. Shit—Dev might as well want to marry Malika's or Rama's daughter.

Dev stood and headed for the door. He turned and looked at Kishore with a plea, "Will you help me talk with Amma and Papa or not?"

After an awkward silence, Kishore asked, "Are you sure you've thought this through, Dev? Sometimes you do things just to annoy the old man. Maybe you're so blinded with infatuation, you don't see the problems such a marriage might cause."

"Bloody hell, Kishore, you too? Infatuation? What the hell do you mean, problems?"

Kishore played with the stapler on his desk. Then he combed his hair with his fingers, lifted his chin, worried that he might hurt Dev. But he knew he had to speak up.

"Well, here's an example off the top of my head. If there was a party at Kalpana, Anita's parents wouldn't come. If they did come, they'd feel out of place and awkward. Shit, they'd feel happier talking to Rama and

Malika in the kitchen. You know, even at Papa's sixtieth, Anita sat quiet most of the time. She was quite overwhelmed with the people there."

"Bloody hell, Kish, she didn't know a soul. I really shouldn't have brought her. Hardly any one spoke to her…"

"Dev, *bhai,* you must understand that she is from a totally different class. No one at the party quite knew what to say to her. What does she have in common with us?"

Dev rose from his chair with a despairing look. "Class! Caste! When will this country grow up? I thought you'd help."

Kishore strode over and grabbed Dev's arm. "*Dekko bhai, look.* This has nothing to do with prejudice but background. You marry someone from a similar background so that certain values and beliefs are taken for granted, you don't have to explain. You say that Anita hasn't had much of an education. Do you have anything in common with this girl besides her looks—and sex? Are you sure she doesn't see you as a way to leave her past behind? A way up and out?" Kishore couldn't believe he was saying such things. Kishore, the calm, tolerant, logical man was letting deeply hidden emotions rise within him, emotions he never believed he had. When his own family was at stake, he was allowing primitive unvoiced ideas overtake him. He was amazingly open-minded and tolerant with other people who were not his relatives.

Rising from his chair, hand outstretched to ward off pain, Dev stared at him. He started backing out of the office, shaking his head. Kishore ran to him to stop him from leaving.

"Oh my God—I'm so sorry, Dev. I don't know what got into me. I'm sorry, *bhai.* Please don't leave. Come, come, sit, sit."

There was a knock on the door. Kishore hoped that it didn't announce another emotional meeting with Jameela. She came in with some papers for him to sign, and he asked not to be disturbed again. Then Kishore turned back to Dev.

"What about Anita's education?"

"Well, Anita went to a convent in Bandra. Besides learning English, she also learned to sing."

Kishore finally asked, "Is she going to continue to sing if you get married?"

Dev looked up and said, "I'm sure I'll be thrown out of Kalpana, so we'll have to find another place to live. You know what rents are like in Mumbai. I don't think we can make it on what I earn, so yes, she'll have to work."

Kishore thought for a few minutes, then said, "Tell you what. Both Anjali and I would like to get to know her better before we talk to Papa and Amma. Why don't you bring her over for dinner tonight?"

After a long silence, Dev finally whispered, "What time?"

Anjali

KISHORE SAT AT HIS DESK, mulling over the news. This was probably the toughest spot Dev had put him in. Sure, getting him through his drug infused problems had been horrendous, but this…what amazed Kishore was that he was thinking like his parents and their friends: that generation. Well, actually, maybe it wasn't just the older generation's mind set; maybe it was common sense. It was true his family would have nothing in common with Anita's. It was also true he didn't find too much to love and admire in Anjali's parents—but at least they were of the same class. Sighing, he reached for the phone and called Anjali.

"Sorry, darling, have to cancel our Willingdon dinner tonight. But before you get mad, guess what? Dev was just here with some astonishing news. He wants to marry Anita—remember the singer he brought to Papa's party? Well, Amma and Papa are dead set against the marriage, so he's asked me to help him."

"Why are they against it? Amma has been after him for years to get married. Oh, please—don't tell me it's a caste thing. She seemed perfectly nice, though a bit quiet. Come on, Kish, this is nothing to think about. Of course, if he loves her, he should marry her. Anyway, what can you do?"

"I asked them to come for dinner tonight. Let's postpone the

Willingdon until tomorrow? I think we should get to know what this girl is like before I talk to Amma and Papa."

"That's fine. Don't worry about the club; this is much more exciting. I'll have Shiva prepare a nice dinner. It should be fun—I'll have a sister finally. What time will you be home?"

"I'll be home by seven so I can tell you what Dev told me. Don't be sure about having a sister, either. See you then, darling."

When Kishore came home, he sat Anjali down and told her about Anita's background. Then he said, "So, don't ask her about her parents and stuff like that."

She looked at him wide-eyed, incredulous, and said, "You mean, we can't talk about her family, college, books, parties, friends—all the things we usually talk about?"

"That's right," Kishore said grimly, getting up to shower.

"I'm sure you're exaggerating, Kish. You know I can talk to anyone, you'll see," she said confidently. And it was true. In these years, Anjali had overcome her chariness about India and adapted to living in Mumbai. She could talk comfortably with Shanti's friends and her own. She could converse easily with Kishore's business associates and with her own servants. It had not always been thus.

She remembered some terrible and frightening times she had when she was still new to Mumbai and India. One time, she had been alone in the car with the driver snailing through choking congestion and noise, almost a riot it seemed. People were yelling, out of control, waving sticks. She stared at the huge crowds walking and dancing with abandon in the streets. Men carried clay replicas of the elephant god Ganesha, garlanded with jasmine and marigolds and shouted *Ganapati Bappa Moraya*. Some played blaring instruments and cymbals, others were gyrating, careless about traffic. Anjali cowered in the car until she reached home safely where Kishore explained to her that it was the last day of Ganesha Chaturthi, the festival for the god Ganesha.

He told her that on this day of the festival, the crowds were taking the idols to immerse them in the sea. There was nothing to be afraid of.

After that first year, her fear changed to delight when the festival rolled around, and she was happy to explain her newly learned traditions to visitors from abroad. Now that she felt comfortable in India, she had become adept at entertaining people from different backgrounds. She was sure she would do fine tonight with Anita, despite Kishore's trepidation. And she went to give Shiva instructions on what to cook for dinner.

Dev and Anita arrived at 8:30, Dev very dapper in black. Anita however, took one's breath away. She was tall and slender with straight dark brown hair hanging loosely to her waist. Her hazel eyes, flecked with green, uptilted slightly, mysteriously, exotically. Her complexion was wheat colored and smooth. Anjali looked enviously at her skin and thought, "Not one zit did this girl ever have to squeeze." The combination of British and Assamese had mingled well to produce this girl, lovely in her green salwar kameez. Anjali had dressed down in a plain mauve silk sari which now seemed positively dowdy.

Dev very nervously talked non-stop about the club and friends. In fact, he seemed to be deliberately ignoring Anita. "Is he high on something?" Anjali silently asked Kishore with her eyebrows slightly arched. "I think he may be, or he's just nervous. Let's get through this evening" he shrugged.

After a couple of scotch and sodas, Anita joined in their conversation. Her heavy Maharashtrian accent made her difficult to understand. It soon became clear to Anjali that she had been wrong about herself. She could not talk to this girl; they had nothing in common. Anjali had been in schools all over the globe, in third world countries as well as highly developed ones. She never had trouble making friends or talking with strangers; in fact, she prided herself on it. But tonight the obvious topics were forbidden. How easy it would have been to ask, "What do your parents do, Anita?" or "What were your favorite subjects in college?" After some awkward silences, Anjali rummaged in her mind and came up with a neutral question.

"What do you enjoy doing, Anita?"

"Oh, I like shopping, Aunty, for clothes, you know. Saris, salwar kameezes, sometimes American jeans. And jewel-ery. But you know, everything's so much, so expensive. Every week it is more and more expensive. I like to only look and try on in the shop."

"But your salwar kameez is lovely."

"Oh, Dev bought this for me to wear to your house only, Aunty. He is so nice to me," she smiled over at him.

Dev squirmed in his seat and helped himself to a large handful of pistachios and began shelling them, looking at neither Anjali nor Kishore.

After a long pause, Anjali tried again, "Anita, you mustn't call me Aunty. I am not your elder. We will be...um, friends." Anjali swallowed, wondering when the evening would end. Then she carried gamely on. "Do you enjoy reading? What sort of books do you read?"

"Oh, the nuns, you know, they make us read so much in St Joseph's. I went to St. Joseph's in Bandra, you know. It is the convent school, no? I said, once I get out of school, what the hell, (she giggled as she said the forbidden 'hell') I won't have to read any more books. Books are boring, no? So I doesn't read much now, only mags like *Filmfare* and *Femina*."

"How about your music? Do you have to practice a lot for your songs?"

"Nai, nai. Dev takes me to Hindi pictures, so I learn the songs from that. The English songs, the band leader, Fred, he only gives me the words and plays piano for me to learn the tune. And I listen to tape or CD."

"You must be very talented to learn everything so fast."

"Oh, yes, I learn songs very fast."

Dev was busy with the snacks, not looking at anyone. A thin sheen of sweat gleamed on his forehead. Maybe he felt they were grilling Anita. Kishore and Anjali looked at each other wondering how someone who was so poorly spoken and with a thick Maharashtrian accent could possibly be successful in a hot night club of Mumbai. Swallowing all her earlier declarations against parental objections to Anita, Anjali now wondered what on earth Dev saw in this woman beside her sexuality. Did she have a brain in her head? How long a conversation could he have with her?

Anjali excused herself to tell Shiva to bring out dinner. Soon they were sitting around the table playing with the rice and dal on their plates, Anita clumsy and inept with her knife and fork. A smiling Shiva brought out piping hot rotis and a fragrant chicken curry. Anita was thrilled with the meal.

She exclaimed, "I never had such good *gobi-alou,* Aunt—I mean, Anjali. How you call this in English? Some kind of flower? Huh? Cauliflower, yah. My mother sometimes cooks it at home, but she puts in too much chillies." Anita screwed up her face fumbling with her fork to try lifting the cauliflower and potato pieces to her mouth.

Anjali thought, I'm not touching that opening about her mother being a cook. Shit. Now what can I talk to her about? Look at Kish and Dev gabbing on and on about the political situation. What the hell, I'll join them. So aloud she said, "So when will this latest hostility with Pakistan be over, do you think?"

Surprisingly, Anita jumped in, "Oh, Anjali. Those men like to shoot boom-boom over nothing. You were here for the riots, no? Terrible— Hindus, Muslims hitting each other with lathis, killing with knives, blood, blood everywhere, screaming. Poor children, women. Two days, nobody go out. Even the policemans joined in… You don't remember?" She had given up on the fork and had started on the chicken and rice with her fingers slurping softly as she sucked in the liquid sauce.

Dev smiled at her. "No, Kishore and Anjali were in America when that happened."

Long awkward silences punctuated their dining. Anjali kept telling herself, I got on with everyone; why am I so dumbstruck now? Why can't I start and continue a conversation? Kishore, help. There is still dessert to get through.

As if he heard her. Kishore said, "Well, Anita, maybe after dinner you will grace us with one of your melodies."

"Huh?"

Dev intervened, "My charming brother means, will you sing a song for us after dinner? I can play the piano for you, okay?" Kisan was taking piano lessons so there was a small piano in the drawing room.

"*Achcha,* I'll sing," and she perked up with a smile.

When Shiva brought in the gulab jamun, Anita clapped saying, "This is my most favorite sweet." After dessert, they gathered in the drawing room and Dev moved to the small piano gently tinkling the keys. He and Anita put their heads together whispering. Anjali looked over at them and thought, "What a gorgeous couple. Why can't she be right in other ways?"

Shiva, Shamala and Lakshmi wandered to the door of the drawing room when they heard the music. They knew there was a concert in the air, and they wanted to see more of Devsab's new girl, the one he was going to marry.

Slowly, Dev's riffs took on a melody and he said, "This is a goodie. I think you'll like it. I know I do." He smiled at Anita and played the introduction to "*My heart will go on,*" the song from the *Titanic.* Anita gently rested a hand on the piano, totally relaxed, and started to sing. Her accent disappeared and every nuance from the original Dion version came pouring out of her throat.

Anjali and Kishore sat speechless.

Anita actually blushed when they and the servants clapped enthusiastically. At their insistence, she sang two Hindi songs. The servants grinned their appreciation and clapped even more loudly when she finished each one. The woman was an oral chameleon. She took on the persona and voice of the original singers. To finish the evening she sang Kishore's favorite, "*Moon River.*" She was dazzling; she was brilliant. Anjali and Kishore could not praise her enough.

When Dev and she got ready to leave, Anjali and Kishore were generous in their compliments for Anita's singing. And the servants came in to smile and nod their approval as well.

As she got ready for bed, Anjali said, "You know Dev is going to call you tomorrow, or come to see you. What are you going to say?"

"I don't know, Anju. You saw how painful the evening was. Can you imagine her with our friends? With my parents' friends?" He looked at Anjali with a plea in his eyes. "Don't you think Dev must have seen it as well? He's not that infatuated, is he? Oh, God, what can I tell him? What should I tell Amma when she calls? I hope the idiot hasn't proposed yet. Do you think he has? What should I do, Anju?"

Anjali was silent. She wanted so badly to speak up for Dev, be on his side, be on Anita's side. Poor girl, she was just trying to improve her lot. Her parents were so poor, and Dev had probably led her to believe that she had a chance to marry him. She had seen his flat at Kalpana Apartments; she had seen how well Kishore and Anjali lived. Of course she wanted to be part of it. Who wouldn't? It couldn't be easy to sing in a ritzy night club where liquor flowed and people threw money around—and then go home to … what? Anjali couldn't even imagine her squalor of her flat with her postal worker father and cook-servant mother. But Kishore was right. She couldn't imagine Anita at the Willingdon or Kalpana Apartments with their friends. It was an impossible picture.

She finally said, "I think you need to be honest with Dev. Poor guy. He's always had it hard compared to you, hasn't he?"

Shanti

SHANTI SAT CROSS-LEGGED ON A mat in the puja room. She had offered jasmine blossoms and tulsi leaves to the gods. Now doing aarti with a small wick soaked in oil burning in the brass holder, she circled the flame around the gods three times and began to feel more peaceful. She laid down the aarti, ran her hands quickly over the fire three times, then bowed her head as she put her hands together in prayer.

She prayed wordlessly from her heart. Hari Ram, Hari Krishna. Please save my son, my Dev, from this karma. If he marries this girl, he will be lost. Vinod will never speak to him again—he will no longer be our son. Please, make them both come to their senses.

After an hour of fervent prayer and meditation, she emerged from the room. Little Bhim had waited patiently outside the puja room for her; he knew entry into that sacred space was banned. As she came out, he greeted her with frolicky leaps and strenuous tail wagging. She petted him and calmed him down before conferring with Rama and Malika about lunch and dinner for the day. Rama was carelessly using more oil and coconut in the cooking, even though she kept stressing to him that it was dangerous for Vinod. Rama would shake his head, not comprehending the idea of cholesterol. Since they were not expecting company for the day, she asked him to cook a simple dal, a chicken tikka, vegetables and rice. Then she went to her favorite spot near the window where she could see an angry grey sea lashing the rocks and shooting spray high towards the darkened sky.

The blackening clouds seemed to her to be enveloping her family as well. Never had she felt so threatened, not even when Dev was using drugs. That had been a difficult time. Vinod never knew how much Dev had stolen from her. She had always been protective of her younger son, her lost sheep. How many sleepless nights she had spent wondering where he was, what he was doing. Too often she pictured him in an opium den, the kind she had read about in books about China. She had begged Dev tearfully to please give up those wicked drugs. At one time, she thought she would have to ask advice from their doctor friends about treatment.

Fortuitously, there came the tragic death of Deepak, after which Dev seemed to emerge from the happy drugged fog he had been in. Vinod and Shanti had tried to help him in his recovery, but since they knew nothing about that world and why their son was in it, they had asked Kishore and Anjali to encourage him to free himself of drugs, and he seemed to have done so. Now Dev had brought a new problem to them.

She and Vinod didn't even know what this girl's—this Anita's—background was; they just knew she wasn't right for Dev. Shanti thought about how she had tried so hard to be open-minded and not let caste dictate the rightness of a match. This was no longer the age when parents consulted astrologers and the stars to help them choose mates for their children. At least, educated people did not. Certainly, none of her friends did. And dowries too were becoming rarer in her social circle.

Actually, she didn't know what that girl Anita's caste was. Was Vinod's and her visceral hostility because she was Anglo-Indian? That was so evident by her fair skin and gray-green eyes. True, many Maharashtrians had blue eyes. Yet, somehow you could tell that this girl was an Anglo-Indian. Vinod, in his exaggerated and blustery way, had called her a nautch girl, relegating her to the class of concubine, or at best a mistress. The few words Shanti had spoken to Anita at Vinod's sixtieth birthday party showed her that the girl was uneducated and a gold digger.

She had smiled at Shanti and said, "Such a nice house, Ma. Must be very expensive." And, "Such beautiful furniture, Ma. Must be very expensive." The way she spoke suggested that she must be after Dev for his money; she saw how he lived in Kalpana on Malabar Hill and thought he was wealthy.

Shanti closed her eyes and tried to regain the peace she had felt in the puja room. She chided herself for thinking malicious thoughts about this Anita whom she did not even know. She remembered when Kishore had told them he wanted to marry Anjali. Both she and Vinod had been overjoyed, even before they met her. Anjali's aloofness at the wedding she could understand. The poor girl was nervous because she had never met her in-laws or any of Kishore's friends. And at first even Anjali had not turned out to be the kind of daughter Shanti wanted.

When Kishore and Anjali came back from America to live in Mumbai and Kisan was a baby, Anjali had been withdrawn. It was almost as if the girl was afraid of emotions, even toward her little baby. Her own mother, Subadra, had been completely inept, flapping her hands helplessly. After Subadra left, Anjali had resisted Shanti's guidance for weeks. How difficult it had been for Shanti not to see and play with her first grandchild every day. Slowly, ever so slowly, Anjali had accepted Shanti's help and advice with Kisan. Even so, Shanti felt a holding back—what she was receiving from Anjali was a beautifully decorated box, empty inside. And then, Anjali prevailed on Kishore to move to his company's office in California—some town called Santa Clara they hadn't heard of. It had been heart-wrenching to see them leave.

Such a void their going left. Of course, Dev was still here, but he was always busy with his friends and his music. Kishore had first thought his transfer to California was for only one year. But it stretched to one more, then perhaps another. Shanti couldn't abide not seeing

Kisan growing up, so after two years, she persuaded Vinod to travel to California. And she remembered how difficult that visit had been.

At first it had been so exciting—they had never been to California although they had traveled to Europe many times, and even to the east coast of the United States. Kishore and Anjali lived in Santa Clara in a nice house. They had three bedrooms (though not as big as the ones in Kalpana), and a lovely kitchen. In the front was a smooth green lawn (only at the clubs like the Willingdon or on the golf courses did one see such lawns in India) and their back garden had an orange tree, a peach tree and flower beds. They also had a bright red and blue set with swings and a slide for little Kisan. It was such a beautiful, clean neighborhood.

Shanti was happy to be with them, watch the baby and play with him on the swings or read to him when Anjali went out. Vinod was content to sit with the newspaper, to watch the business news on CNBC and to take his daily walks. Within a week, he became acquainted with the neighbors and built a small circle of retired friends.

Shanti did all the cooking and baby-sitting. One day she was doing Vinod's and her laundry. There wasn't much, so she got Kishore's, Anjali's and Kisan's clothes to add to the load in the washer. When she took them out to dry she was aghast—all the clothes were pink! She looked for the offending garment. Her sari. It was pale blue cotton, but it had a thin red border which she hadn't considered. As she looked at Kishore's undershirts, his underpants, Anjali's bras, Kisan's t-shirts, she was reduced to tears. How could she have been so careless? Just then Anjali came home.

"Amma, what have you done? Oh, my God!"

"I'm sorry, Anjali. I was only trying to help. I didn't notice the red border on my sari. Oh, I'm so sorry."

Anjali bit her lip to keep harsh words to herself. If it had been a nanny or housekeeper, she could have fired her. This was her mother-in-law.

She said, in oh, such a controlled way, "That's all right, Amma. Things happen. I'd better get to the mall to replace these. Let's see, three t-shirts for Kish, three for Kisan, three bras and altogether nine pairs of underwear. No problem. I'll go after lunch while Kisan has his nap."

Shanti swallowed. She wanted to add that Vinod also had pink underwear, as did she, but she was so humiliated that she couldn't speak. Vinod would have to put up with it. How could she have been so stupid? Even when she thought of it now, she squirmed. Thank God, when she showed Vinod what she had done, he had laughed heartily, danced around the room waving his pink shorts, then sat down still laughing and shaking his head.

One day, Anjali took Shanti to the market so that she could pick out what she wanted for the meals. When they were in the store, Shanti had been rather surprised at Anjali's behavior. Santa Clara's population of Indians was burgeoning because of the high-tech industry, and Indian engineers had a propensity for computer technology. Shanti was happy to see some women in salwar kameezes and saris and eagerly went toward two who were conferring about some spices. Anjali grabbed her arm and whispered, "Don't talk to them."

"Why, Anjali? Maybe they can tell me where I can find some *haldi*."

"Look, Amma. Kishore has to maintain his higher executive position in the company. These people are in the lower level of any company they work for, and I can't be friends with them."

"What's wrong with a little talk in the market? You don't have to be friends with them."

"Amma, you don't understand. They'll invite us over and then we'll have to ask them. I can't do it. Come, let's just get what you need." And she hustled her out of the market. Shanti felt disturbed by Anjali's behavior. Was she turning against Indians? Embarrassed by them? Their clothes, their accents? Had this Anjali remained hidden in Mumbai? Wherever Shanti and Vinod had gone in Europe, Shanti had proudly worn her saris and felt flattered when asked about her homeland. Here Anjali seemed almost eager to be non-Indian, to wear American clothes and fit into the American "life-style" as they called it.

Shanti's venture with Anjali on a "play date" for Kisan was equally embarrassing. They went to Sue's home, and Katie and Janet were there with their kids. Apparently everyone just had a first name. The ladies seemed happy to meet Shanti, shook her hand, saying slowly and loudly, "So...nice...to...meet...you." Then they turned to Anjali and asked, "What does she think of the United States? Does she like it here?" Anjali smiled at Shanti, dressed in a lovely lavender silk sari, looking a bit befuddled, and spoke for her, "Oh, yes. She's having a good time."

Sue asked, "Would you like something to drink? Some coffee? Some iced tea?"

Shanti nodded, "Some coffee, please." And those were the only words she spoke. She watched the children play while the mothers talked about nannies, day care, the hours their husbands worked. Shortly, Anjali said they had to go, so they scooped up Kisan and went home.

"Did you enjoy that, Amma?" asked Anjali, sincerely pleased that she had taken Shanti out.

"Yes. It was nice to see Kisan playing with his friends." How could she say she had felt humiliated, treated like one of the nannies they were talking about? She had been invisible. Anjali's friends had acted like she was uneducated, that she didn't speak English. Anjali, happy to have taken her mother-in-law to see how nicely her family fit in, prattled on about Sue, Janet and Katie and their husbands' positions in the company.

The closeness she had developed with Anjali when Kisan had been a baby had dissipated. In this place and at this time, Shanti felt that Anjali unwittingly treated her as if she were out of place and irrelevant. So Shanti more and more opted to stay home and care for Kisan. He was now an active almost three-year old, running around and getting into all kinds of mischief. While Shanti cooked the meals for the day, Anjali took Kisan for play dates or to the park. Shanti never wanted to go along after that first debacle. One day when Anjali got ready to take Kisan on a play date, she said "Amma, the lunch and dinner are all ready for the day, why don't you come with us?" and Shanti's face lit up. Anjali looked very smart in her black jeans and white tee-shirt. She stood dangling her car keys, biting her lip. She continued, "Actually, Amma, I don't know these people very well. In fact, this is the first time I'm going to their home. Perhaps it would be best if you came another day. Would it be all right?"

Shanti felt as if she had been slapped, and she lowered her eyes. Even though she might have refused to go, she would have welcomed the invitation. "Of course," she said. "I am in the middle of a good book, so I can read. You go and enjoy yourself. Bye, my little pet," and she hugged Kisan. She took her book and sat by the window. Her book lay unread on her lap as she stared outside.

Such clean streets, trees, houses and gardens, all immaculate; not one person to be seen. Occasionally cars would glide by, silently. What a contrast to the raucous scene she usually saw from her window in Mumbai—pedestrians jabbering, cars honking, bumping gently into each other, dogs and bikers narrowly squeaking past fruit vendors, and vegetable sellers pushing their carts laden with green and red produce, garland makers hawking their jasmine or marigold strands. And behind it all, the eternal, gray Arabian Sea. It was indeed the chaos and turmoil of living. Here in Santa Clara, it was tranquility—the chaos probably being played out behind the walls of the immaculate homes. Was it all illusory? Did the quietude on the streets hide unhappiness and despair inside the houses? Was the noise and tumult in the roads of Mumbai a façade for quiet and emptiness, or was it a reflection of the chaos inside the homes there? Ah, this was a paradox for Vinod. All Shanti knew was that she found the silence here oppressive. And she felt terribly alone.

At dinner that evening, Kishore noticed a tension at the table. Amma was subdued, and Anjali was not her bubbly self. Before they went to bed, he asked, "Is everything all right between you and Amma? You were both so quiet tonight."

Anjali buried her face in his chest. "Oh, Kish, I don't know what to do. I feel so guilty about her here. In India it was fine when my friends came to visit, they included her in all their talk because everyone knew the same people. Here it is so different. I don't really know these girls very well, and I don't want to take her with me. It is too awkward. The one time I did, she did not seem too comfortable."

Kishore's jaw tightened. "Are you saying you are embarrassed by her? Of taking her places and introducing her to your hoity-toity friends? Come on, Anju, it's not as if she doesn't speak English. In fact, she speaks it better than many of the people here who say stupid things like "between you and I" and "Do you want to go with?" Tell me. Is it that she wears a sari? That she's not wearing clothes from Banana Republic or Nordstrom's? What would be so awkward? Tell me."

"God, Kish, I don't know. These girls are so sophisticated…"

"What rubbish, Anju. Sophisticated, my ass. Most of them are hicks from Fresno, Bakersfield, Chino and places like that. Many of them have never been out of California. Don't you see that?"

"Well, I have to make friends, and it was hard for me to break into their circle. Anyway, you know, I loved having this house to myself and learning to do everything. Oh, sure, at first I missed Shiva, but I enjoy cooking. Now, she has taken it over entirely, and the care of Kisan. The whole house smells of curry all the time. My large cooking spoons are turning yellow with turmeric. I'd love to have a pizza or pasta one day."

"Sweetheart, she's doing all the cooking for us; well, actually for me—all my favorite dishes. Why don't you get a pizza when you want it, or pasta, or Chinese, for that matter. I'm sure she won't mind. But you have to include her more. What's happened? When we were in Mumbai, you were getting along so well, no? Now this."

"Well, in Mumbai, that was her territory. She knew everything and she was teaching it to me. She was marvelous. Here, I am the one who knows things—and she doesn't seem to fit into this territory. Oh, Kish, I'm so ashamed and guilty. What can I do?"

"Surely you can take her some places with you. She hardly goes out unless we make a big deal of taking them sightseeing on the weekend. Come on, Anju, you must do better than this. Take her with you tomorrow."

And through the paper thin wall, Shanti heard it all. Slowly, her tears wet her cheeks. She thought she was helping, but Anjali was finding her a hindrance. Of course, when they had been in Mumbai, Anjali had really needed her teaching. Now, Anjali was the one in charge, and Shanti was just a useless appendage. Kishore was right—because she wore a sari all the time, she was conspicuous. Vinod didn't stand out in his pants and shirt. Maybe Anjali felt her mother-in-law's conspicuousness was awkward. Well, it was time to leave.

The next day, she talked to Vinod about their VUSA ticket. This ticket, Visit U.S.A., which they had bought in Mumbai, allowed them six or seven flights anywhere in America. Vinod and Shanti had several relatives scattered all over the country—doctors, engineers, business owners—all urging a visit. Even though they had planned a longer stay with Kishore and Anjali, apparently three weeks was long enough. However, she couldn't tell Vinod the real reason for her sudden desire to go to Houston almost immediately to see their nephew.

Vinod was reluctant to leave—he had begun to make some interesting friends, and he enjoyed talking politics with them. But Shanti was persuasive; she wanted to leave right away. Kishore was bewildered by the sudden turn, as was Anjali who had determined to try harder with Shanti. And so they had left the young couple not knowing when they would see their grandson again. Thank God Anjali became pregnant again, and they moved back to Mumbai. Because of Shanti's forgiving nature, she and Anjali became close again. When Shanti asked them to live at Kalpana when the baby was born, Anjali gratefully accepted. So once more, the roles were reversed and Shanti was the guru to a willing Anjali.

Even now, remembering the visit to Santa Clara, Shanti felt humiliation and hurt. However, she recognized it as a temporary and specific problem. Here in Mumbai, it disappeared. Dev and this Anita and the problem they presented would not evaporate in the same way—they were permanently in Mumbai, and the family would have to endure the cruel tattling and chatter that would inevitably besmirch their good name.

So, what could she do about this Anita? Vinod was so intransigent and opposed to Dev marrying her. She had never seen him so unreasonable. True, she herself would not be happy if Dev chose to marry Anita, but she was willing to invite her for dinner to get to know her better. Vinod had forbidden that. With only two sons, she could not afford to lose one. She was almost afraid to speak to Vinod again on the matter for fear of causing another heart attack. But she must—she must keep her family together. Tonight she would approach him. She had her wiles, and she could gently throw water on the flames of his anger.

Vinod

V INOD SAT WITH HIS ELBOWS on the chair's arms, his fingers laced, and he rested his chin on them. Occasionally he shook his head. Sometimes he snorted. What could he do about Dev? What should he do? Shanti, he knew, wanted to invite that girl for dinner. He would not allow it. Never in his house. If she were some other young man's kept woman, then all right. But as his son's intended, never. He would not countenance the marriage. If Dev continued with his disobedient mulishness, he would turn his back on his son. It had taken thirty plus years for him to consider disinheriting the scoundrel. And it pained him to the core.

It had always been this way. He rubbed his eyes then rested his hands on the book he had been pretending to read for an hour. Dev had been trouble right from the start. He never made an effort in school causing the teachers to call Shanti to complain about his lack of motivation. However, Dev's irresistible charm seduced the same teachers to give him passing or even good grades. When Kishore received his SAT scores—and how good they were—Dev completely gave up. He began running with a fast crowd of very wealthy boys. It was that pack of rats who introduced him to drugs. The only thing the boy was passionate about was the drums. Vinod supposed he was good. He didn't know; he had never been to any of the clubs where

Dev played, nor would he go. As far as he was concerned, it wasn't even music, just noise. Anyway, what sort of career was that for a man? There was nothing he or Shanti could do. Vinod's tirades only brought on further rebellion. Did the boy not respect him at all? He could not imagine himself going against his father's wishes.

How old had he been when he himself was enamored of a lovely young classmate? About eighteen? What was her name? Rekha? Rukmini? Radhika. That was it. Radhika. They would sometimes talk after classes when she waited for the bus. He was so skinny then, but debonair, leaning nonchalantly against the bus stop sign. She was having difficulties in her physics class and asked him questions, and one day he was emboldened to invite her to a coffee house to continue the explanation. He supposed the tightness in his chest, the dryness in his mouth, and the way his stomach turned a somersault when he saw her was a form of love, the kind he had read about.

At their coffee, casually stroking his upper lip with its sparse mustache, he asked her what her full name was. She was Radhika Susie Abraham. She didn't have to say anything more. He knew she was a Syrian Christian from Kerala. He could not pursue this further. Even if his parents did not object (and of course they would, vehemently) hers certainly would. Kerala Christians kept a very tight grip on their community—even subsects tried to remain separate and pure. He knew the minute she said "Abraham" that this would be their last meeting alone. Her eyes beseeched him to understand—she liked him too and wanted at least this one stolen half-hour with him. He had wordlessly sacrificed what might have been a grand passion, the sort that Russian novelists wrote about. He had suffered, (surely, the Russians did not suffer more than he had) but he had survived. Thinking about it now, he couldn't help but smile at the tender bittersweet memory Radhika had left him

And wasn't it for the best? Just a couple of years later, his parents had found Shanti for him. What a treasure she was, his better self. She had uncomplainingly lived with his parents when they were first married and learned how to run a household from his mother. She cooked, handled the dhobi who did their laundry, told the mali what flowers to plant and when. Shanti added such sweetness to their family. She even studied German and French so that she could help him in his career. After Dev was born, she began to prod him about moving into their own flat.

Vinod shook his head with a smile recalling the beguiling way she had done that. He himself was comfortable in the flat where he had grown up. As the oldest son, he knew he would inherit it. But Shanti was so wise. She pointed out that they should find another apartment since the one they were in, which they shared with his parents, was too small for two families. Besides, she said, now that we have two boys, shouldn't we have two flats to bequeath, one to each of them? Of course, she'd been right. Although, Vinod thought sadly, he didn't feel like giving Dev anything right now except a hard kick in the arse, the no-good bugger.

Chalo, he shouldn't waste any more time on something he had made up his mind about. He knew Shanti would spin her filmy web around him and try to get him to soften. Dev had always been Shanti's favorite, rather like a stray puppy she had to protect. She never had to worry about Kishore and Anjali. They were the joy of life.

Maybe he should have evicted the tenants who lived in his parents' flat long ago and told Dev to go and live there on his own. Every time he had hinted at that, Shanti protested.

"Dev will surely go back into drugs, and haven't we worked hard to get him away from that?" she said.

"Come on, Vinod, can you see him looking after a flat even with servants? And the servants, they will steal everything from him," she said.

"He'll have too many noisy parties, with too much drink and loud music, and all the neighbors will be angry. Until he marries, he will be hopeless on his own. He is not at all responsible," she said.

Vinod pointed out, "In America, youngsters find their own flats as early as eighteen; they learn responsibility or suffer the consequences.

Here this bugger is close to his thirties, and you are always there to look after him. He is not a child any more, Shanti. Let him learn."

Shanti was adamant, her trump card being, "Vinod, without him in the house, it will be too lonely for me. Just knowing he's here gives me comfort."

And that was that.

With strands of the past and the present weaving together in his mind, Vinod nodded off in his chair. He jerked awake when a stray thought wormed its way into his consciousnesses. God, what if that woman was pregnant with Dev's child? Vinod became agitated. He got out of his chair, teetered and almost fell, so great was his dismay. When he steadied, he began to pace in the drawing room. What could be done? If there was another grandchild on the way, he knew Shanti's position already. Dev and Anita should marry and come live in Kalpana Apartments. After all, hadn't Kishore and Anjali done so when Priya was born?

Vinod began to run through his list of doctor friends. Surely, one of them would know someone who could perform abortions. He could pay Anita a good sum to have an abortion and leave Dev alone. Shanti need never know. He shook his head. No, no. He had never kept anything from Shanti. He would have to tell her, persuade her. He had been reading lately how abortions were becoming more common in India. With the introduction of ultrasound, parents knew the sex of their child early. In many households, where girl babies were not desirable, the young mother was forced to abort by her husband and her in-laws.

He'd had a discussion with Dr. Sharma on this very subject just last week at the Willingdon Club.

"I say, Doc, no abortions should be allowed unless to save the mother, otherwise the practice is barbarous. Where is the sanctity of life? How can doctors play God?" Vinod argued.

"Listen, Vinod. These things are not so easy to judge" Dr. Sharma said, shaking his head.

Vinod disagreed. "What is there to judge, Sharma? A baby is a baby—a gift from God. How can anyone want to kill a baby because it is a girl? Yes, yes, I know about farmers wanting boys so they can work. But this is Mumbai, a city; where are the farms here? Yes, I also know that the dowry system beggars some families, so they don't want girls. Dammit, Sharma, how will this country progress if we allow such archaic customs as the dowry to dictate our humanity?"

"Yes, I agree, Vinod. But surely you also know what happens when the husband wants the abortion but the pregnant woman refuses? We cannot turn a blind eye to what will happen to her. She will be so ill-treated, she will probably be beaten by her husband and his family so that she may spontaneously abort. Even worse, she may be starved and she may give birth to a premature baby or a severely malformed one. In such uneducated families, where is the money to care for such a child? In all of India, where is the money? That poor woman who wanted to bear her daughter will be further disgraced for bearing a deformed child. She will be sent back to her parents who won't want her because of her shame. Her life will be over. And that poor baby girl...her life will never begin." Dr. Sharma spoke compassionately about a moral and ethical dilemma he faced every day. "It is all very well for people to speak about babies being from God. I too believed that when I was in medical college. Now I've seen what some people do with God's gifts—they throw them on the rubbish heap."

Vinod remembered the conversation, and now here he was thinking of abortion as a solution. Damn that Dev. Because of him, Vinod was losing his mind, thinking of violating his principles, his morals. God, what had he come to? He had grown up in a strongly religious home where his mother, like Shanti, did a daily puja. While he did not practice the rituals, the fundamental morality of his religion formed the foundation of his character.

Rama brought him a cup of tea, sweet with sugar. He knew Shanti would be close behind. Sure enough, she came in bearing some biscuits and cheese, followed by a tail wagging Bhim. She knew Vinod loved cheese; she also knew it was bad for his cholesterol. She must have some devious plan. He couldn't tell her where his thoughts had taken him. If she knew, she would be appalled.

"As usual, our Dev has landed in another fine mess. What should we do, Shanti?" he began.

"I've asked Kishore and Anju to come for dinner tonight with the children. They saw Dev last night. Let's hope that he realized how out of place Anita is in our family."

"Shanti, you always hope for a miracle. The boy is besotted with that girl, and he is stubborn, as you well know. Even if he sees it, he will stand by his guns. If he's already mentioned marriage to her, he will feel he must do the right thing, you know; it wouldn't be cricket to break his promise."

"Vinod, would it be so bad…" she said pleadingly

He raised his hand, palm outturned, "Shanti, don't even mention having her in this house again. When my son marries, he must marry a decent girl, one of his class."

"What if he agrees to marry a girl we pick for him, but keeps Anita, you know, on the side…?"

He stared at her as if she had punched him in the stomach. A nightmare from his youth floated into his mind. It had haunted him at the start of his life. Then he had repressed it. Was it going to echo in his old age? He shuddered as the memory he had suppressed all these years surfaced, bringing the searing agony of the day he had seen his larger-than-life grandfather shrivel. Now he saw Shanti looking at him anxiously.

"Are you all right? You've gone pale. Oh God, is it your heart again?"

"No, no. I'm all right. So, little Priya and Kisan are coming tonight. Jolly good. I'll have to show Kisan my magic trick and bring a rupee coin out of his ear. He's such a clever boy, isn't he?" He turned his face from Shanti and called out, "Rama, bring another cup of tea."

And thus, he diverted Shanti's attention. He was not ready to even acknowledge the memory of one of the worst days of his young life.

He was certainly not ready to share it with Shanti. But share it he must, because she had inadvertently thrown a vital complication into the puzzle, and he needed to think of it.

That evening, Kisan came running through the door. He was nearly six and bubbling with energy. His dark hair and smile were Kishore's. He shared a special bond with Vinod.

"Papa, Papa, do you have a new magic trick? Look what I'm doing in school," he yelled, and he flung himself into his grandfather's arms, smiling at him with shiny brown eyes. Vinod looked at his grandson and thought, "I'm glad I have not betrayed the boy's image of me."

Shanti was cuddling Priya and crooning to her. The little one had a head full of dark curls and a heart-wrenching smile. She was almost ready to walk. Vinod gazed around the drawing room and thought of all the articles they would have to move off the low tables to higher spots when she began to toddle—a small price to pay. The pleasure that Kisan and Priya brought to them was priceless. Carrying Kisan, he walked over to Priya to give her a kiss.

It was sad that such demonstrative affection dwindled when the children grew. When they had been with Kishore in America, he had seen grown men and women hug and kiss their fathers and mothers. This would not happen in India. Perhaps Anjali would change that. He would sorely miss not being able to kiss Priya and hug Kisan.

Once they heard the voice of Kisan, Malika and Rama came out to see the children. Little Priya held out her arms to Malika who smiled broadly and took the baby from Shanti. Malika had always been a favorite with the children with her gentle manner and soothing tone. Kisan, on the other hand, was Rama's favorite and the young lad, without a shadow of doubt in his voice, asked Rama if he had cooked his favorite dishes. And the grandparents and Rama and Malika played with the kids and fed them dinner while Kishore and Anjali quietly caught up with their day.

When finally the tired youngsters were tucked in bed, Rama brought out dinner for the adults. After Rama had served everyone,

Shanti and Anjali looked at each other with trepidation, knowing what was coming. Silently, they formed an alliance with each other.

Vinod and Kishore were equally vigorous in their denouncement of Dev. Vinod was pleased to see how right thinking Kishore had become. Yes, Kishore understood that Dev could not marry a woman, beautiful though she may be, so completely without background and class.

Anjali timidly suggested, "Surely, if he loves her…"

Vinod interrupted loudly, "What is this love, love, Anjali? Love can be born and grow after marriage, as Shanti and I can tell you. How long do you think Dev will love that girl when she goes with him to parties and cannot even talk to his friends? Huh? She is beautiful only. What about her parents? Huh? I haven't even asked him about them. Shanti, do you know what her father does?"

Shanti didn't know, and Anjali and Kishore assiduously looked at their plates.

"Do you know, Kishore? Anjali?" And Anjali and Kishore filled their mouths with roti and shook their heads.

"Well," he continued, "I'm sure they won't be of our class. Shanti, you saw how awkward she was when she came to my birthday party? Huh?"

"She can sing beautifully," Anjali tried again.

Vinod snorted. "Achcha. Good, good. So, she can sing. So could a nautch girl. And the rajas listened, used the girl for pleasure, and that was that. How will that help this Anita when our relatives come to stay with us for a holiday? What do you say, Kishore?"

Kishore stuffed a big forkful of food into his mouth and nodded some more. Finally, he swallowed and said, "You're right, Papa. I cannot see her fitting into this family at all. At dinner last night, even Anjali found it hard to talk with her. And Anju can talk to absolutely anyone. Isn't that right, Anju?"

"Poor girl, Kishore, give her a chance, I say—she was on display. She must have been nervous…"

"Come on Anju. Can you imagine, Anju tried to talk to her about books and found out she doesn't read. Nothing except those silly women's magazines, what're they called? *Femina*? We don't have the same friends or the same interests—nothing in common. What do you think, Amma?"

"I know what you are all saying, but I just want Dev to find some happiness. He has had such difficulties…"

"What difficulties, Shanti? He made them all for himself. We did not ask him to take drugs. We wanted him to do well in college, not waste his time. But he had to make friends with all those idle rich boys who don't have to work because their fathers give them all they want. Well, I can't provide for him like that. Why can't he take his example from Kishore—work hard and do well? No, he has to play drums. Che! I ask you. What kind of job is that for a man? Huh? Tell me. But what to do? He's a good-for-nothing bugger and always has been. I'm telling you, if he marries this girl, he may be happy for one, two months— because he won his fight against me. But, mark my words; very soon, he will tire of her. He will begin to leave her at home and go back to his old friends. Come, Anju, tell me what you think—you bring new ideas into this family. What would happen in America?"

Anjali swallowed hard. "Well, Papa, in America I think Dev would already have married Anita. Living in India, he is showing you respect by asking your permission. In America, his parents would let him make his mistakes and suffer for them."

"All well and good, *beti*. Let him make his mistakes—but here, in Mumbai, in India, his mistake smears the whole family name. I cannot let that happen. What he does will hurt you and your children too."

"How will it do that, Papa?"

"Listen, *beti,* we are a small community in this city of fifteen million. What he does will come back to hurt us all," he paused as once more his grandfather's face filled his mind. Suddenly, he straightened, nodded his head to Shanti. Then he called for Rama to clear the table. Kishore and Anjali looked a bit bewildered, but clearly Vinod had decided to close the subject.

"I want you all to understand, and I say this once and for all. If Dev marries that girl, he is no longer my son. He will not enter this house again," and he looked at Shanti who was wiping away tears and said, "I'm sorry, Shanti, but that is final."

It was a subdued Kishore and Anjali who left with the sleeping children draped on their shoulders. No one could speak much after Vinod's pronouncement, especially since it came from such a reasonable man. Kishore had never known his father to be so adamant, so obdurate.

Much later that night after Shanti fell into a fitful sleep, Vinod started talking quietly. "Shanti, are you awake? I cannot sleep. I must talk to you."

"What is it, Vinod? Is something paining you?"

"No, no. I feel the hand of my grandfather reaching out across all these years and touching Dev."

"Which grandfather? Your father's father? The one you who was like a god to you, the police captain?"

"Yes, the same one. You already know that when I was a young boy, the most important figure in my life was my grandfather. How strong he was! What stories he told us! When I was sick, he would tell me of faraway places and transport me with his words, and I forgot my pain and fever. You know, we lived in his house in Karnad when I was little, and he was an important man. It was only when my father got a job in Mumbai that we moved away. For a long time, I was sad and lonely, missing my grandfather and his stories. Do you know, Shanti, I've forgotten what my grandmother looked like; her personality faded next to his flamboyant one. But he is clear to me still."

"I never met them; they were both gone before our marriage."

"I know. I have not told you how deeply my beloved grandfather betrayed me. I've never told anyone."

"What happened?" Shanti was wide awake now and sitting up in bed.

Slowly, he recounted the time when he was about nine years old and opened the door to a man, a stranger who came to the flat in Mumbai.

Vinod said, "He was wearing a ragged and dirty kurta pajama, and he wanted to speak to my Papa. He called my Papa Arun, which shocked me. How could this scoundrel, this beggar call him by name? At least he should say "sir" or "sahib", nai? Before I could say Papa wasn't home, my mother was at the door. She gasped when she saw him; then she asked, 'Oh God, Prakash! Why have you come here? What do you want?'"

"He said, 'I must speak to Arun; I need money.' He began to shout things like 'they owe it to me. We will not be thrown away—my mother and I go hungry, but I can't be silent any more,'" Vinod continued.

He told Shanti how he shrank in the corner, scared, trembling. His mother said she would give the stranger some money and went to fetch it. Vinod's eyes were riveted on that moment from the past. He went on, "When my amma left the room to get the money, this crazy goonda came up to me, and took my chin in his hand and tilted my face to look at me. His nails were black with dirt and his eyes were shiny, like he was mad. I thought he was going to kill me."

Vinod paused and looked at Shanti's puzzled face. He was compelled to continue. Swallowing hard at the memory, he shook his head in pain, then went on,

"He looked into my eyes and smiled a sweet smile, just like my Papa's. My mother came and gave him what money she had in the house, asked him to come in to the kitchen and eat some lunch. I thought now she had gone mad. He ate like he hadn't seen food in days. When he was ready to leave, she packed him some food for his mother and begged him not to come back. He looked at her with such pain and asked, 'Am I so unworthy, Mira? Do I not share the same blood? Why am I tossed on the dung heap? *Achcha*—I won't bother you again. My poor Amma is sick with hunger; that is why I came.' And he ruffled my hair and limped away," Vinod finished his story.

"Hari Ram. Who was he?" Shanti asked, her eyes round.

"That was the day my god-like grandfather was reduced to a mere human. My grandfather, my hero, had a village woman as a mistress, and this man was his son. The man who had come to beg for money was my father's half-brother, my uncle I met only that one time. My beloved grandfather did not provide well for his other family; he was ashamed of them. He never acknowledged them—he really tossed them on the dung heap. They did that in those days," Vinod said in a faraway voice

"Why are you thinking of this now, Vinod?"

"I don't know. When you asked me that question this afternoon, this all came back to me."

"What did I ask you?"

"You asked 'what if Dev marries a girl we pick for him but keeps Anita on the side.' That will never allow for happiness, Shanti. Everyone in Karnad, everyone in our community, knew my grandfather's other son, even though he never spoke of that family. When it came time for Papa's sisters, my aunties, to marry, somehow there were not as many good offers…I am sure now it was because of him. Dev must not have illegitimate children. Can't you see they'll be cousins to our Kisan and Priya? They will be our grandchildren, and we will have to turn our backs on them if Dev is not legitimately their father. I don't know what to do, Shanti. Tell me, what should we do?"

And Shanti stayed silent.

Dev

THIS MORNING DEV WAS FEELING very practical. Yes, he was besotted with Anita, but his whole family was adamantly opposed to her. Up until this week, even he hadn't thought of marrying her. Kishore and Anjali were avoiding the topic. The last time they spoke, Kishore had said, "I don't have time right now, *bhai*. Why don't I phone you when we can sit down and talk about it?" Dev had the distinct feeling that Kishore had talked with Papa and also objected to the marriage. He wished he could speak to his father as easily as Kishore did, but nothing had ever come to him as easily as it had to the 'golden boy.' Kishore was a role model for him—except he never followed the model.

Dev walked into the drawing room and sank into a comfortable chair. He wondered where his mother was; he wanted her company. As he sat back, he wondered what kind of magic Anita had woven to hold him in such thrall. Was he being stupid and foolish, like his father said?

He closed his bloodshot eyes and laid his head back on the chair's soft pillowy upholstery. His hair was a tangle of unruly curls, and he hadn't shaved or showered. He had woken up determined to make some sort of decision that very morning. Maybe he needed to be a bit less mule headed and more rational. He should really think things through. Last night he'd had too much to drink, but this morning he was thinking clearly. Okay, he could be practical.

He was barely making pocket money with his drum playing, and he wasn't interested in taking a job like Kishore's. He had always counted on living at home, rent-free. Heaven knew there was room for him in this flat. He didn't feel guilty about it; all his rich friends lived at home and most of them didn't even work. His mother would be miserable without him at Kalpana, he was sure of that. Vinod, on the other hand, well, Dev tried to stay out of Vinod's way as much as possible. Especially now, the tension between them was so acute, it was impossible to be in the same room. Shanti was definitely the softer touch. Dear Amma—he loved the way she took his chin in her soft lime-scented hand, and looked into his eyes as if willing him to be reasonable. He knew she must be having a hard time because Vinod must be raging, and she was the only audience.

He needed to weigh the pros and cons of his situation. That was a Kishore kind of thing to do. He groaned out of the chair and picked up a notebook and pen from the desk. He would make himself a two-columned list. On the pro side of marrying Anita was his lustful desire of her. Bloody hell—she could turn him inside out when they had sex; she was the most exciting woman he had ever slept with. Having written that down as politely as he could, he tried to find other reasons for the pro side. And the more he thought, he could find none. Not a single one. Shaking his head with a sigh, he knew he had to look dispassionately at the opposing side. And he had to be honest with himself.

He knew that if he went through with this marriage braving all the objections, his father would disown him. Vinod had shouted as much during a rage-filled scene, spittle spraying out of his red-hot mouth. Dev had cringed before such wrath, and Shanti had been silent and trembling, too afraid to intervene. Even now, Dev shuddered at the memory. So, if his father disowned him, that would mean he would have no place to live. Even the ancestral flat, Vinod's parents' home that he knew had been set aside for him, well, Vinod would not give it to his disinherited son. Not only the property, he was sure he could kiss any money goodbye, except small sums his mother could smuggle to him. Was he willing to give up his inheritance for Anita? Well, no. That was a big mark in the con column.

He moved his mind systematically on to Kishore and Anjali, whom he was counting on for support. They both seemed very tepid in their acceptance of Anita. Bloody hell. He had been so sure that Anjali would be beguiled by the romance of the whole story. With her American background, she should have been entranced by the fact that he was willing to defy his parents, give up his easy lifestyle, all for love. And then, shouldn't Anjali have enthusiastically cheered on the sidelines that Dev was not only willing to sacrifice his family's blessing, but he would break through the caste and racial barriers to do it? The more he thought of that, the prouder he felt about himself—he was a white knight in shining armor saving this beautiful damsel from a lackluster life in the spurious glamour world of night clubs.

But, Anjali too had been strangely aloof. The dinner at their flat had been a disaster. It was clear that Anita did not really fit into their circle. Dev had just been too unwilling to accept that. Now remembering the evening, he squirmed as he remembered that Anjali tried hard to make conversation, but Anita didn't have much to say that was relevant or sensible. She talked a lot, but she didn't *say anything*. It was only when she sang that Anjali and Kishore seemed to appreciate her. Up until then the atmosphere had been thick with tension. Anjali had talked about shopping, clothes and even books, but nothing had caught on. He realized, of course, that Kishore had warned her not to talk about friends, family, college or all the other subjects that their social circle usually jabbered on and on about. As for Kishore himself, he'd assiduously avoided speaking directly to Anita all evening. Frankly, the whole time, Dev had seen disapproval simmering in his eyes.

Dev shook his head again. God, it was so humid. Why was it always so fucking hot? He called for Rama to bring him an ice-cold lime juice and turned on the overhead fan. For several minutes, he watched the blades spinning robotically, click, click, click. As he sipped his lime juice, he closed his eyes again so he could think better.

So far he had blinded himself to reality—in truth, Kishore and Anjali were uncomfortable with the idea of Anita in the family. There, he'd admitted it. While his parents may object on grounds of caste and status, Kishore and Anjali did not like the idea of *Anita herself*. Looking at that in the cold light of truth, Dev saw that maybe he was being too stubborn and opposing everyone just to prove a point. One more mark in the con column—the disapproval of Kishore and Anjali.

Finally, Dev looked at the situation from the viewpoint of his friends. Sure, all his bachelor friends envied him for his gorgeous girlfriend and were always lasciviously seeking details about the evenings he spent with her. And how he enjoyed giving them those salacious details and watching them drool. However, the girls in his group couldn't find anything in common with Anita. When he took her out with his friends, she always was left out of the conversation, the in jokes, the shared experiences. It was quite pathetic to watch her try to throw in the odd irrelevant and inappropriate remark. Dev winced as he recalled some of the eye-rolling expressions on his friends' faces as they ignored Anita's comments and returned to their animated blather. Uncomfortably, he recalled that he hardly ever tried to rescue her, but instead ignored her and laughed and continued talking. There, family and friends all vote no to his marriage.

Dev opened his eyes. He needed to call on his will, give up this weakness. Anita was another drug for him—forbidden, intoxicating and addictive. Looking at himself honestly, he admitted that he had not been entirely successful in giving up drugs. He still smoked pot, he still drank too much rum, and he still took Valium when things got too "rough." Would he have the will power to give up Anita? He knew intellectually that she was completely wrong for him; if he stayed with her he would lose his family, his friends and his inheritance. Was she worth it? No. He had to sacrifice the pleasures of her body (and how long could his lust for her last?) so that he could live a reasonably happy life. If he were to be brutally honest, he wasn't really in love with Anita—he just desired her flesh and the hundred and one ways she was able to pleasure him in bed. Today he would break up with her. He would be a weakling no longer. Yes, he had the strength to do it. If after the breakup, it became too hard to work with her in the same nightclub, he would get himself another job somewhere else. He had talent. He had a reputation.

He continued to sip his lime juice thoughtfully. What lay ahead? He could do what so many of his friends had done—they'd married girls that their parents had chosen for them. He knew he could count on Shanti to choose a suitable girl for him. Even his friend Rohan, who had been such a wolfish bachelor, had succumbed and married that vacuous, pretty and rich woman. What was her name? All she could talk about was shopping and movies. But Rohan seemed happy enough. Dev admitted that if he married Anita, he would soon run out of common ground with her. Then, knowing himself, he would stray into other arms and there would be a divorce, family eruptions, general unhappiness. Is this what was in store for him? No, he could not put Shanti and Vinod through all that. He was not that selfish.

And, what about his friend Naren? Poor Naren. He was small, rather sparrow-like, timid and faltering. His father was determined his son earn a degree from America, so he paid a fortune for Naren to be admitted to the University of Alabama. Naren was not very bright, but he had done well enough to be offered some job opportunities to work in Alabama and adjoining states. This in turn brought several families eager to make a good match (or was the word really catch?). Before he went to work at a local bank in Montgomery, he came to Mumbai for two weeks.

During that time, he surveyed eligible girls his parents paraded as possible brides, chose Smeeta, became engaged, had a splendid wedding and took his new wife back to the U.S. All in two weeks. And of course, her father had paid another fortune so Smeeta could accompany her new husband to America. So, if his friends could do it, he could too. He had no right to split up his family, break the hearts of his parents. No, he wanted to continue to live the comfortable life he enjoyed now.

Willing himself the strength, he wondered where his mother was. Then he heard the soft tinkle of the prayer bell and knew she was doing her puja. Damn, he wished she would hurry so he could see the happiness break out on her face when he told her his decision. He began to play the scene of his breakup with Anita in his mind.Oh God, she would be heartbroken. He saw himself being kind and gentle as he told her that because of his family's violent objections, he just couldn't marry her as he had been hinting. He didn't want to hurt her, but what could he do? The demands of society were really stringent.

Just then his cell phone played its annoying little tune. He must remember to change the tones.

"Hello?"

"Dev? Dev? Oh, my God…" Anita dissolved into sobs.

"What's the matter, Anita? Has something happened? What's happened? Tell me."

"Can you come over? Please? Can you come *now?* Come to the club. Please, come soon," Anita was sniffling and could barely speak. Dev was alarmed.

Dev snapped his cell phone shut and raced out of the flat. What the hell could have happened? She sounded very distraught. Last night had been quite wonderful, even though there had been tension between them. This tension was due to him, his inability to ask her unfalteringly to marry him, to take her proudly to his parents' flat. Surely, she must feel inferior to his family. Then another thought struck him. Fuck, she wasn't pregnant, was she? No, no—she couldn't be; he'd always used protection.

He slapped the steering wheel, placing his finger firmly on the horn as the traffic crawled in the crowded city. Godammit, at this rate, it would take him half an hour to get to the club. What had happened to make Anita so desperate?

Finally, twenty minutes later, he reached the club and rushed in to find her. She was sitting curled up on a chair, her face all smudged, kajal streaming down with her tears. She ran into his arms unable to speak because of her sobs. He soothed her, patting her back and smoothing her hair. He impatiently yelled at and waved away all the curious spectators who had gathered to witness the drama. After a few minutes, she quieted down enough to speak.

"Oh, Dev. Oh, why has this happened?"

"What is it? Tell me, Anita. I'm going crazy wondering why you are so upset."

"This morning after I woke up, my mother and father started to talk to me. They looked so happy. Do you know that Mr. Amarnath who keeps coming to the club all the time? Sometimes, he has sent me flowers after I have finished my songs. You don't know who he is? He's about sixty years."

"Why are we talking about this old man, Anita? I have no interest in him."

"Listen, Dev. Just listen, please."

"Okay, okay. Now how did this Amarnath upset you so much?"

"Last evening, Mr. Amarnath spoke to my parents and asked if they would agree to my marriage to his son. His son lives somewhere in America."

Dev's heart lurched to his stomach. Relief flooded him. His dilemma had solved itself. Now he wouldn't have to break up with her. Almost simultaneously he was overcome with anger. How could she break up with *him?*

"What the hell are you saying, Anita?" Dev's eyes were wide with shock and he held her at arms' length. He was losing her. This could not be happening. Was she going to slip through his fingers? Shit. He couldn't lose her to an anonymous jerk living "somewhere in America".

"Surely, you can't agree, Anita."

"Mr. Amarnath promised to pay for the wedding and everything, saris and jewel-ery for me. And," she whispered, "he offered my mother one lakh in cash and a nice flat in Bandra so that they could live in comfort."

"Oh, my God."

How could he compete with that? The wedding all paid for and her parents given a flat and one hundred thousand rupees as a kind of reverse dowry. Bloody hell, he was definitely losing her now. He would elope with her and to hell with everyone else.

His mind became a confused tangle of hurt, relief, and loss. All his morning's thoughts and resolutions melted away. He couldn't remember a single logical thought he'd had just hours ago. He knew he could not let Anita reject *him*. He just kept murmuring over and over into Anita's hair, "It'll be all right, baby. I'll make it all right."

She turned her face to him, her eyes accusing, anguish lurking in their depths. "How will you do that, Dev? Have you asked me to marry you? You've taken me to your parents' house once only and to your brother's house once only. Do you think I am stupid? Do you think I am blind that I didn't see the looks in their eyes when they spoke to me? They don't think I'm good enough for you or your family. They don't want me in the family. Isn't that true, Dev?"

How could he deny it? He tried to placate her, saying "I'm sure they'll come around, Anita. I just have to keep working on them. Give me a little time, please."

"How much more time should I give you, huh, tell me? It's been more than a year since we met. And what do you mean, working on them? Whatever you do, whatever you say, they will never accept me. Do you think I don't know that? And how do you think I will feel if we get married and your family treats me like a servant? And what will they do to you? Will your father throw you out? Tell me the truth now, Dev. At least now, for once tell me the truth."

"Darling, they will grow to love you like I have."

"Tell me the *truth*, Dev. What will happen to you? What has your father said? What will happen to you?"

"Well, you know, he's very stubborn, but I am sure…"

"For once, can you just tell me the truth?"

Dev hung his head, "Please, please don't leave me" he whispered.

When he finally looked up, he was shocked to see scorn in her eyes, not the adoration he was used to. She straightened her spine, grew taller and stronger. When she began to speak, she was a stranger. Her tears had dried and there was purpose in her features.

"Dev, I have waited for you to ask me to marry you for one year. But now I've been given a chance. I'll go to America and who knows? Maybe I'll become a singing star. And my marriage to Mr. Amarnath's son will also make my parents comfortable. In this whole year, you have not once met my parents. I know that they are not rich like yours, living on Malabar Hill. But Mr. Amarnath is also rich, but he came in his big car to my house and begged my parents to permit me to marry his son. He said if he was younger, he would have married me himself. He told them how he comes to the club just to see me and hear me sing. He also promised that his son would be coming back here after a few years, and I would be near my mother. Now tell me, Dev, what can you give me? How long should I wait for you only?"

"Anita, let's run away and get married today."

"No, Dev. I am tired of waiting for you and listening to your lies. I know your brother and sister-in-law don't like me, and your father won't even look at me. My parents already agreed and the wedding will take place in a few months when a hall is available."

He couldn't believe he had lost her—and with no warning. This could not be happening to him. Why was he always so damn weak? He had lost her.

He tried to pull her back into his arms as tears started to his eyes. Shocked, he felt an icy resistance. Never before had she been anything but supple and eager to fit into his embrace—but this? She stood ramrod stiff in his arms, her face a mask. Gone were the tears, the desperation he had heard on the phone. This was a new Anita, and she was stronger than he had ever been.

She looked at him with a wistful regret in her eyes. Then she said, "This is the last time I can see you, Dev. I'm sorry, but my kind of people have to look after ourselves. My mother always told me that no one would look after us—and I can see she was right, especially about you. So even if Mr. Amarnath's son is not handsome like you, even if he is short and ugly, I am going to marry him and go with him to America."

"My God, Anita. How can you be so callous and just forget this past year."

"I don't know what this 'callous' means—you see I didn't go to all those fancy schools like you and your friends. Tell me the truth, Dev: you were always ashamed to take me to your friends' parties, no? Oh, yah, I saw the looks in their eyes whenever I said something. They would roll their eyes and look at each other. Maybe Mr. Amarnath's son won't care …" Suddenly, her eyes filled with tears." I won't be singing here any more. Now I have to go. Mr. Amarnath is sending me his car and taking me shopping for jewel-ery."

He watched as she walked out without a backward look. And he watched his heart break. The pain of losing her seared him viscerally with an intensity that he didn't expect. He damned his parents, Kishore and Anjali, his friends; they had stopped him from marrying her. He forgot his recent decision to break up with her. Now all he felt was the anguish of grief and guilt. It was his fault. He had been too weak to stand up for what he wanted. He had allowed his domineering family and his silent friends dictate his future and snatch away his chance at happiness. He headed for the bar, walked behind the counter and poured himself a drink to dull the pain even though it was morning yet.

Two hours later, he sat nursing a large rum and veering between remembering the idyllic moments he had shared with Anita and the bitterness he felt at her betrayal. She was so mercenary. How could she have so quickly tossed aside the wonderful times they had shared, their surreptitious love making in friends' homes and hotel rooms? Was she really willing to marry a total stranger? Well, she was doing it for money. Hah, his father was right. She was a nautch girl, selling her body. She had turned out to be a slut after all.

Then he remembered her words "people like us have to look after ourselves." She was not about to inherit any money or jewelry from her mother, and Mr. Amarnath had certainly made his offer irresistible throwing in the lakh of rupees and the flat. If she married his son, she made her future financially secure. As the rum coursed through him, he woozily recalled his morning's inner debate. He vaguely remembered that he was planning to break up with her because of his parents and friends. Well, she'd made breaking up easier for him. He had been dreading telling her…but, bloody shit. How could she break up with *him?*

He slammed the glass down on the counter, grabbed his car keys and headed for home. Maybe now Shanti would have finished her puja. He could tell her his decision not to see Anita again and watch the happiness replace the worry lines on her face. Even Vinod would be pleased with him. He rang the doorbell to the flat, said good morning to Malika when she opened the door. He called for his mother, who by now was sitting and reading.

She looked up, alarmed, since he was never home in the early afternoon.

"What is it, *beta*? Is everything all right?" she asked, worry entering her eyes.

"Never better, Amma. Shall I ask Rama to bring lunch for us? Come, let's have lunch together." Then he called for Rama to bring the food to the table.

Shanti could not contain her happiness. It was so rare that Dev ate lunch at home. When she saw his red-rimmed eyes, she knew that all was not well with him. And she smelled liquor on his breath. She knew better than to accuse him of drinking. As they ate, she questioned him gently. "What is troubling you *beta*? Something has happened, isn't it?"

"Amma, I know you and Papa, and even Kishore and Anjali, have not approved of Anita. What could I do? I thought I was in love with her, but I know it made you and Papa very unhappy."

Shanti looked very distressed. "I know, *beta*. I tried talking to your father, but he is very firm in his objections."

"What about you, Amma?" Dev had no idea why he was even asking her.

"*Beta,* all I want is your happiness. I know that this Anita is not of our class and caste, but nowadays that doesn't seem to matter so much. I am only afraid that you won't be happy with her..."

"It's all right, Amma. I thought it over for a long time, and today I told Anita that I could not make you and Papa so unhappy, and I would not see her anymore. So I said goodbye to her this morning."

Shanti stopped eating and stared at him. "What are you telling me, *beta*? Is it true?" She could not believe her ears.

Dev smiled at her—he had made her happy. "Yes, Amma, it's true. I finally told myself that I shouldn't make you and Papa worry so much. Haven't I given you enough to worry about? After all, you have showered me with so much and let me do whatever I wanted. You have your reasons for objecting to this marriage. Even Kishore and Anjali seemed to object. All of you are smarter than me, so you must have seen something that I have been blind to."

Shanti could not stop her words from flowing now. She felt such a huge boulder lifted from her chest and the lightness made her dizzy. She said, "My Dev. You have made me so happy. I did not like being torn to pieces between you and your father. You know, I also did not feel she was the right girl for you. I thought she was after your money."

Amma was right, he thought, Anita did sell herself for money, didn't she?

Now he covered her soft hand with his and said, "Well, I thought all of you can't be wrong. Most important, I knew I couldn't hurt you, Amma. You have always been on my side. But this time, I knew we would lose. Papa was too stubborn about this, wasn't he?"

Shanti nodded silently. Then she looked up at him and said, "Don't worry, *beta*. We will find the right girl who will be suitable in every way for you. She will fit into this family and into your life. You will be happy, I know it."

After they finished lunch, he knew she would head for the phone to speak to Vinod, and then to Kishore. In a small way, with the help of the rum, his pain was eased. Certainly, seeing a smile break through her clouded features was worth it. Yes, he had made the right decision.

Dev headed into his room and closed the door. He threw himself on the bed and let the conflicting emotions flow over him. What a day! He wondered what to do to ease the pain he felt. After a few minutes, he sat up. Then he rummaged in the drawer for his chillum pipe and tamped in the marijuana leaves. This would not desert him. This he could depend on. Just as he could depend on his family's support of him and their approval now. Yes, it would feel good. As the hazy smoke soothed him, he gazed through the grayness of it, dizzy with relief. Things were going to be all right now. No more fighting his parents, his brother, Anita—aahh. Yes. He had made the right decision. It wouldn't take long to forget her.

That night Dev stayed home for dinner—he couldn't stand to go to the club just yet. Vinod was in an expansive mood before the meal, so evidently happy with the news. Never had Dev felt his father's grace warm him so palpably. With each passing moment, he felt more and more pleased. When Kishore and Anjali came over with Kisan and Priya, Dev felt almost like the prodigal son. Everyone made a big fuss over him, but no one mentioned Anita and the turmoil she had caused in their family. It was only Anjali who whispered when she kissed him good night, "I can only imagine what you're going through. Call me and we'll talk, okay?" He nodded mutely.

For two weeks, his family left him alone as he swung violently between feeling utterly bereft about losing Anita and feeling so relieved of the tension caused by her presence in his life. Yes, he sank deeper into drugs and drink, and everyone knew it, but they did not chastise him. He was going through a crisis; it would soon be over and he could be eased into normal life without those crutches.

Meanwhile, Shanti was not idle. She let her friends and relatives know that Dev was finally available for marriage. Of course, being the modern family in Mumbai, she did not resort to the traditions that were still common, especially in the south of India. Shanti remembered when she and Vinod got married, their families were among the first not to have the bride's and groom's horoscopes read by astrologers. In those days, horoscopes were studied for ten spheres of compatibility, and if seven or eight matched, it was assumed that the marriage would have a good chance of success. So, even though Shanti's and Vinod's horoscopes had not been "matched" she was sure that compatibility would have been found in more than seven or eight spheres. Of course, for Dev Shanti would not go through astrologers. She was content to rely on friends to suggest eligible brides. That grapevine was strong, and she knew the results would be better than anything predicted by the stars.

Thus it was one day that Shanti asked Dev, "*Beta*, tonight your father and I want you to go with us to a small cocktail party at Mrinalini's."

Dev was puzzled—when had he ever gone out with his parents?

"I want you to meet their daughter Jaya. She is very pretty and fair and she has a degree in architecture," Shanti went on to explain.

Dev smiled; so it was starting. Nubile young women were going to be introduced to him, and he could take them out and choose one to marry. He understood that he was a good catch. Vinod and Shanti would never ask for a dowry from the young bride's parents. Some families, even in this day and age, demanded that the bride bring jewels, a new car, thousands of rupees. Dev thought that the dowry system was archaic and barbarous. Families went deep into debt to get their daughters married. No wonder Indian families wanted only sons.

Anjali wondered how Dev could submit to being on show. Kishore had put it in a context that she could understand, "Well," he said, "it's rather like a blind date. Don't friends set up couples in the U.S.? Here the parents do it. And there is the safeguard: the parents check into the prospective bride or groom and the family. The backgrounds will have much in common. In the good old days, it pretty much assured a forever marriage, but nowadays, even an arranged marriage has the same chance as any other."

Anjali said, "I still can't see how Dev can put up with this parade, this *galata.*" Kishore laughed and said he thought Dev was enjoying every minute of it.

That first cocktail party at Auntie Mrinalini's introduced him to Jaya. Of course, Mrinalini was not really his aunt, but in the Indian way, he called all his parents' friends, all his elders in fact, Uncle and Auntie. While the parents and their friends chatted, Dev and Jaya found a quiet nook to talk to each other. However, there was no spark between them and after a few minutes their conversation dried up. As they sat in the awkwardness of silence, the ever-observant Shanti rescued him by including him and Jaya in the parental conversation. The evening came to a close, but no one felt rejected buffered as they were by the guests at the party. It was clear to Dev that Jaya felt the way he did—relieved when the evening was over.

And thus the search continued. Dev enjoyed meeting all these new girls. Where had they been hiding? Some of them were attractive; some were plain—all were intelligent and had college degrees. Some were working at good companies; others were involved in social and community service. Dev's life style seemed lightweight by comparison. For a change he did not feel inordinately superior to these girls as he had to Anita. Sometimes on his outings he really worked hard to not sound shallow.

Dev had moved from playing in the international hotels to the newly sprouting bars and nightclubs. He'd played at Cyclone and the Abyss, and he was now a regular at Athena. He took some of the girls to all three nightclubs to see how they would handle the smoke-filled atmosphere and the music. At each, the bands played the latest American music, from hip-hop and soft rock to heavy metal, interspersed with Hindi pop songs. The crowd was young, well-dressed, eager to drink and dance. Dev watched carefully to see how his companions enjoyed the scene. Whenever he went with them to the Athena, he excused himself and joined the band for a set. From his perch behind the drums, he could see if they genuinely appreciated his talent.

After a whirlwind six weeks, choices were made. Dev and Shilpa became officially engaged. She was a perky young lady, unfailingly good humored. She enjoyed visiting the nightclub and thought his drum playing was inspired. She worked in a financial firm and knew so much more than he did about investment and the economy. It was as if he provided the fun and she the substance—and together they fit as snugly as yin and yang. Dev genuinely enjoyed the time he spent with Shilpa, and now that the die had been cast, he became impatient for the wedding.

That was not so easy since the wedding halls were reserved so far in advance. Shanti and Vinod wanted the wedding to be at the Taj Hotel, just as Kishore's had been. That required a year's wait, and neither family was willing to do that. Finally, it was Kishore who had the brilliant idea of asking for the house at Juhu Beach that Sun Micro provided for foreign visitors. It was large and had a beautiful garden with palm trees that went right down to the white sand. The setting was tranquil and lush, the perfect solution. After the wedding, the couple could spend the night at the beach house. The reception the next night was to be at the Oberoi Hotel.

Of course, they had to wait for the auspicious months—certain times of the year were definitely considered not good for weddings. Obviously the monsoon months brought their own restrictions. The heat of the months before the monsoon made them also undesirable. Finally, a date was chosen, only four months away.

Anjali was as excited as if it were her wedding. This one was more traditional than hers had been. Now that she had been in Mumbai for several years, she was wholeheartedly involved in the rituals. She was an eager participant in Dev's and Shilpa's wedding preparations. It was she who persuaded Shilpa to do the mehndi the night before the ceremony. It was great fun having all the women gather, sing songs, tell jokes and watch Shilpa's hands and feet painted with elaborate saffron designs.

When Vinod, Shanti and family went to the Juhu house on the morning of the wedding, they found a fairyland—garlands of jasmine and marigolds had been strung between the coconut palms. That evening, twinkling lights encircled the trunks of the trees and hung in the fronds. Shilpa wore a green silk sari with intricate gold work. A string of diamonds in her part ended in a pendant of rubies on her forehead. She wore beautiful gold necklaces and heavy ruby and emerald earrings. Like Kishore before him, Dev rode in on a white horse, handsome in a white turban. The ceremony was performed in the garden under the stars in a sheltered corner so the priest could light the fire around which the young couple walked. Later the guests went inside for cocktails.

Silent servants quickly set up tables in the garden for dinner. The caterer had outdone himself. In the center of the elaborate buffet was a mountain of splendid mutton biriani. Pakoras, crisp and hot, kept the guests munching as they heaped their plates with the biriani, the chicken kofta, the pork vindaloo, eggplant and other vegetable dishes too numerous to count. The dessert was the rich sweet gulab jamun, smelling faintly of roses. Anjali surprised the young couple with a traditional wedding cake. Kishore happily made a funny toast to his younger brother. Meanwhile, inside the house a band played music for as long as anyone wanted to dance. It was past two in the morning before everyone left the young couple to themselves.

Alone at last, Dev approached Shilpa with something akin to shyness. He had never felt like this when he was seducing other girls. His palms felt damp and his throat dry. He watched in wonder, standing awkwardly and gazing at her.

As she eagerly shed her gold, her jewels and her silks, he wondered if she were a virgin. She wasn't and she passionately followed him wherever he led. After making love multiple times, they finally lay sweaty and tousled on the rumpled sheets. Dev's last thought before falling asleep was "Why did I ever think Anita was the only woman who could satisfy me? Shilpa is the one—oh my God, I am so exhausted and so happy."

Four years later

Anjali

Anjali picked up Kisan and Priya at Kalpana where they had gone after school. Kisan was now eleven years old and Priya six, both attending Cathedral School. Priya was in the infant school close by on Malabar Hill, and Kisan had moved on to the junior or "big" school as he called it. Their grandparents welcomed the opportunity to see the children two or three times a week, and the children had a solid bond with the old couple.

"Hello Amma, were the babies good today?" Anjali asked after Malika let her in.

"Mummy, please don't call me a baby anymore. I've asked you a thousand times," said Kisan.

"Sorry, my big boy. Did you get any homework done, or were you bothering Papa to tell you stories?"

"I finished all my maths and history. I only have to do some science and English. I hate grammar, Mummy. Why do we have to parse sentences?"

"Sorry, *beta*. We all had to go through it. So are you ready to go home? Go, get Priya. Come on, *jaldi, jaldi*. Daddy said he is coming home early today." Anjali was beginning to intersperse Hindi or Maharati words into her speech because sometimes those words seemed the most appropriate. When Kisan disappeared to fetch his sister, Anjali turned to Shanti who seemed exhausted and whose hair was slightly disheveled.

"Amma, are you all right? You look tired. Are the children making you tired? Tell me, and they can go straight home from school." Shanti waved away Anjali's concern. Anjali looked surreptitiously at her mother-in-law. She was now approaching sixty and noticeably slower. Perhaps she could be persuaded to have a check-up. Of course, she vigorously resisted seeing any doctors.

"Why should I go? There is nothing wrong with me. I am like a rock," was her chant.

Anjali did not worry about Vinod. He was energetic as ever. After his heart attack those many years ago, he took his doctor's advice seriously. He walked every day in Kamala Nehru Park, near their flat. During the monsoon, he went to the gym at the club and used the treadmill. Next to Shanti, he looked fit and trim; she, on the other hand, walked more slowly, her hair was almost completely grey, and her skin seemed sallow. Anjali determined to talk to Kishore about it that night.

She was eagerly awaiting his coming home wanting him to explain his mystery. This morning he had called and said, "Anju, I want to make sure we are not going out tonight. I have something important to discuss with you." All her cajoling did nothing to break his silence and his repeated, "Just be patient; you'll know soon enough."

"Mummy, Priya is taking too long. Make her hurry up," said Kisan as he ambled back into the drawing room carrying his book bag.

"Just be patient, *beta*. She must be finishing something important," said Shanti, echoing her son. Soon Anjali and the kids left Kalpana for their own flat. After making sure that they did their homework and had their baths, Anjali allowed them a half hour of television. Indian TV was so awful—violent, unreal and with no redeeming value. She preferred to buy the latest DVDs for children.

She made sure that Shiva would have dinner hot and ready for Kishore, then sat with the kids to watch their mindless DVD. By eight o'clock, Kishore was home answering Kisan's rapid fire questions. After

Kishore had a quick shower and changed out of his suit into a cool white cotton pajama, they had dinner together. The children were growing so fast, and Kishore was glad that his work now allowed him more time with them. What was his news going to do to this little family?

After the children went off to bed, Anjali could wait no longer. Kishore got up from the dining table and led her into the drawing room where he sat down next to her on the sofa. He smiled as he brushed her hair off her face with the back of his hand.

"Now, tell me, or I'm going to burst," she cried, catching his hand.

"Okay, here it is. Today I got an offer from Microsoft to work for them in their Seattle headquarters. Anju, this is really big—the salary is two hundred thou, and stock options…"

"Two hundred thousand *dollars?* Not rupees?" she dug her nails into his hand.

He smiled at her excitement. "With a company car like we have here and all sorts of other perks. So, beautiful lady, do you want to move to Seattle with me?" he asked.

Anjali took a deep breath. "Oh my God, Seattle…I've never been there. It's supposed to be beautiful. Did this just happen today?"

"Well, actually, it's been going on for weeks, feelers here and there, hints, suggestions. Anyway, I didn't want to tell you anything until I knew for sure. The final firm offer came in today. I asked for a week to give them my response since this is not like moving to another city in India. So, what do you think, Anju?"

"I can't think—this is so exciting. My Kish being wooed by a Bill Gates surrogate."

"We should think of letting the children live here in Mumbai with Amma and Papa so they can finish school…" Kishore suggested.

"Are you mad? I want the kids with me, especially during their teen years."

"Think about it Anju. They have good friends here. In America there are so many temptations, drink and drugs, violence in schools."

"Come on, Kish," she interrupted. "Don't tell me those temptations are not all round the streets of Mumbai. Look at your own brother," she said. She went on to tell him how good the private schools were in the U.S.; when her father was posted to Washington D.C. she had gone to St. Albans. This was comparable, if not superior, to Cathedral because it offered myriad opportunities for arts and music. Tomorrow she'd surf the net to find an appropriate school in Seattle and download all the requirements for entrance.

Kishore sighed. "Amma and Papa will miss them very much. They live for the days when the kids visit after school."

"I know. Kish, Amma looked so tired today. Don't you think she has aged a lot recently? I'm worried about her."

"I'm sure she's fine. Papa would have told me if he was worried."

"You know who else is going to miss us all? Good old Rustum. He's become such a part of our family now, nai?" Anjali could say this fearlessly since the menace of gossip had worn itself out, and the tattling tongues had moved on to other subjects.

"Right you are, Anju. He does depend on us for companionship and the warmth of family. The kids will miss their Rusi Uncle as well," said Kishore.

After hours of talking, they agreed that he could not give up the opportunity; he would take the job. Kishore worried about what it would do to his parents. He suggested that they break the news to the old couple gently. What did Anjali think of taking them to dinner at the Zodiac Room at the Taj Hotel? She clapped her hands, delighted to be going to the hotel where they had been married, renovated since then.

In bed that night, Anjali was so excited that she couldn't sleep. Seattle, the city with the Space Needle, the Olympic Mountains, the Pacific Ocean—or was it Puget Sound? She remembered *Sleepless in Seattle*, the movie with Tom Hanks, which showed that some people lived on nearby islands and commuted on a ferry. How wonderful that would be. Then suddenly, unaccountably, an alien feeling rose from deep in her: she didn't want to go!

Where had this come from? She'd loved living in the U.S., but over the years, she had grown to love Mumbai. It was a feeling that had crept into her so stealthily, she hadn't even recognized it. Sure, like everyone else she complained of the heat, the monsoon, the intermittent riots, the corrupt politics, but she'd made good friends and more important, she had learned to think of people other than herself.

As she had always suspected she would, she'd become good friends with Sonali. Sonali, the girl she thought of as the conservative traditionalist, was really someone who took action in a quiet, unassuming way. She would have to meet Sonali to break the news to her. She did not relish the thought.

Anjali felt the blood rush to her head, and she sat up so she could clear her mind. Careful not to wake up Kishore, she crept out of bed and tiptoed to the lounge chair. She sat with her legs drawn up, her chin on her clasped hands. For the past few years, she had helped Sonali work with abused women in the city. She loved the work she was doing, but she had to go with Kishore—her loyalty belonged to him. The face of the battered woman who had come to see them yesterday came into Anjali's mind. She shook her head to dispel the image and willed herself to think of the pure snow-topped peaks of the Olympic Mountains and the clean, clear blue waters of the Puget Sound.

It took Anjali several days to find the right school in Seattle and arrange for the entrance exams for Kisan and Priya. This allowed her to postpone telling Sonali that she would be leaving. Finally, she invited Sonali to lunch at the Willingdon. As she sat on the verandah overlooking the lawn, she sipped her gin and tonic and thought about how much of her self she had invested in the abused women project. Sonali had proved to be a powerful persuader working on Anjali until her reluctance to get involved evaporated. It had been four years ago that Anjali had first gone into the slums of Mumbai to tackle the pervasive problem of wife abuse. She remembered that experience vividly.

Women, the poor and the helpless, whether they lived in villages or in cities, existed with silent resignation and acceptance of perpetual beatings.

Often the men demanded bigger dowries from their wives whose families had already gone into abysmal debt and had no more to give. The demands were usually accompanied by beating. At other times, the husband was a sot who beat his wife routinely when drunk. Anjali had taken a long time to inure herself to the pain she saw. She had taken even longer to understand the passive resignation which these women displayed.

The abused women believed it was their lot, their karma. They accepted that they had nowhere to turn. Their families did not want them back. While divorce was becoming more acceptable in the modern India, it was not a viable option for the poverty stricken.

Sonali and Anjali ventured into these areas to offer some hope, some relief. The first time they had gone into a slum, Anjali had been scared and nervous, much to the amusement of Sonali. "What do you think, Anjali? They're not going to attack you, for heaven's sake," Sonali said.

Still Anjali felt so alien—she who had traveled and lived in so many cities in the world, including Tashkent and Abu Dhabi. Yet this slum, in the heart of the big city of Mumbai, her *home*, was more threatening to her. When she traveled to a foreign city, she felt safe everywhere, whereas at home she knew where dangers lurked. She swallowed her fears that seemed absurd in the bright sunlight. Through the squalid assortment of huts, children followed them with large velvet eyes bright with excitement and teeth flashing white against their dark skins.

At first the women did not leave their hovels but continued to tend to the small fires over which they cooked their dal for the day or fried their chapattis. Slowly their curiosity lured them out. When a few gathered, Sonali began to speak to them while Anjali distributed sweets to the children. More women drifted nearer, covering their heads with their saris and sitting down on their haunches. Some nodded as Sonali spoke, and some slowly showed their bruises. Others cried. Sonali tried to urge them to go to the police if they were beaten, but at this they all scoffed, shaking their heads. One spoke up mockingly, "What do you think will happen? Our husbands will only beat us more for reporting them."

Anjali's heart ached for these women, inescapably trapped. And how anomalous it was that in the midst of this pain and grief, the children lifted their voices filled with the raucous laughter of life. As they left, Anjali turned to wave, and the children waved back, grinning with their shiny white teeth.

When they first started, Sonali and Anjali met with passive resistance from the women who did not really believe that these obviously rich women were coming to help them. With perseverance, Anjali and Sonali attracted more and more women to listen to their talks. Slowly, gradually, they gained the confidence of the victims. Slowly, gradually, women with bruises and haunted, hopeless eyes came forward to ask questions. It took months to build up the trust of the oppressed women to the point where they felt they could actually go to the police, report abuse, and not be further abused because of the report.

The two ladies worked tirelessly, pulled strings and bullied the police to make sure that complaints would be heard and acted upon—without reprisals. And more and more women gathered the strength to file police reports. Anjali was so proud of the work she was doing. If she left, she would be betraying and abandoning these women. Especially now. She and Sonali had persuaded a philanthropist to give them a large warehouse. This was where they were housing their most ambitious project.

There they planned to set up sewing machines and hire someone to teach the women tailoring so they could earn some money on their own and not be forever yoked to an abusive brute. When Sonali and Anjali talked excitedly together, they saw their project blooming into a cottage industry. Some people spinning jute, others sewing, still others painting. After all, hadn't women in—what state was it? Up north? Bihar, that was it—yes, the women in Bihar used to draw very stylized depictions of gods, mythological creatures and village scenes. From drawing on their walls to commemorate dates, they had begun to draw on paper and parlayed their primitive drawings into now much sought after Madhubani paintings.

It would be so fulfilling to continue this work Sonali and she had started. Looking up, she saw Sonali approaching her, waving excitedly. She had big news. So did Anjali—and she felt sick.

Kisan

KISAN KNEW THEY WERE TELLING some secrets; that's why he and Priya had been shunted off to bed so quickly. Why couldn't they realize he was growing up? When would they stop treating him like a baby? Why did he have to go to bed the same time as Priya? He tossed restlessly first kicking away the sheet that covered him and then sitting up and shrugging off his pajama top. Ten o'clock and it was still so bloody hot. The ceiling fan was whirring at highest speed, just moving the hot air around. He would go and ask Daddy to turn on the a.c.

Mummy and Daddy had a strict rule. Nobody but the two of them could turn on the air conditioner. They said if he did, he might blow a fuse, or he might overload the circuits of all the flats in the building. They were so ridiculous. If he had to teach Mummy how to use programs on the computer, surely he was smart enough to turn on the air conditioner without blowing a fuse. Maybe it made parents feel like parents when they made rules. So ridiculous!

He was eleven years and two months; he knew if he felt too hot. He swung his legs over the side of the bed and wiped his dewed upper lip and his arm pits with the sheet. He was beginning to get some hair under his arms (maybe), and he wondered when he would start sprouting a moustache. He was just beginning to hit a growth spurt and his body had the awkward lankiness of a giraffe. As he stood up, his knees clicked; they were doing that a lot lately. Amma said it meant his bones were growing. He walked confidently to the door in the blackness. A gecko on the ceiling went tic-tic-tic before it scurried to the other wall. If Priya had been here she would have screamed; she was terrified of geckos. Such a baby.

Feeling his way in the dark, he continued to grouse about the unfairness of his parents. If he were with Amma and Papa, they would let him do anything he wanted; that's why he loved visiting them at Kalpana. Besides, Rama made his favorite snacks every day for after school—hot cheese straws, samosas, pakoras.

Brushing his hand along the wall, he slowly tiptoed in the dark toward the light in the room where Daddy and Mummy were talking. As he neared the drawing room, he held his breath. Maybe he could listen to their secrets first. He heard only snatches of what they were saying, but a few words were enough. With his back against the wall, he slowly slid down until he was sitting on the floor with his knees under his chin, arms hugging them tightly. No! It couldn't be true. Bloody hell, they were talking of moving to America.

When they had spent some years in Santa Clara in California before Priya was born, he had not even been in school. He remembered Mummy taking him to play with some other kids. He'd had a red and blue swing set in the garden of their house. And an inflatable swimming pool. That had been fun, but he didn't need a swing set. And now he swam in the sea or the pool at the club. He had all his friends here—he didn't want to go to America. He bit his lip to keep from crying. Wait, Daddy was saying something about leaving him and Priya with Amma and Papa. Oh, please, please…No. Damn. Mummy squashed that idea. He wiped his cheek with his open hand.

As he crept back to his room, again groping his way in the dark, he knew exactly what they would say when they decided to tell Priya and him: It will be exciting. It's a part of the world you've never seen. You'll make new friends. Mummy will put on her too-wide smile, and even Daddy will talk logically about good opportunities.

He didn't want opportunities. He wanted to stay here and go to school with Goutam and Anand and all the other boys. What fun they had together. Goutam especially spent almost every day after school with him, playing chess or Scrabble after they did their homework. Kisan helped Goutam in maths, while Goutam was good in explaining history and English, especially stupid grammar. Who cared about parsing sentences anyway?

As he lay in bed, now sweating with anxiety, he thought of the afternoons they had spent at the beach at Juhu with Goutam's family. Both Goutam and he had learned to swim in the sea there. When the grown-ups weren't looking, they teased their little sisters, splashing water on them, calling them fraidy cats and sissies. And what fun they had flying kites on windy days. He saw himself and Goutam running on the yellow sand with the red and the black diamond shaped birds with their long tails swooping and diving behind them. When the boys collapsed laughing on the beach, they let their kites fly free. Whenever he thought of America, all he could think of was tall buildings, traffic,— hell, every movie had some kind of car chase. No school would be as good as Cathedral, and no boys could replace his friends here. It just wasn't fair. Why should he go just because his parents wanted to? What could possibly be as good as Juhu? He'd seen pictures of beaches in America—people lying on towels trying to get brown. Well, he already had a nice brown skin.

Kisan laced his fingers under his head so his armpits could be dried by the whirring fan. Even his curls were getting damp with sweat. Why was it always so hot? He kicked off the sheet again and tried to think. Mummy and Daddy were always talking about schools; maybe he could persuade them that his education was better here. He could remind them of the violence in schools in America. Yeah, what about all that stuff he read about in the papers, which Daddy and Papa talked about? Boys bringing guns to school, or fighting over skin color, having food fights in cafeterias. He was sure the food in any school cafeteria would not equal Rama's cooking. Rama's samosas…

He would miss even Suresh, the vendor on Juhu Beach. Kisan loved seeing him scale the tree and pluck coconuts. Goutam and he would run to Suresh's stand, but Suresh never gave them what he already had plucked. Grinning, his weathered skin set in permanent wrinkles, he would hitch his pants and fold them above his knees, loop a rope around his ankles and shinny up the tall branchless palm. Wielding a sharp scythe, he would hack off two large green coconuts and throw them down. Were there such coconuts in America? Where was the man who could, like Suresh, slice off the tops with sure strokes, stick a straw into the hole and hand over the sweet milky drink? Where would he get such right-off-the-tree fresh coconuts in America?

He and Goutam had always talked of going to Disneyland—that would be super. The Small World and the Matterhorn rides seemed exciting—but wait! Could they compare in surprise and wonder to a live camel ride at Juhu? Bloody hell! Riding a "ship of the desert" (he had just learned that phrase in school) on a beach had been more than super. Well, actually not. Maybe the camel was pissed off to be out of its Sahara desert and near an alien ocean—even if it was called the Arabian Sea. Anyway, the animal was repulsive, chi chi, dirty!

Kisan smiled as he recalled the mangy fur and the nauseating stink of the camel. Even more disgusting was the way it had fixed Kisan with its vindictive beady eye, bared its huge yellow teeth and spat. Then while loping on the sand, the creature began a series of farts which enveloped Kisan in a stomach-curdling vapor. Kisan wrinkled his nose at the memory. However, when he and Goutam talked of it, they only remembered the thrill of riding a camel on sun-warmed sand lapped by the Arabian Sea.

Slowly his eyes closed. He would lay his plans tomorrow to prevent this terrible move. Yes, many of his friends would envy him going to America, but he loved it here in Mumbai, and he loved his grandparents. As he drifted off to sleep, a thought hit him which would become his best argument. They didn't play cricket in America! That should be a trump card with Daddy who loved the sport as much as he did.

Vinod

VINOD WISHED KISHORE AND ANJALI would not waste their money. Why did they all have to go to the Taj Hotel for dinner? But Shanti's eyes sparkled at the name of the grand hotel in the shadow of the Gateway to India, where an evening's stroll of a few dozen yards took one to the shores of the gray sea.

So, Vinod surrendered, inwardly shaking his head. Kishore wanted to share his success, and it gave Anjali and him such pleasure to take the old folks to dinner. On that evening, Shanti wore a gold embroidered blue sari and Anjali looked splendid in a turquoise silk pant with a matching kurti embroidered with kundan work. This was indeed to be a special evening. As they were ushered in by the red turbaned Sikh doorman, even he could barely suppress a gasp, and Shanti's eyes widened with delight. The foyer had been redone since Kishore's wedding.

One wall was a carved wooden fretwork in white depicting the tree of life. Continuing the pristine look, the white marble floor, inlaid with colored marble, formed the illusion of Persian carpets. In the foyer, American and European businessmen and their wives sat chatting with their Indian counterparts. Several Arabs in their flowing robes, unaccompanied, sat sipping their colas and lemonades, eyeing the women. Of course they never had their several wives with them. Vinod knew that more Arabs would come during the monsoon season. He had been told they came from their desert kingdoms to see and enjoy the rain. Looking around, Vinod was struck by the wealth in the room. Such opulence and so many in rags on the streets, just outside the doors.

Tonight was not the time for such thoughts. Tonight was the time to celebrate—celebrate what, he did not know. Kishore and Anjali had brought them to this splendid place to give them some big news. Maybe another baby on the way? Maybe a promotion? Each day he thanked God that Kishore and Anjali had settled down in Mumbai. He and Shanti could revel in and enjoy their grandchildren.

Another doorman opened the door to their hushed dining room. A middle-aged Goan man played the piano softly, concentrating on Sinatra and Louis Armstrong numbers.

As they sat at their table in the Zodiac Room with its star-filled blue dome, the chef herself came out to tell them about the specials. Vinod was surprised—first that the chef was a girl, a young girl. And second, that she came out to meet them. Anjali talked to her easily and learned that her name was Nikki, and she had trained in a culinary school in France. She assured them that all the fish was fresh and advised them on what to order. Before she returned to her kitchen, Nikki told them she was trying out a new avocado soup and a new lychee infused custard—she offered it to them with her compliments only asking for their honest opinions of her creations.

Kishore ordered a bottle of wine. Yes, Vinod thought, I am right. They had some good news. Kishore raised his glass and smiling at his parents said, "We have big news. I've been offered a great job with Microsoft." Vinod smiled and raised his glass to toast his son. Shanti looked so proud. As he looked at Kishore, slowly Vinod's happiness dissolved. An emptiness, a void opened in him as he realized what was coming. His hand holding the wine glass began to tremble, but he steadied it and fixed his smile. He knew what Kishore would say even before he said it. After clinking glasses, Kishore went on, "We have to move to Seattle."

Seattle, 5 years later

Kishore

T HE RUDE JANGLING OF THE phone woke up Kishore and Anjali. He groaned and looked at the clock with one slitted eye. Who could be calling at three in the morning? He groped for the phone, mumbling, "'lo? Who's this?" Anjali opened her eyes, willing him to finish the conversation, go back to sleep.

Now he sat up, wide awake, "Amma? What's wrong?" Kishore said. Anjali too sat up, fear in her eyes, speculating, listening to Kishore's "un huh, un huh. God, when?"

Worry spread across his face, wrinkles honeycombing the corners of his eyes. "Amma, I'm coming. I'll be there as soon as I can. Don't worry; Papa'll be fine." And with a few more assurances and soothing words, he hung up and stared at Anjali before reaching for her.

Embracing her, he choked hoarsely into her hair, "Papa's in the hospital with another heart attack. I must go and be with Amma. This one is bad."

Anjali stroked his back and said, "Tell me what happened."

"Let's see. If it's three in the morning here in Seattle, it's about three in the afternoon in Mumbai—so it must have happened in the morning. Amma is incoherent; she sounds very distraught."

"Aren't Dev and Shilpa there to help her? Poor Amma, she must feel so frightened."

"I'm sure that somehow Dev is in the middle of this. Sweetheart, can you make me a cup of coffee? I better get on the net and book the earliest flight I can find."

After Anjali left the bedroom, he sat at the side of the bed and let the guilt take over. To further his career, five years ago he had taken his family to Seattle, snatching from his parents the pleasure they derived from their grandchildren. They had not shared in Priya's successes in elementary school, her scribbling, her vivid red and green crayoned flowers and fruit that Anjali stuck on the refrigerator. Now eleven, she was getting ready to enter the middle school at Lakeside, where Kisan was a junior. And Kisan—Papa's eyes shone every time he looked at the boy—and Kisan in turn adored his grandfather. Both grandfather and grandson had felt the wrench the most with the move to Seattle. Even though Kisan had been at the difficult age of twelve at the time, his good-nature and friendliness helped him adjust quickly and he was doing brilliantly at the exclusive Lakeside School. Now seventeen, he was taking all the advanced classes the school offered and thinking about universities. Kishore was so proud of him—he was tall and lanky with dark curls and large brown eyes. When Kishore looked at him, he saw himself.

Kishore sat immobile on the bed, torn between his father and his children. He felt wretchedly warm guilt rise in his throat, reaching out to his fingertips. He grabbed Anjali's pillow and hugged it to himself. What a choice! He needed to be by his father's side, a stable support for his mother. He needed to continue to work in Seattle for Kisan and Priya to finish school at Lakeside. They had visited Mumbai every summer, but these sojourns only served to widen the distance between the children and their Indian friends. And when they had to return to America, the pain in his parents' eyes each time was palpable.

Kishore combed his fingers through his lightly graying hair and dragged himself to his laptop just as Anjali brought him coffee. He was sure that Papa's heart attack was brought on by Dev. What the hell had Dev done? Damn him. He logged on to the internet to make his flight arrangements, showered and dressed to go to work. Both kids were at breakfast; Anjali had obviously told them the news. They looked at him, Priya, with eyes large and round, too afraid to talk.

"Tell Papa I'll beat him at chess next time." Kisan said stoically, staring at his Cheerios. Finally, Priya whispered, "Daddy, is Papa going to die?"

He hugged her tight while his heart lurched at her question. "No, sweetheart. We must all hope and pray that he'll be fine. Now you two, be good and look after Mummy. I'll be leaving today before you come home from school."

When he said goodbye to Anjali, she asked, "Should I email Rustum and ask him to pick you up at the airport?"

"No, no. The plane gets in at some ungodly hour in the middle of the night. The customs take forever—I wouldn't ask him to wait in that crush of people. I'll just take a taxi; it's easiest. Thank God I kept several five hundred rupee notes from our last trip, so I won't have to change money. Just email and tell him I'm coming and what's happened." And he gave her a hard hug and was gone.

He cleaned up his desk, delegated some work at his office, and Anjali took him to the airport. On the United flight to Los Angeles, he agonized over his dilemma. Anjali and the kids were happy in Seattle; how could he uproot them again? However, Amma could not manage Vinod as an invalid. From Los Angeles, he kept trying to call Mumbai on his cell phone. No response. What the hell was going on? Where was Dev and why was his cell phone turned off? Finally, just when he was about to give up, he reached Shilpa, apologizing to her for calling when it was so late in Mumbai.

"Hi, Shilpa. I just wanted you to know I'm on my way. I'm on Singapore Airlines and will arrive in Mumbai tomorrow—no, wait. It'll be the day after, at one o'clock in the morning. What's going on? How's Papa doing?"

All he heard was Shilpa crying. Finally, she said, "Kishore, I'm so sorry. It's all my fault, all my fault. I'm so sorry."

He couldn't comprehend. What on earth did she mean? Her fault? "Calm down Shilpa, and tell me what's going on," he asked.

She sniffled and controlled her sobs. "This morning I went to the flat to tell Amma and Papa that I couldn't take Dev's habits any more. I've really tried, Kishore. He's promised so many times to get off drugs and drink, but he just can't do it on his own, and he won't go to AA meetings. I don't know what to do. I don't want my little Arun growing up like this. Anyway, I went to tell them—Dev, naturally, was sleeping off a hangover."

Tearfully, she continued that when she told Amma and Papa that she had to leave, Papa got furious with Dev, cursing and calling him names. Right in the middle of the tirade, he collapsed. Amma was petrified, couldn't do anything.

"Papa is resting easily now, but they did an angiogram today to see if he needs a bypass or if they can do angioplasty. The doctor will tell us in the morning. Kishore, I am so sorry," she said.

Kishore was stunned. So it was Dev's fault. He consoled Shilpa as best he could, said she shouldn't blame herself and asked her to look after Amma. Waiting long hours at the Los Angeles airport he got more and more furious—not just with Dev but himself. How could he have thought that Dev would become responsible and care for Amma and Papa? Ultimately, as the older son—and especially knowing Dev's proclivities—he should have stayed in Mumbai and not let grandiose ideas of his career tempt him. To distract himself, he tried to work on his laptop, but couldn't concentrate. Finally, Singapore Airlines boarded.

During the twenty-four hour journey, Kishore's mind swung between two poles. He damned Dev; he damned himself. He recalled his conversation with Shilpa; the frustration he heard in her voice was an echo of all he had felt when he lived in Mumbai. She'd probably gone to Kalpana to tell Amma and Papa that she wanted to divorce Dev. Shock for the old man. A blow to Amma too. He could vividly imagine the scene Shilpa had described, with Papa cursing Dev and falling down unconscious. To erase that picture, he tried watching the onboard movie. Finally, he dozed, wishing the plane could take him to Mumbai faster.

After the tedious red tape, always maddening in the Mumbai airport, he cleared customs and grabbed a taxi. He went straight to Breach Candy Hospital and arrived there about four in the morning. He knew Amma would be sleeping in the room with Papa, as she had after his last operation. He hoped that the bypass surgery, if it was needed, had not taken place yet—he wanted to be present. He hoped and prayed that Papa would receive the less invasive angioplasty.

A young nurse—he had to remember that all nurses were called sisters in India whether they were nuns or not—led him down the dimly lit hall whispering that Vinod sahib was asleep and Dev sahib was also sleeping in the room. Shanti had been persuaded to go home, sister said.

Kishore stood at the foot of his father's bed. Papa looked so frail, so withered. Could he have shrunk so much in just a few months? Brushing the tears from his eyes, he sat down in a cold hard chair by the side of the bed and took his father's hand, touching him gently, trying to pass some of his strength to the man who had been the axis of his life.

When Dev and Vinod awoke, Kishore was too tired to talk, so tired he felt nauseous. All he cared about was that they had waited for him before doing anything. He comforted Vinod, called a cab and went to Kalpana.

Shanti greeted him at the door, bursting into tears when she saw him. She was followed closely by the Lhasa Apso, Hari, that had taken the place of Bhim when that little dog had died at fifteen. Kishore had never seen his mother like this—her hair unkempt, face ashen. She could barely speak as the twin emotions of joy and relief at seeing him mingled with her fear for Vinod.

Taking her gently by the hands, he led her to the sofa. As she sat, Hari jumped up and laid his muzzle on her lap. She stroked his silky head as she incoherently told Kishore how Dev had slid into his old habits. She recounted how much she prayed that when Dev married Shilpa he would straighten up. After their son Arun was born, the young couple moved from Kalpana into Vinod's ancestral flat. Shanti and Vinod saw the boy and Shilpa often; they saw Dev less and less.

"We were so blind," she said. "It was a great shock to both of us when Shilpa came and told us that she could no longer live with Dev because of what it was doing to her and Arun. Tell me, *beta*, where did I go wrong?"

"Amma, nai, nai, you did nothing wrong. Now we must concentrate on Papa."

She told him how Vinod had turned red with anger as he cursed Dev, and she shuddered at the memory. "Never have I seen him like that, *beta*. When he fell down…" she couldn't talk. She shielded her eyes with her right hand and pulled Hari closer to her; Kishore waited wretchedly, guiltily. "*Beta*, I wanted you here, I wanted your strength. Vinod lay on the ground, his glasses swinging on one ear, and I could do nothing. I forgot Dr Rajan's phone number—I even forgot Rama's name. Oh, I should tell Rama to make you some breakfast, no?"

"That can wait. What did Doc Rajan say?"

Shanti looked bewildered. She could only shake her head. "I don't remember. Why don't you call him, Kishore?"

She padded to the bedroom to find the number. Kishore leaned back and closed his eyes. What a mess. Was it his imagination or had Amma aged terribly in the past year? She could not look after Vinod. Dev certainly was useless. Kishore would have to hire a nurse to see Vinod through recovery.

Shanti returned with her small phone book. He remembered it from Vinod's first heart trouble twelve years ago. With trembling hands, she fumbled trying to find the number. She sat down on the leather chair and lifted the border of her sari to wipe her eyes, annoyed at her helplessness. Kishore tenderly took the book and found the number written in her precise hand.

Speaking to Dr Rajan, he found out that Vinod needed a triple bypass. Dr. Rajan said that angioplasty was not a good option because Vinod's vessels were very narrow and too many of them were diseased. Dr. Rajan assured Kishore that he had done many bypasses: "It's just routine. Don't worry." The surgery was scheduled for the afternoon and would probably be a four or five hour operation.

Kishore's head was spinning with this spate of bad news. He desperately needed to sleep off some of his jet lag; needed to call Anjali and the kids; needed to comfort and support his mother and father; needed to talk to Dev. He chose to sleep first—then all the other duties would be easier.

As he lay on the hard bed of his teen age years, he saw the faces of Kisan and Priya. Kisan was ready for the SAT and APs; he and his friends spent all their time comparing universities. And Priya, his artistic pet, with her large eyes…he drifted off to sleep.

Too soon he felt his mother shake him awake. They needed to get to the hospital—the operation would start soon. Wiping the sleep from his eyes, he stumbled into the bathroom for a quick cold shower and changed into clean clothes. He was still groggy from the plane ride until he got to the hospital. When Dr Rajan came to shake his hand, he became alert, listening attentively.

As Dr. Rajan explained how he was going to take a large vessel from Vinod's leg and use it to bypass the blocked portion of the arteries, Kishore was glad that modern medicine could do such unimaginable procedures. Reassured that Dr. Rajan was expert at the operation, Kishore shook hands before the surgeon went into the operating theater. Dev stood passively by his side letting Kishore take over, roles they had both played since childhood.

And then the waiting began. Kishore looked around the room. Nothing much had changed since Vinod's last visit twelve years ago. His mother sat praying. Dev lounged half asleep in a chair. And he paced, checking the time on his cell phone, waiting for morning to arrive in Seattle. Finally, he was talking to Anjali, describing Vinod's condition, his mother's helplessness, and the situation with Dev and Shilpa. He spoke to Priya and Kisan, assuring them that Papa was with a good doctor who was doing his best. He asked them to say a prayer for Papa. Anjali returned to the phone, told him to stay as long as he needed to. Just before hanging up, she suggested he have Shanti checked out by a doctor as well.

He girded himself for a talk with Dev. He sat down next to him and asked, neutrally, "So, what's going on, *bhai?*"

And Dev looked at him with anguish, saying, "I've really fucked up this time, haven't I? I may have lost my wife, son and father all at the same time. It's a record even for me, right?"

Kishore shook his head, held his temper and asked Dev again what had happened. He knew what to expect—Dev would not defend his actions, he would plead weakness, vow to do better—not one word would be changed.

Kishore was right, of course; the only difference was now Dev had to include Shilpa and Arun in his monologue. Dev protested that he loved his wife and son; he was weak and however many times he tried to give up booze and drugs, he just didn't have the strength.

"What should I do, Kishore? Tell me what to do. I can't lose them. Without them, I will really be finished, *khatum.*"

Shanti looked over at the two of them talking, made a move as if to rise from her chair, but shook her head and went back to her prayers.

Kishore glanced at Shanti, glad that she wasn't coming to Dev's rescue again. Sighing, he said to his brother, "Tell you what to do. Well, fuck you, Dev. What else have we all been doing all these years? At some point, you have to show some gumption. God, man, you are close to your forties! You think only of yourself and probably don't realize how many lives you have affected, not just yours and Shilpa's. I know now I can't depend on you to look after Amma and Papa. This means I have to move my whole family again, even though it's Kisan's senior year. It'll be hard for all of us because we've succeeded in Seattle, made friends, done well in school and at work."

With more than a tinge of bitterness, Kishore continued talking, almost more to himself. He'd have to break the news to Anjali and the children; he'd have to job hunt again; they'd have to move again; make friends again, readjust to living in Mumbai again. As he spoke, Kishore realized his decision was crystallizing. He hoped Anjali and the children would understand—he could not leave Amma and Papa to the care of Dev. They would have to adapt.

He looked at Dev's tear-stained face and at that moment, he hated his brother. What a weakling. Papa was right—from the start, Dev had been nothing but trouble. How often had they listened to his excuse that following Kishore was hard for him? How often had they smiled indulgently when he got into scrapes in school and college? Now in his late thirties, he still expected someone else to provide him a ladder so he could climb out of the pit he was in. Filled with repugnance at the sight of his brother, Kishore walked over to his mother.

Shanti raised eyes filled with hope. She knew Kishore could make things right. He sat next to her and held her hand, knowing this was not the moment to tell her his decision. He had to think about it some more, tell Anjali first.

"How long can you stay, *beta*? How I wish you were still living here. I am so afraid," she said, clutching his hand.

"Don't worry, Amma. I'll stay until Papa comes home from hospital. I'll also arrange for two orderlies to stay in the house day and night, so you won't have to do anything. You'll see. Papa is strong. Doesn't he go for walks every day and follow a good diet? He'll come through this operation with flying colors, as Dr Rajan would say."

"What are we to do about Dev and Shilpa, Kishore?" she whispered.

"Amma, that's their problem. Please don't worry about it. You concentrate on Papa now; I'll take care of everything else, *achcha?*"

And she gripped his hand and knew he would make things right. Kishore sat at her side, glad that Anjali had urged him to have Amma checked out as well. With the focus on Vinod, Shanti could easily fall through the cracks. He tried to recall his conversation with Anjali. Yes, of course. He had mentioned how frail Shanti had become, how she was forgetting things, even the names of her servants. He remembered how she kept calling Hari by the name of his predecessor Bhim. Yes, after Vinod was out of hospital and at home, he would have his mother examined by—what kind of doctor? A geriatrician? A neurologist? A psychologist? He'd have to speak to Dr Rajan about it and Anjali too.

Shanti

S HANTI CHANTED HER PRAYERS ROBOTICALLY in the puja room. She offered tulsi and jasmine, bananas and coconuts to the gods, lit the wick in the brass aarti and circled it in front of the idols three times. She did not feel the deep tranquility that her puja always brought her. Kishore had told her that he was taking her to a new doctor today; he wanted to make sure she was all right before he left.

"I know you're a rock, Amma, and I know there's nothing wrong with you. Just go with me for my sake—I don't want to go to Seattle and have you fall sick after I leave. Anjali is worried about you too; she made me promise to make sure you were all right," he cajoled. What a good boy Kishore was. Anjali too was very sweet. She wished they did not live so far away. She would try to persuade them to return quickly.

Meanwhile, now, on the verge of visiting a new doctor, she was afraid of what he might find. She had gone through menopause over ten years ago. While it had been difficult and uncomfortable, no one had even known about it. When she had hot flashes or night sweats, she blamed it on the miserable Mumbai weather, so even Vinod had no idea what she went through. She was proud of not making a fuss over a natural aspect of life. Then she had been in control—she could conceal or she could reveal. She chose to conceal as her mother and grandmother had before her. And it had hurt no one.

Now she was losing control. She worried about the many simple things she was forgetting. Where had she left her keys? Had she told Rama what to cook for the day? Was Arun coming to see them? One time she was mortified when she asked Malika to get her bath water ready, and Malika, amused, told her she had already bathed. Shanti managed to laugh it off—but that was the first time she began to worry about her memory.

Everything else was going right. Vinod, thank God, had come through his by-pass "with flying colors" and was now home. Rama, so scared that his cooking had caused Sahib's heart attack, checked with Shanti several times about cooking for Vinod. Kishore had been in Mumbai for almost three weeks; as promised, he had hired two young orderlies from a medical agency to take care of Vinod, one for the day and one for night. Though these young men were not trained as nurses, they gave Vinod his bath, helped him walk to the bathroom, massaged him daily, made sure he took his medicines, and kept him company. Certainly, she could not do all those things.

After her puja, she dressed carefully in a peach silk sari. She dreaded going to see a new doctor. Was she not as well as she had always been? But she had promised Kishore, and she wanted to make him happy regardless of her inner fears.

Driving with Kishore to the doctor's office, she asked him, "What kind of new doctor are you taking me to see? What is wrong with Dr. Sharma? He looked after all of us, you also when you lived here."

Kishore smiled at her. "I just want you to see this lady that Dr. Rajan recommended. I thought you'd be more comfortable with a lady doctor. Her name is Dr. Kumar."

Dr. Rajan's name appeased her, and she was mollified by Kishore's thoughtfulness about getting her a lady doctor, but she continued to grumble. When they arrived at the doctor's office, he whisked her past the board that proclaimed that the Dr. Kumar they had an appointment with was a psychiatrist and a geriatrician. As they waited, she kept worrying about Vinod. Uncharacteristically, she wondered if young

Ganesh, the orderly tending Vinod during the day, could be trusted. She asked Kishore, "*Beta,* did you make sure that all the cupboards were locked? You can't trust anyone these days." Kishore put this fretting and suspicion down to nervousness and reassured her as best he could. After a few minutes, Dr. Kumar came out smiling and invited them into her office.

Dr. Kumar was young, personable and friendly. She checked Shanti's blood pressure, ("excellent, excellent; you're in good shape") her heart and lungs—all the usual things any doctor would do. Kishore was invited into the office after the examination, and the doctor assured him that Shanti was fine. Kishore was glad that this seemed to be a waste of time.

Then, Dr Kumar sat back and started a friendly chat with Shanti. "I see from your form that you are in your mid-sixties. I hope I am in such good condition as you when I reach your age." Shanti looked triumphantly at Kishore, liking this young doctor more and more.

As she was making notes, she offhandedly asked Shanti, "So, madam, did you have breakfast before you came?"

"Of course," Shanti said; "I always have breakfast by 9:30."

"So tell me, what did you eat this morning?"

Bewildered, she looked at Kishore, then back at the doctor. What a stupid question, Shanti thought. But she was frantically searching her mind to remember what she ate. All she could see was fog. What did it matter?

"I had breakfast," she said.

"Did you have toast, cereal, eggs, or upma and idlis?"

"No, no. Kishore, what did we eat this morning? Was it French toast or scrambled eggs? Why is it important?"

"Amma, we just had cornflakes and fruit today."

"*Achcha,* now I remember. Rama was making porridge for Vinod."

"So, you live alone with your husband?"

"Yes, Doctor. This Kishore, my older son, lives in America, you know, working with Microsoft. He has two lovely children—the little boy, he's eleven and so clever. His sister is also clever, isn't she Kishore? Their names are…" again she looked over at Kishore, becoming agitated as the names eluded her.

But Shanti was so happy to be talking about her grandchildren, she glossed over their names and went on to tell the doctor what the children did. "The little boy will be going to college next year and…" she frowned as she realized that Kisan was no longer eleven. "I'm sorry, doctor, did I say the boy was eleven? That's how old he was when he left Bombay and went to Seattle. Now he's much older, nai Kishore?

She didn't notice Kishore staring at her with alarm. Dr. Kumar, however, pleasantly continued asking questions about daily family life, and Shanti spoke about her dog.

"He is such a sweet Lhasa Apso, doctor. Bhim follows me around everywhere. When I am reading, he sits next to me. You know, after Bhim died, I didn't want any other dog. But I felt so lonely, so Vinod got me another dog just like him. We named him Hari."

Shanti's comfort with the doctor rose in direct proportion to Kishore's discomfort. She was mixing up the dogs' names again. She turned and smiled at Kishore, assuring him wordlessly she was no longer angry that he had brought her here. As she continued to talk to the gentle Dr Kumar, she felt compelled to say, "Kishore's wife, Anjali—you will meet her one day—she was the one that suggested he bring me to you, doctor. Such a sweet daughter-in-law I have. I am hoping and praying that they will come home soon."

"I'm sure that will be a big help for you, madam. Especially now that your husband has had an operation, it's nice to have family close by, isn't it? Now, my examination is over. Sir, would you take your mother outside so she can sit comfortably. Then you can come back and I will give you some prescriptions and tonics for her. Madam, it was very nice to meet you. You are in fine shape, but I want you to take some tonics to give you more energy and strength, *achcha*?"

Shanti nodded happily and went to the waiting room with Kishore. She thought nothing of it when he returned to see the doctor and get the prescriptions. She worried about Vinod and Dev the whole twenty minutes Kishore was with the doctor—never for one minute did she worry about herself. She was in fine shape. She didn't worry on the way home when Kishore was so quiet.

That evening, she sat in the bedroom reading to Vinod. He was restless, so she went to the kitchen to ask Rama to warm a little milk to soothe Vinod before dinner. She was crossing the drawing room, when she heard Kishore talking. Funny, the doorbell hadn't rung. She went to the door of his bedroom and saw that he was talking on the phone. As she turned away, she heard her name mentioned—and the pain in Kishore's voice. She paused. What was wrong? Was it something she did not know? Was Kishore worried about her because Vinod was in serious condition?

Then she heard his words, muffled but understandable to her straining ears.

"You were so right, Anju…No, Amma doesn't know! …Yes, she was clear…she said it is possibly early onset Alzheimer's…I don't know what to do. We can't leave them alone…memory loss is the first…she couldn't remember Kisan's and Priya's names…No, I can't tell her; what will she do? The doc said there are some tests, but there's nothing…"

Shanti couldn't move; she felt the blood rush from her head leaving her dizzy and weak-kneed. Ram, Ram! So she was sick after all. Her forgetfulness was a symptom. She had read about this terrible illness, but never for a moment did she think she had it. She waited patiently until Kishore finished his conversation before entering the room.

Kishore sat with his head in his hands. Shanti put a gentle hand on his back and asked, "So, *beta*, there is something wrong with me after all. I heard bits of what you were telling Anjali. Why don't you tell me also?"

"Oh, Amma, I am sorry you overheard. I wanted to spare you until I decided what to do. Dr. Kumar suspects only—doesn't know for certain. Anyway, we'll come back to be with you; I just have to talk it over with Anjali."

Her eyes filled. "Hai Ram, why is this all happening now? First,

Dev and Shilpa—what is going to happen with them? That sweet little Arun. Will I see him like before? Vinod is sick; you are so far away—hai, Ram, Ram. This is our karma. What will happen, *beta*?"

"Don't worry, Amma. Papa is going to be fine—the doctor said that his operation was a success. We just have to worry about his diet and make sure he exercises. I promise you Amma, we'll all come home within a year, maybe sooner."

She clasped his hands. "Kishore, you are always the one. What would I do without you? *Chalo* now, tell me what the doctor said about me. What is this Alzheimer's? What will it do to me?"

As Kishore shielded her from the worst ravages of the disease, she listened, nodding. Then she said, "So, it is something that attacks my mind, not my body. I will start to forget things more and more. Is there nothing that can be done?"

She watched as Kishore shook his head miserably. Then he said, "But there is new research every day. I'm sure they'll find a cure."

She tried to be brave for him, but her eyes glistened with fear. How could she cope with a heart patient if she was slowly losing her mind? Then she did what she had vowed she would never do. She asked him.

"*Beta,* do you think you could come home to Mumbai and live here with us? This flat is too big for two only. The children will make us happy. What do you say?"

Kishore rocked wretchedly. Of course this was the way things were done in India—the son and family moved into the ancestral home. "We'll see, Amma. We'll do what's best. Now, I don't want you to worry any more. Go take care of Papa."

Anjali

ANJALI TUGGED ON HER BLACK yoga pants and hoped that the hour and a half of "meditation in action", as her instructor called it, would calm her down. Alzheimer's. Poor Shanti—why did such a terrible thing happen to such a good person? And Kishore. Anjali knew he would feel wrenched. Guilty about living on the other side of the world. Really, what could he do? His job and career brought them to Seattle. And look what the move had done for Kisan and Priya. Kisan was brilliant; he had his heart set on following Kishore's footsteps and going to MIT. Dreamy Priya was not studious at all, happy with B's but excelling in art and dance. And she and Kishore never pushed her.

Driving her silver Lexus to the yoga studio, she wondered when Kishore would return. He had so much to take care of in Mumbai—his parents, the caretakers for them, and the problem of Dev and Shilpa.

As she drove in the gray mist that was always Seattle, she pondered the differences between Kishore and herself. Despite spending so much time in the U.S., Kishore was innately Indian, holding strongly to Indian customs and beliefs. He felt an indissoluble family tie, an unswerving responsibility toward his parents and even to the weak-willed Dev. Which did not mean that he subjugated his own little family to his parents—no, no. Anjali smiled as she thought of his dedication and devotion to herself and the children, and she felt blessed. How many of her friends here in Seattle were consumed with doubts and suspicion about their husbands: doubts about their fidelity or discontent about their ungodly hours at work.

As she parked the car and ran into the studio, she felt an overwhelming premonition that their family was heading for a crisis. In the pit of her stomach, she knew Kishore and she were going to be tested. She entered just as the instructor began chanting.

Today the class had unusually few students so they could spread out. As always, they started with *surya namaskars*. Anjali loved this beginning to the yoga routine, the sun salute, which got her heart going and engaged all the muscles. Today, she just couldn't get her rhythm. *Triconasana*, the triangle pose, another of her favorites, found her losing her balance and unable to hold the position for the requisite time. Then the instructor gave the instructions for *Virawadrasana 1*, saying they would do all three warrior poses in succession. Anjali always felt powerful doing these warrior poses—they were so strong, calling for enormous concentration and balance. She did them well and thought that she had overcome whatever weakness she had felt at first.

However, when she found herself toppling when doing the head stand and shoulder stand, she went over to the side of the room to regroup. Finally, it was time for *sevasana*, the corpse pose which ended the session. Supine, arms away from her body, she breathed deeply and tried to relax, telling herself that everything would continue to be fine, like it always had been. But strange feelings stirred during this most meditative of poses, the agitation disturbing her minutes of total submission. Relieved at the chanting of the last mantra, she rolled up her mat hurriedly and left without even her customary thank you to the instructor.

When she reached home, she found two messages on the machine. One was from Bridget, the first friend she'd made in Seattle. Bridget's call reminded her about the committee meeting for the school fundraiser. Ansuya, the second caller, was her favorite Indian friend, smart and fun loving. Since Kishore was out of town and her husband was working late, Ansuya suggested that they go to a movie that night. Anjali thought it would be good to talk to both of these women and get their perspective.

She called Ansuya and made a date for dinner and a movie. That evening, leaving the children doing their homework and school projects, she picked up her friend early and drove to a local Italian restaurant. As they sipped their Chardonnay, she answered the question about when Kishore was due back.

"I'm not sure yet. He found a bigger mess than he had bargained for when he left."

Ansuya dipped the warm, crusty bread in the rich golden olive oil and asked, "Why? What else? You only told me his father had a heart attack."

"Well, yes, his father had to have a bypass operation and is now home. Kish had to arrange to have two nurse-types to care for him day and night because his mother can't do it all. But, remember I told you about his charming brother Dev? Apparently, he's gone back to drinking and using drugs, and Shilpa, his poor wife, can't take it any more. So she went to tell my in-laws that she and Dev were separating—that's what might have brought on the heart attack. Now Kish feels he can't rely on his brother for anything. To add to that, whenever Kish spoke to me, he said his mother looked so frail. You know, I always think of her as a take-charge woman, in a soft and gentle way. Anyway, I urged Kish to take her to see a specialist, and guess what?"

"Oh, the usual thing in India. Everyone has high blood pressure or high blood sugar. Which one, tell me."

"Neither—the doctor said she has early Alzheimer's."

"Oh, my God! What will you do?"

"I don't know. I'm still in shock. Poor Amma—you know, she was more of a mother to me than my own mother," Anjali shook her head and took another sip of wine.

Ansuya munched on the bread for a few moments in silence. "So, Kishore will have to go back to look after his parents. Do you..."

"What do you mean? He should just give up his job here and uproot us all again?" Anjali was indignant.

"Come on, Anjali. His father has just had a second heart attack, his mother has Alzheimer's, and Dev, you say, is useless. Who else will look after the old folks?"

"But, Ansuya, Kisan will be in his senior year in high school, Priya will enter middle school next year. Will he expect us to give it all up and meekly go to Mumbai?"

At this moment, the waiter brought their steaming plates of pasta. Twirling her fork through the fettuccine, Ansuya murmured, "My, this smells so good. And, yes, Anju, Kishore's an Indian through and through. He's the oldest son. It is his duty to look after his parents in their old age. As for the children, believe me, the schools in Mumbai are just fine. I'm sure it'll be hard on Kisan and Priya, but Kisan can get into MIT or Harvard from Mumbai just as easily as from Lakeside. Didn't Kishore?"

Anjali sat staring. Listening to Ansuya's voice put her own uneasy fears into words. And the sound of the words made those fears true. This is the crisis, she thought. This is what was bothering me in yoga. I couldn't articulate it because I couldn't bear to.

"You don't know what you're talking about. Surely we can wait one year while Kisan finishes, don't you think? I mean, they don't have AP's in India, do they? Kisan wants to graduate with his friends, and so does Priya." Anjali was reassuring herself. Ansuya shrugged, swallowed a mouthful and said, "Of course, you could stay here with the kids while Kishore goes, gets himself a job and gets things settled."

"What? That's crazy."

"Anju, what's the choice? Put his parents in a home? There aren't many good homes for the elderly in India because older people live with their children or other relatives. It's the tradition." She paused, then asked, "Did Kisan ever do community service through Lakeside at a retirement home?"

"No, he never did that—feeding the homeless was his big thing."

"Well, my Sujatha did. She always came home feeling so sad for the people there, but glad that she had spent some time with the lonely ones. She had such stories. Some of the old folks were active, playing cards or doing crafts, but others just sat staring vacantly, waiting to die. They had visitors on the occasional weekend. Sometimes, even when their children lived in town, they didn't come to visit." She shook her head and continued, "I tell you, Anju, I don't know what the answer is. In this country, some young couples put their parents in these homes and abandon them and their responsibility for them. In India, young couples sometimes sacrifice their careers and privacy to live with and look after their parents. I'm not saying the Indian way is the right way. Sometimes it can have terrible consequences: old people are neglected and verbally or physically abused, but at least they have a place to stay and food to eat and family noise around them. This sense of duty I've rarely seen here. You know, I have no brothers. I know I will bring my parents to live with me when they get older. Which is the better way? You tell me."

Anjali pushed her fork around uselessly in her ravioli. She had lost all desire for food. She could picture Shanti, helpless and lost, trying to look after a bedridden Vinod. She knew she was exaggerating the severity of the situation, but still, could she allow it to develop into that? She couldn't bear the picture in her mind; equally she couldn't bear the suppliant, silent voices of her children asking to stay in Seattle.

Anjali poured herself another glass of wine. Thus mellowed, she could tell Ansuya about her lonely childhood. When her mother died some years after Priya was born, Anjali had gone to Delhi but felt nothing. Her father's presence at the funeral was perfunctory. Because her relationship with both her parents was so tenuous, she had gratefully wallowed in Shanti's and Vinod's love and acceptance.

"Do you know, my father has come to see my children only four or five times? I can't even dream of asking him to come and live with us when he gets older. But, you know, I would gladly live with Kish's parents." She paused. "Just not now."

At the movie, she left the darkened theater three times to call Kishore, but he wasn't answering his cell phone. By the time she dropped Ansuya home, Anjali had even forgotten the name of the movie she had just seen. Kishore did not call that night. What was happening?

The next morning, after the kids had gone to school, she sat in front of her mirror looking at the dark bags under her eyes. She lifted a chunk of her dark hair. Yes, the gray was returning. She was getting a second chin, she thought, as she put two fingers under her ears and pulled back the sag under her chin. She leaned into the mirror to look for wrinkles—not too many. Anjali was in her early forties now and keeping the crawl of the years hidden as best she could. As she massaged moisturizing anti-aging cream into her cheeks, she envied how Kishore's gray hair, at the temples and smattered in patches, made him look younger. He didn't have a wrinkle that was not flattering. Now that he wore glasses, he looked even more handsome. Why didn't he call? She reached for the phone to try him again. No, it was late at night in Mumbai.

Sitting with the phone in her hand, she kept hearing Ansuya's words playing over in her head. The drizzly gloomy weather didn't help her mood. Slowly, she began to punch in Bridget's phone number to invite her to lunch. Once that was arranged, she felt better—she'd taken action of some kind. She looked out the window at the steady rain and remembered how she'd felt during the Mumbai monsoons, the claustrophobic feeling that made her want to climb the walls. She even got the memory of the clothes and their damp, mildewy odor despite the soap and the natural scented fabric softener she imported from the U.S. God, she'd hated it, especially that first year of her marriage. But the gray bleakness of Seattle was much more pervasive; it got under her skin and sucked her energy. She shuddered. She must do something. She pulled on her black tights and scruffy "Lakeside Parent" t-shirt, grabbed a towel and went to the gym to make the morning hours pass until lunchtime.

The workout at the gym made Anjali feel better. As she put the last touch of gloss on her lips, the doorbell rang. Trust Bridget to be on time! She greeted her friend with a wide smile, and in the car, they chattered about the upcoming fundraiser and the donations they had received for the silent auction.

"Imagine, this year a couple of our new Asian families have donated two first class tickets on Singapore Airlines, a limo, and a week in the best hotel in Hong Kong. Isn't that great? I wonder which lucky couple will bid on that?" Bridget was excited about the auction which was her responsibility.

They went to a restaurant which boasted a view of Mt. St Helen's on the two or three days of the year when the snow-topped mountain actually showed herself. Today was too overcast and drizzly, so they sat inside and ordered salads. Inevitably, Bridget asked when Kishore was returning, and Anjali told her about the situation Kish had found in Mumbai.

"I know Kishore will feel a strong sense of duty that will tug him back to Mumbai. But he will also want to let the Kisan finish out his senior year at Lakeside. I tell you, I've been going crazy for the past few days."

Bridget nibbled on the romaine lettuce and took a sip of her Perrier water. "So, you think Kishore will feel compelled to return to India because of his parents? And you want to stay here because of the kids? Quite a dilemma."

"You know, I feel fine, really, about going back—but not now, not when Kisan is about to enter his senior year. He deserves the chance to finish with his friends, go through the college admission process. I don't know what to think."

Bridget gazed out the window, looking into the distance. "About four years ago, my mother was diagnosed with Alzheimer's. She'd lived alone since my father died—in Nashville, far away from here. I visited her often, but each time I went, she drifted further from me. The light faded from her eyes, and the woman I'd known disappeared into bottomless darkness. I couldn't have her live with us because of my own small family—how much it would be affected by someone needing constant care. If she'd lived with us, I knew I couldn't deal with her wandering from the house and nobody knowing where she was. We finally put her in a home in St. Paul where my sister lives, a place with trained personnel. Now at least we know she's safe."

Anjali looked at Bridget wide-eyed. She hadn't known. "Oh, my God, I'm so sorry. How is she doing now?"

"Well, it's very hard to see her—harder each time. She knows none of us. I feel guilty whenever I see her, but I know I couldn't..." Bridget cleared her throat, then continued. "It's a terrible disease, Anjali, and it only gets worse. You'll have caregivers twenty-four seven, which will make it easier. But be prepared for an emotional abyss you never dreamed of."

Anjali looked away from the anguish in her friend's face and took her hand. "I am so sorry. Thank you for telling me," she said slowly.

Bridget dabbed a tissue to her eyes, tried a wavering smile, and said, "Let's talk about your options. To go or to stay."

Seeing that Bridget wanted to change the subject, Anjali spoke of the Indian custom where older people in India lived with children or other relatives. "At this time, Kishore's parents are basically fine. His father is recovering from surgery, and she—it's early, I think she's functional. I don't know where her disease will take her. I know they'll be expecting us to return to Mumbai soon to take charge."

"These people who will look after them—can't they be hired for a year? Then you can go after Kisan graduates."

"I know that sounds logical and reasonable, but I see her getting more and more afraid, losing her confidence. She is the heart of that home, the spine." As Anjali listened to herself, she knew where her duty lay. It would be impossible to describe to Bridget the life that Shanti and Vinod led in Mumbai, a life that she fully understood only now. It wasn't just having someone to look after them that they needed. It was the daily chatter of children, their own children, the voices of the servants, the visitors who dropped in daily. It was family and life.

That's what they knew. That's what they needed. Without the anchor of family, Vinod and Shanti would get more and more isolated as her disease progressed. In the midst of the neighbors, they would be on an island of solitude.

Anjali looked over to Bridget and said, "You've no idea how much you've helped me. I'm pretty sure that Kishore will want to go back as soon as possible. I'm not sure about myself—I want Kisan to graduate from Lakeside. I have to think things through. Thanks for your help, Bridget." And she squeezed Bridget's hand.

At home after lunch, she tried to read a magazine, but she was restless. In a few weeks, the school year would be over, and they could all go to Mumbai for the summer. Then Kishore could stay in India while she could come back with the children so they could finish their next school year. It wasn't too long if you thought of Christmas break and Spring break. Surely Kishore would agree.

Kishore

Vinod had been home for a couple of days when Dr. Rajan came by to see him. Since Dev was visiting as well, the two sons and Shanti gathered in Vinod's bedroom to hear what the doctor had to say. Vinod looked gaunt and pale lying under a white sheet, and Shanti sat on the bed next to him. Kishore sat in his father's favorite chair, with its faded blue upholstery, threadbare where Vinod rested his arms and hands. The back of the chair had a dark spot where Vinod always laid his head, often nodding off to sleep. Next to an open book, his brown rimmed glasses on a chain sat ready on a small table by the side of the chair. Kishore's heart filled with the days and years of sitting and listening to his father in this now weary, drab room, filled with the smell of his parents, with their spoken wisdom and their unspoken love.

Dr Rajan reassured them that the bypass had been a success, and Vinod was good for at least another fifty years. He asked them to be careful with his diet and make sure he exercised daily.

Kishore interrupted, "Doc, I know he is very good about taking walks, but what should he do during the bloody monsoon—no one can walk then."

"Walking is the best exercise, of course. What, Kishore, have you forgotten what he does when it's raining? He does what you all do in America whether it is sunny or raining. Come on, Vinod, tell him what you do."

"And what is that?" smiled Kishore.

"I go to a gym and walk on a treadmill for half an hour or so."

"Of course, you're right! I'm so used to seeing you set off at six in the morning for your walk in Kamala Nehru Park, I never thought of you using the gym. Yes, the Willingdon is quite close, and even the Bombay Gymkhana for that matter. Will you do it, Papa?"

"What do you think I've been doing all these years during all the monsoons? Of course I will—don't I want to see my grandson graduate from MIT like his father? I will keep myself in tiptop condition for that occasion only," Vinod said.

Shanti smiled, encouraged. Dev offered to drive him whenever he needed to go, but Vinod ignored him. Dev might as well have not been in the room. It was obvious that the old couple blamed him for the fact that Shilpa was not there with them.

Rama was called into the room to listen yet again to the doctor's instructions about meals for Vinod. Kishore looked at the cook, now a little stooped and thin, his hair entirely gray, but still with the magic touch for great food. He'd learned all the family favorites and aversions for three generations. Besides, he carried their secrets, and he held them close. Of course he knew all about Dev's drinking and drugs. He was the one Dev called in the mornings when he was hung over. He had a remedy which made Dev functional in a short time—all Kishore knew was that it contained garlic and red chili peppers. He remembered it from his own college days.

Rama was carrying a tray, offering glasses of freshly made lime juice to everyone in the room. As Kishore drank his, he thought that it was more refreshing than the lemonade in the U.S.—tangier. Dr. Rajan drank his juice in one long swig, set the glass down and talked to Rama. As Kishore listened, he was struck by the fact that Vinod and Shanti treated Rama as a member of their family. He admired his parents for their acknowledgement of Rama and his talents and acceptance of him into the family. As long as Kishore could remember, Rama had never been like a servant, even during the years when servants were, well, servants. Now he was like a wise elder in the family. Malika, the maid, had been retired some years ago after she had a stroke; she had gone home to her village with a generous sum of money. A young woman named Jyostna had taken her place.

Now Rama stood listening intently, nodding in agreement, asking questions. He wanted to be sure to give Vinod the best of care—an important aspect of Vinod's recovery had been entrusted to him. Dr. Rajan assured him that Vinod was doing fine, and if he followed the diet he would continue to do so.

After Rama collected the juice glasses and left, Dr Rajan made himself comfortable and stayed to chat with the family. "Yes, yes, of course I have to see other patients—but surely I will always have time to spend with you. So, Kishore, tell me what is happening with the family? Doing well in Seattle?" he rubbed his hand over his bald head, smiling like a gnome.

And Kishore recounted how the kids were doing in school. Dev was being studiously ignored. Dr. Rajan knew what was happening with him, and knew that Vinod did not want to talk to him or about him. Unable to break through the barrier of ice that encased him, Dev got up, knocking a side table over. Loudly saying, "Well, call me if you need anything," he abruptly left. Kishore wondered for a fleeting moment if Dev was going to a bar. That was the way he dealt with pain—and pleasure too.

Finally, Dr Rajan got up to leave and Kishore saw him to the front door. Slowly, he closed the door and turned and looked at the drawing room of the apartment where he had grown up, everything just as he remembered it. The large sofas, the polished brass idols and oil lamps that Shanti collected—only the television had been recently replaced. He wandered to the window to look out at the street, congested as always with bicycles, taxis, cars and pedestrians. In this fourth story home, he was elevated above the tumult of the city. The altitude protected him from the fray in the streets, filtering out the noise.

Further out, he saw the spray of the waves as they crashed on the rocks. He compared it to his comfortable life in Seattle. But this mélange, fusing spices and people, mingling the raucous noise of street life with the chant of mantras and prayer bells, all colored brilliantly with the dazzling hues of the saris—this, this was where his heart belonged. He hoped that Anjali and the children would understand.

He heard Shanti call him, and taking a deep breath, he returned to Vinod's bedroom. Vinod gestured to him to sit in the blue chair. This was reminiscent of the many talks he'd had with his parents in this room. Shanti asked Ganesh, the orderly, to go get some tea for himself from Rama. Now Kishore knew it was important; it was a private family matter. Kishore leaned forward, ready to listen.

And Vinod, who liked to draw things out, told the story of how Shanti and he had lived for twelve years with his parents before they could afford to buy a place of their own. Kishore had heard the story many times but he indulged his father. Vinod continued the familiar tale about how Shanti nagged him until they bought this flat in the new Kalpana building. And now it was worth several crores, ("remember, Kishore, one crore is ten million rupees"). Even in dollars the value was staggering. As always, Kishore complimented his parents on their astuteness—this flat was a priceless asset.

"Which is why I have asked Govinda to come tomorrow," Vinod said. Kishore had no idea who Govinda was. Vinod said he was a new young lawyer who had drawn up some papers. Kishore was quite confused—what was his father talking about?

"*Beta*, we are growing old. It is getting harder and harder for us to look after this flat. As you can see, there are water stains on the walls, some windows don't open. Lots of repairs to be done. To us it doesn't matter because we don't have dinner parties like we used to. As the traffic in Mumbai gets worse and worse, people our age don't want to go out much. And so we get along and don't look at the problems as urgent. We live quiet lives. But, really, the repairs should be done before things get worse. This flat is too valuable to deteriorate, don't you think?"

"Papa, I'll get someone to come in and repair everything," said Kishore.

Vinod chuckled. "*Beta*, you must have forgotten how long it takes in India to get any work done. Workmen don't show up when they're supposed to. They can't find parts they need. Someone in their family gets sick or dies. They say they can't work in the rain. They can't work when there is a festival. There are strikes, riots and so on. Always something. Do you remember?"

Kishore nodded at each excuse his father recounted, grinning. "Yeah, that's true. So what can I do, tell me."

"This is why Govinda is coming tomorrow. As you've always known, this flat will be yours when Shanti and I are gone. I want to deed it to you now. This way it will be good for taxes. When you and your family return, you can move in here. I also turn over the maintenance of this place to you and Anjali—Shanti and I are too old and tired to do it anymore. You young ones do what you want."

"Papa, this is a surprise. Are you sure you want to do this? What about Dev?" Kishore stammered.

"Dev has the other flat though the damn bugger doesn't deserve it. But he is our son, and I hope he comes to his senses and does whatever he needs to do to get Shilpa and Arun back. Stupid boy."

Kishore changed the subject so as not to agitate Vinod. "Papa, are you sure you want our whole family to move in here? The children are wonderful, but as you know, they are young and bring with them the noise of teenagers. I need to give parties for my business, and Anjali also likes to be social and have people over."

Shanti smiled. "It will be so nice to have that kind of noise in this house again. We've been too quiet for too long."

The three of them continued the discussion of bequeathing the property now. Vinod had done his research and knew the Indian tax system and the advantages for Kishore if he inherited the flat now rather than later. Vinod wanted all the papers drawn up and signed while Kishore was still in town. After some time, Vinod became visibly exhausted, and Kishore and Shanti left him to sleep. As Kishore reached the door, Vinod called out, "So now you'll be our landlord and we'll be your tenants. What d'you think of that, huh, Kishore?"

In the same joking manner, Kishore replied, "Don't worry, Papa. I won't evict you if you don't pay rent," and smiling went to his room to think about this momentous development.

Kishore wasn't surprised that the flat was his. He had known that all his life. He was surprised at the timing. He could understand that Vinod and Shanti did not want to do the painting and repairs that the place sorely needed. That's hard enough when you're young and healthy.

He remembered the remodel of the kitchen Anjali had insisted on doing in Seattle. All the cabinets, appliances, counters, and lights were replaced—it had been a six month nightmare. He multiplied that tenfold; that's how horrendous it could be in Mumbai.

He became more and more excited about moving back into Kalpana. He looked at his watch and saw he couldn't call Anjali until later that evening. He picked up the phone and dialed Rusi.

"Guess what, *yaar*? My father is giving this flat to me now—which means that soon I will bring my family back to Malabar Hill."

Rusi was ecstatic at the prospect of their return; he missed them sorely. He promised to drop in that evening to celebrate with Kishore over a drink.

Nostalgically, Kishore looked around his old bedroom. For the first time, he looked critically. Gray walls, faded in places. Certainly, these hard beds and mattresses would have to be replaced—and the beds for the kids too. As he thought of it, he became more and more uncomfortable about the bed in which he had spent his youth.

That's just it, he thought. I slept in this bed forty years ago. Nothing has changed. Look at the curtains—thinned with age, held together by dust and determination. A wash might shred them. Did he really keep his clothes in the steel cupboards? He unlocked one and found an old school blazer hanging limply on a wire hanger. It was part of the uniform—navy blue with a crest on the breast pocket that proclaimed he was a prefect. The scratchy serge fabric had made him bloody hot! A few of his old shirts, his too small shorts and pants were folded neatly on the shelves. Why on earth hadn't Amma given them away? She couldn't have been saving them for Kisan—or, God forbid, for little Arun!

As he looked through the other cupboards, he realized that his mother was a squirrel, hoarding everything. He shook out clothes hopelessly out of style, saris that smelled musty, Vinod's old pajamas and kurtas—he wondered if his mother would be willing to part with them. Would she give up the old steel cupboards with their solid locks? He rubbed a finger over the chipped blue brand name on the door: Godrej, the best brand of all. He remembered with a wry smile how Amma had kept these cupboards locked, and had always hooked a bunch of keys into her sari at the waist. Even so she constantly misplaced them, and how many hours he and Dev had spent looking for them when they were little. So many keys to so many cupboards! How different it was living in Seattle where closets were open, where the housekeeper was trusted. Now in Mumbai, especially with the two new young men in the flat looking after Vinod, Shanti would once more make sure that everything was locked away tight.

And, of course, in a country where so many were so poor, it was cruel to put temptation in the path of these men whom they didn't know. Who could blame the casual workers from filching small items from a home where they might not even be missed? He wondered how Anjali would react to keeping her clothes and jewelry under lock and key. He knew without doubt that Priya and Kisan would hate it.

Kishore got up and drifted into the drawing room. God, he hadn't realized how huge it was. He looked at the walls, splotched and water stained, and thought: Anjali would like to paint them a peach or sage to warm the room and bring the walls in closer. All the lumbering furniture was set against those dreary walls. On one side was the divan, piled with cushions to lean against, terribly uncomfortable for sitting but providing an extra bed when needed. The coffee tables were probably antique—he remembered Vinod telling him how he and Shanti had bought them from British families who were going home after India's independence. Nice rosewood and teak. They could keep those, but the faded gray couches would have to go.

He found himself getting excited about the prospect of tailoring the flat for his family's needs. He stepped back and swept a stray lock of hair from his forehead. Looking around the room he could see it with pale green walls, with new furniture arranged intimately, conducive to conversation. Glowing ceramic lamps, brilliant red and orange flowers in vases and Shanti's beautiful shiny brass icons. How gorgeous that would be!

He did not hear Shanti come quietly into the room. She knew what he was thinking, and she smiled and nodded. "Yes, *beta*. You should probably paint this room and put new covers on the sofas."

"What d'you think, Amma? I was looking around my old bedroom and thinking we should get rid of the Godrej cupboards and make nice new built-in closets. Do you know you still have my school clothes from so long ago? We'll give those away."

"Give away the Godrej cupboards?"

"Yes, yes! And I was thinking of painting the walls in this drawing room a green or blue. We'll need new curtains and, Amma, not just new covers on the sofas, but we'll get new sofas. You'll see it'll look very nice; you'll like it. Come see, look with me." He put his hands on her shoulders and steered her around the room. "See, this is where we'll have a table lamp, and one on the other side of the room. Maybe we'll even keep some of your divas around and put in some oil and wicks and light them for special occasions. It'll be prettier than candles. You know the light in this room is so dim—I don't know how you and Papa read here at all. I should go and look at the bathrooms and the kitchen also, just to have an idea what we'll need to do. You know, Amma,

Anjali loves decorating; she'll love doing all the work here. She has very good taste, so I'm sure you'll like whatever she does."

He was so excited with his vision, he babbled on. He was looking at this flat, his heritage, his eyes seeing its possibilities and potential. He was waiting for it to be night time so he could talk to Anjali. He was insensitive to Shanti's silence, her numb eyes and her sudden pallor. He was oblivious when Shanti said, "I'll tell Rama to bring you some snacks and tea." And she turned away.

Shanti

Ｈｏｗ ｌｏｎｇ ｓｈｅ ｈａｄ ｗａｎｔｅｄ this! How fervently she had prayed
for the day when Kishore and his family would move in with
them. As she walked back to the kitchen, she felt dizzy and had to
steady herself by leaning against the wall. She told Rama to bring some
tea and biscuits and went back to Vinod's room. He was still sleeping,
thank God—if he saw her, he would know something was wrong.

But really, there was nothing wrong. For months, Vinod and she
had talked about Kishore's family moving in and how nice it would be
to have young voices in the house again. A few weeks before his heart
attack, Vinod had told her about seeing a lawyer to draw up his will.
Did he somehow sense how things were going with Dev? Vinod always
knew more than he talked about. When he told her what his plans
were, Shanti's joy ran deep. Now she wouldn't have to worry so much
about looking after Vinod by herself. Since Kishore had told her about
her Alzheimer's, she was even more anxious. How could she look after
the house and her husband if her mind was failing?

Always the picture of Kishore was before her. He was so steady,
so reliable. He would come and save her. She had not expected him
to want to change everything. No, no. What had happened was only
natural. She went into the puja room, picked up her *rudraksha* beads
and began to murmur some soothing mantras.

By the time Vinod woke from his nap, she was sitting in her chair in their bedroom with a smile on her face. She asked Ganesh to tell Rama to bring the tea. Rama brought in the tray and laid it on a table. She removed the tea cozy, then lifted the pot and poured the hot tea into two cups, added sugar and milk. She put two salt biscuits on the saucer and passed the steaming hot cup to Vinod. Then she settled down for a chat. Vinod told her how happy he was to be arranging the transfer of the flat to Kishore. "I don't want to put pressure on them, but it would be good if they returned soon. How long does Kisan have before college?" he continued.

"One more year, Anjali said. That boy is just as smart as Kishore; I'm sure he'll go to the same college. And that sweet Priya, what a little pet; she's a real artist, always painting. How long it has been since we saw them!"

"So, tell me, what did Kishore say about my plan?"

"I found him in the drawing room while you were sleeping. He said we should give away the Godrej cupboards. Then he has an idea of painting the drawing room green. And he wants to give away our sofas also."

Unaccountably, Shanti's eyes filled. She looked down and sipped from her cup, and taking a biscuit dipped it in the hot tea. She couldn't say what was bothering her. Hadn't she been happy about giving up the responsibility of the house? She would love having the children running around, chattering on the telephone, inviting their friends over. And surely Anjali would also give big parties, the kind she and Vinod used to have. She hadn't thought Kishore would want to paint the drawing room. She saw bright emerald green walls—they would look so cheap, like a bordello. Who on earth had green walls? Not for one minute did she imagine the walls a soft, pale green. And her Godrej cupboards—so many memories they enclosed. How could he want to give all that away?

Vinod sipped his tea in silence and after a while said, "Do you remember, Shanti, when we bought those sofas, huh? 1955 was it? We searched all around Bombay—yes, it was Bombay then, nai?"

179

"How can I forget? We couldn't find anything that suited us."

"Every week-end you took me to one furniture maker after another. Our drawing room was so big, we had to get really big sofas made. And what little choice we had for the covers, isn't it? I'm so glad you changed that ugly material we first had, that horrible dull gray. Now I'm forgetting. When did you get new material to cover the sofas? It was before Kisan was born, wasn't it?"

Shanti nodded. "Not just before Kisan was born, but we did it before Kishore's marriage. I wanted everything to look nice and fresh."

"And it did. Can you believe it was more than twenty years ago, isn't it?" He looked at her knowing exactly what was in her mind. "Shanti, for so many years we've lived here, and you've made it comfortable. You made everything just the way you wanted it. And it has been splendid. Remember how you used to complain about the furniture in my parents' house? You wanted to furnish a new house in your own way? Huh?"

Shanti nodded grudgingly. "But Vinod, he wants to give away the Godrej cupboards. We've had them for so long and they keep everything so safe. Can you imagine painting the drawing room green?" She wanted Vinod to see the walls the same bright shimmering emerald green that she saw in her vision. "It will look so cheap."

Before Vinod could respond, she continued, "You know what else? He says the lights in the drawing room are too dim. We need table lamps, and he's going to light divas also. He was going to look in the bathrooms and the kitchen to see what else should be changed. Is there anything he likes?"

Vinod gazed fixedly at a picture of a raja mounted on a horse on the opposite wall. Gently he spoke, understanding the unvoiced pain behind Shanti's words, "Kishore is doing just what we did more than forty years ago, isn't it? Who can blame him for wanting to have his own style, his own way of doing things? This will now be his home. We'll make sure he doesn't touch our room, *achcha?*"

"You're right, I know. They should leave our room and my puja room alone—let them do whatever they want, *nai?*"

"Don't worry, Shanti, you'll see the changes will happen more slowly than he realizes. This is not America where all work is done on schedule—this is Indian Standard Time. We'll probably be dead and gone before even one change happens." He laughed, hoping to find an echo in her. Nothing.

"But really, I'm more worried about you and me. How will we live with workmen in the house daily, with banging hammers, paint, dirt and everything? Well, at least, until all the workmen are finished, we should keep the cupboards with the good locks, nai?" He was smiling.

Shanti smiled reluctantly. She could see that Vinod was right. Of course, Kishore and Anjali should make this their home, just like she had. She understood that, she knew that.

But deep inside, why did she feel her son was ripping away all she had built, all that made her comfortable? Every sofa held memories of the visitors over the years, the family gatherings, the parties. Every cupboard held pieces of the past, pieces that defined her and her family. Yes, even Kishore's and Dev's old clothes. She could look at the small shorts and shirts and see the mischievous boys. The happy times. So soon, Kishore was making changes so soon, too soon. She would never tell him how she felt. Because, as Vinod said, it was only natural. She herself had done the same thing all those years ago, as Vinod reminded her. Vinod knew. So he gave her comfort by telling her that their room would be sacrosanct. She nodded to herself, and her chin lifted a little.

Let them do anything in the drawing room, the dining room and their own bedrooms. No one would be allowed to touch Vinod's and her bedroom and her puja room. After all, these two rooms had everything she needed, and she would keep these two most important rooms pure. What else did she need?

Then why did she feel an ache, a pain of loss? Her life was slowly, gently wisping away between her fingers and forming a silken pool at her feet. She was being slowly erased. Her mind was gradually becoming a blank. And it seemed that the page on which the story of her life had been written was also fading into nothingness.

Slowly she opened the door which led to the small verandah outside their bedroom. There was room for a chair and a few plants in pots. Shanti used the space to plant her tulsi, marigolds and jasmine she used during her puja. Now she stood against the hip high wall of the balcony looking up at the gray sky, the lowering clouds. And she felt an inexplicable void in her heart. When she heard Vinod call her, she turned and walked in slowly.

Priya

SHE KNEW THAT SOMETHING BAD was happening to her Amma and Papa. Daddy had just returned from Mumbai, and he had gathered them all around the table to hear the news. He looked so tired with dark circles under his eyes. His hair was greasy and uncombed, and his shirt was crumpled. He even smelled all sweaty—he hadn't yet taken a shower after his plane trip. Mummy was biting her lip and looking very worried.

Then Daddy spoke in a blustery and fake cheerful voice, "Papa came through the operation with flying colors." She was so glad to hear that. She adored her grandfather. Of course, now she was too old to sit on his lap, the way she used to before they left Mumbai. He would tell her stories, some of them true, of experiences he'd had when he was growing up in Bombay (that's what he still called it).

She had planned the picture she was going to paint for him—mostly red for his heart. She knew he liked red, liked her paintings. She would make it cheerful and bright. Now Daddy was talking about Amma, saying she had something called Alzheimer's which was making her forgetful. He said we must go back and live with them in their flat. He said that's the way it was done in India; children looked after their parents in old age.

Oh no, did that mean they would have to move again? She'd hated leaving Mumbai five years ago; now she didn't want to leave Seattle. She'd had some difficulty making friends when they moved here because she was so shy. Now she had a small group of girl friends, and they even had sleepovers in each other's houses. Those nights were always fun—the girls loved Priya's long, almost black, curly hair, and they used her as a model for styling the latest updos. In her pink pajamas, hair swept up in a sophisticated twist, dark eyes accented with mascara, Priya would look in the mirror and think, "Wow! Maybe I'll be as pretty as Mummy when I grow up."

Now Daddy was saying they would have to go to India and these fun times would end. After all these years of living in Seattle with just Mummy, Daddy and Kisan, it would be weird to live with Amma and Papa as well. At none of her friends' homes here was there a grandparent.

However, thinking about her friends in Mumbai, she remembered meeting a grandfather or grandmother, sometimes both, in most of their houses. Whenever she visited, she used to always pay her respects to the old people first, like she had been taught to do. She knew to sit with them for a few minutes and ask about their health. Sometimes it was easy when they were friendly; sometimes they were nasty and acted as if the kids were a nuisance. Yes, the children made a noise, laughing and talking, but sometimes they quietly did their homework. Where else could they go? There were very few gardens attached to flats in the heart of Mumbai.

Now, as usual, Kisan was asking a million questions about something. She stopped listening to Daddy answer Kisan as her mind wandered to Shalini's grandmother with a shudder. What a witch!

Shalini's family was not wealthy, and they didn't have a separate room for the grandmother. The divan in the drawing room was her bed, so she was there all the time. She wore white saris, strictly following the Indian tradition of widows wearing white. The old lady had lost most of her teeth, and she constantly made wet sucking sounds as the drool slowly slimed down her chin. When the children came home from school, she yelled that they were too raucous, that they were disturbing her, giving her headaches. Shalini, her brother and sisters, even her parents, all ignored the complaints. And thus the family lived in a permanent state of flux, with an uneasy truce, trying to give each other space where there was indeed none.

After going to Shalini's just twice, Priya couldn't stand the apprehension she felt because of the witchy old lady. So she invited Shalini to her grandparents' flat to play and do homework. What a difference. Rama had freshly made snacks ready; Amma welcomed them with a smile. Even Papa came in to say a cheerful hello. Priya could see the envy in Shalini's face and felt sorry for her friend who had to live with a loud whiny old bag.

Daddy was still talking—he was saying that they couldn't go until he found a good job. That meant that she and Kisan could finish the next year of school right here. What a relief. She wanted to graduate from elementary school into the middle school at Lakeside. Oh, wait! She'd probably go to the middle school in Mumbai—the Cathedral School. She wondered if any of her old friends were still there. But she loved it here in Seattle. She had her best friends, her art classes, her everything.

"It's not fair; why do we have to move again?" The words came out before she could stop them. Nor could she stop the tears that accompanied the words.

Daddy pulled her over, sat her on his lap and hugged her tight. Although she was almost eleven, he didn't think she was too old for his lap. "I know how hard this is for you, sweetheart. Right now though, Amma and Papa need us. They have always given us everything, haven't they? Now it's our time to be with them, to help them."

Priya swallowed hard. It's not that she didn't want to help her grandparents. No, it was just that she didn't want to leave Seattle. She looked over to Kisan for help. He just sat there like a miserable lump, head bent. He was probably thinking of how he would graduate from Lakeside and then go on to some fancy college he was always yakking about. But they were both being forced to do something they didn't want to do. She badly wanted to get up and go to her room, and she looked around to see if she could excuse herself. But Daddy seemed so sad, and Mummy was biting her lip the way she did when she was almost crying. So Priya snaked her arm around Daddy's shoulder and snuggled into his neck.

Daddy kept talking about how much they would enjoy being back in Mumbai, with Rama and his cooking, with someone to make their beds and fold their clothes. And what about Amma's dog? They were going to love this new dog Amma had named Hari. Then Mummy chimed in about their friends. Remember Goutam, she asked. Remember Lata and Shalini?

"Yes," Kisan said, dejectedly. Priya just nodded not trusting herself to speak.

Soon after, Kisan asked to be excused, so Priya could leave as well. She went straight to her room and began dabbling in her paints. She painted furiously, slashing the canvas with brilliant reds and oranges. Gritting her teeth, she drained herself of her emotions until she was spent and threw herself on her bed.

After some time, she crept to Kisan's room and knocked on his door.

"Go away," he growled.

"Please, I want to talk," she begged.

"Oh, all right. But make it quick; I'm busy."

She saw him staring at the computer screen. That's what he did most of the time.

"What are you doing?" she asked.

"I'm checking out Alzheimer's. That's what Daddy said Amma has. It's quite terrible, Priya. I'm scared about what's happening to her, to them both."

"What will Alzheimer's do to her?"

"Well, first she will start to forget things, y'know like her keys, her book, her glasses. Then she'll start to forget people, like her friends, then, like, even her children..." and he looked at her wide-eyed. "I think she will forget us too."

"No," Priya whispered. Then she screamed, "Just shut up, Kisan. You're saying that to frighten me. She can't forget us. She can't forget Mummy and Daddy. You're wrong. Shut up, shut up! I hate you and your stupid computer!" And she stormed out of the room wailing.

Mummy and Daddy came running to see what was happening. She rushed into Daddy's arms. He had just showered and was wearing his sweat pants and an undershirt. He smelled of Dial soap and her favorite Herbal Essence Shampoo. She buried her face in his chest, sobbing, unable to stop.

After a while, she quieted down, the whole family clustered around her. Then Daddy led her into the living room, and Mummy and Kisan followed and sat close together on the sofa. Daddy sat in the big lounger and took her in his lap. Kisan was contrite, and Mummy and Daddy looked worried. Kisan confessed that he was researching Alzheimer's on the internet to find out more than what he vaguely knew and described to his parents the ravages of the disease. By this point, he knew more than the adults. As they listened to Kisan, they inched closer together, touching hands, loosely hugging, drawing and giving comfort as they stared into an unknown future.

Priya knew that in a year she would be saying goodbye to her friends here and would probably never see them again. And it made her sad. But she knew that if they did not go back to India, she might never ever see her grandparents again—and that she couldn't bear. She wiped her nose and eyes on her shirt sleeve.

"Let's go back soon, Daddy. I want to see Amma and Papa again," she said. She felt Mummy's hand caress her back. Then Daddy gripped her in a tight bear hug and dropped his head, and she felt his shoulders shake. She stroked his wet hair.

Mumbai, three years later

Anjali

ANJALI WAS ON THE PHONE, trying to control the anger in her voice. "You said someone would be here by eleven today. Now it's one o'clock, and no one has come."

"I'm sorry, madam. I'm sure he's coming quickly. You see, it's raining..."

"Yes, I know it's raining. It's always raining, but I have a big problem and the electrician promised he'd come. If the problem is not repaired today, we won't have any lights, no T.V. no a.c. Call him on his mobile and tell him this is urgent," Anjali demanded.

"Yes, yes madam. I will phone him and tell him to come quickly. Thank you, madam," said the unctuous voice on the other end.

Anjali was ready to throw the phone out the window, completely frustrated with what Vinod called the *"chalta hai"* attitude. When she'd asked him to translate for her, he had explained it literally meant "it's going along" or, more broadly, "don't worry. It'll happen...someday." Chewing on a cuticle, she flung herself into a chair. She'd wanted to get the bedroom ready for Kisan's summer visit, and she'd bought a couple of nice lamps. When she'd plugged them in, she'd caused a blowout.

She placed her right ankle on her left knee knowing how unladylike it looked. Drumming her fingers on her thigh, she looked around the room. She'd done an amazing job in two years. The drawing room in which she sat glowed with peach walls with one accent wall in a muted orange. It diminished the cavernous feel and made the room more inviting and intimate. Original paintings from India's up and coming artists—street scenes, abstracts, black and white drawings—mingled with the art she brought back from Seattle. Eclectic, a mish-mash, but it worked gloriously.

The large couches had been replaced by smaller sofas upholstered in a sea foam green fabric contrasting nicely with the walls. Pillows in varying sizes and shapes echoed the oranges of the walls and the reds and blacks in the paintings. Anjali had reveled in picking the fabrics from the multitude of silks and cottons available in the stores. The sofas and armchairs had been placed strategically to allow for small conversation groups. In one corner of the room was a round table with four chairs where people could play chess, Scrabble or cards. Until the finishing touches of paint and wiring were done in the dining room, the family ate their meals at this table.

She glared out the window—rain, rain, rain, a convenient excuse for the electrician. Was she ever destined to live anywhere where the sun dominated? Los Angeles, for instance? Forget the sun, what about a city where it didn't rain so bloody much? It was so depressing. It had been grey and dreary and raining in Seattle, and it was grey and angry and pelting in Mumbai. She picked up *Time* magazine from the side table, flipped through it before tossing it aside. Even more depressing.

The transition to Mumbai had not been bad at all for the family. She had been so fearful that Kisan would be yanked from Lakeside in his senior year—that didn't happen. When Kishore returned from Mumbai and told them about the condition of his parents, the kids were old enough to understand. They'd all agreed that Kishore should look for a job in Mumbai and move there as soon as feasible. Kishore insisted that Kisan finish his senior year and Priya her final year in elementary school with their friends. Anjali blessed him for his understanding and devotion.

He told them how Papa had bequeathed him the Kalpana flat.

Slapping Kisan on the back, he'd said, "Now you have an ancestral piece of India to return to anytime."

The children had reacted to Kishore's news quite predictably. Kisan browsed the internet to learn all he could about Alzheimer's, printing out reams of pages over which he pored with single-minded concentration. Priya withdrew into herself and her room where she painted until she had produced a beautiful acrylic abstract in cheerful colors to send to Vinod and Shanti.

It had taken Kishore more than six months to land an appropriate job with India Infomatics, Ltd. He did not leave Seattle until March, after which only three months remained for Kisan's graduation. Kisan had graduated in the top seven percent of his class and did not make valedictorian. Junior English, concentrating on American literature, had brought him his only B+. Since Vinod was so eager to attend Kisan's graduation, Kishore had flown him and Shanti first class to Seattle. Anjali and Kishore were happy to have the parents there on such a memorable occasion. It was also a time to celebrate Kisan's entrance into Harvard which, in a last minute decision, he chose over MIT. Kishore was disappointed, but how could one argue with Harvard?

Anjali and the kids moved into the Malabar Hill flat that June, and Kisan spent the summer reuniting with his grandparents and traveling around India with his friends. He left for Boston in August, and Anjali had been busy remodeling ever since. She heard Shanti's footsteps padding toward the drawing room and quickly lowered her leg. Shanti had just finished her puja, and she looked perky and cheerful, smiling, so much better since the younger family moved in. Her face was unlined and placid. She stopped for a minute, looking befuddled as she searched for her favorite chair. Then her memory clicked in and she moved to one of the new sofas.

Having that chair moved was the hardest thing Anjali had done. When the new furniture had arrived, she had worked around the ugly chair, leaving it in place. There it sat, upholstered decades ago in a dowdy khaki-gray, faded in splotches from the full glare of the afternoon sun. For days, even weeks, Anjali said nothing. Daily Shanti moved from her puja room somnabulistically to her chair, where she sat gazing at the Arabian Sea. From this elevated perch, she could a part of the Mumbai scene and yet apart from it. It isolated her but also made her a silent player. It had been her refuge for forty years.

The eyesore grew and grew in Anjali's mind. It began to overwhelm the room and her thoughts. She found herself annoyed with Kishore for not caring and with Shanti and Vinod for not understanding what she was trying to do. Finally, one night, she provoked Kishore into an argument over an inconsequential matter and burst into tears.

Engrossed in his work, Kishore had been pleased that Anjali had something to keep her occupied. He was delighted with all she'd accomplished. Especially since she had accomplished it all without involving him. To him, her tears now signaled her frustration with dealing with the vagaries of Indian workers.

"I'm sorry, Anjali," he said. "I know that these workmen can be frustrating and you've done an amazing job so far..."

"God, Kish! You don't see it, do you? You don't see what it does to the room? You don't notice how it is like a magnet pulling everyone's eye. It's so hideous and ruins the rest of the drawing room."

"What are you talking about? I think the drawing room looks fantastic—the colors, the furniture, the art. What is it? Here," he pulled open the door of their bedroom where they'd been talking, grabbed her hand and led her into the drawing room, "now you show me."

Fortunately, Vinod and Shanti had gone to bed so she was able to point to the offending chair without embarrassment. She saw Kishore's face tighten and a tic appear at his jaw.

"Oh, Anju, we can't ask her to give up her special chair. She has sat in this chair as long as I can remember. I'm not going to do it—sorry. Damn. How about if you reupholster it in the same color as the sofas?" He chewed on his lower lip, looking at the chair critically. "No, you're right, it just doesn't fit. But how are we going to tell her?"

But of course, Anjali had coaxed and nagged until he'd talked to his mother, and she had acceded to his request with hidden pain. The chair had been moved to her bedroom to sit next to the window with a view of the water-streaked walls of the neighboring building. Anjali had felt wretchedly guilty for weeks although neither Vinod nor Shanti had said anything. Even so, every time Shanti came into the room she looked for her chair—*every time*. She meant no malice, but Anjali always felt a twinge of remorse.

Now Shanti smiled warmly at Anjali; she was so happy to have the young family in the flat. She asked, "What time is Dev coming, Anjali?"

"I don't know, Amma; did you speak to him?"

"Yes, yes. He said he'd come for lunch today."

"It's only one o'clock—he'll come later."

It was the same every day. Shanti waited for Dev who did come to lunch at least once a week, always when his father was not there. And today Vinod was at the club using the treadmill. It was sad to see how much Shanti missed seeing Shilpa and Arun, though Shilpa was very good about bringing the little boy over a couple of times a week. But Shanti felt the irreparable wrench that had happened in that little family

Anjali looked at Shanti and wondered how she felt to be losing control of her mind. While Anjali had bravely told Ansuya and Bridget that she was happy and willing to move in with her in-laws, she was basing her feelings on her long stay with them when Priya was born, and she had been needy. Now, however, there was a more than a subtle difference—now it was her flat. She could look around it and change things. Shanti and Vinod were family, but they were like guests—what were the roles now? In her childhood and youth, Anjali had never had much family interaction, and she had spent most of her life out of India. She was unsure of her behavior in this new and permanent situation. Again, Shanti and Vinod made it easy for her.

After a few weeks, Vinod broached the subject. "Anjali, I'm sure your taste in furniture is very different from ours, just like ours was from my parents. You should make changes any way you like."

And Shanti put her soft hand on Anjali's and said, "Yes, *beti*. These pieces hold memories for us. Now it is time for you to make your own memories in your own home."

Anjali did not find caring for her mother-in-law onerous at all. Occasionally Shanti forgot things—her keys, whether she had eaten—trivial things. She had not reached the stage Anjali had heard about from her friends and was dreading: the one where Shanti might wander out of the flat and into the streets at night, or where she would want her bag packed so she could return to the childhood home. Having Priya around seemed to ground Shanti, and she was happy talking to the teenager and listening to her chatter.

To divert Shanti's attention from Dev, Anjali said, "Amma, Kisan is coming day after tomorrow. He enjoyed his second year in college and is anxious to see you and Papa."

"Kisan. What a sweet boy that one is, isn't it?" Anjali realized that Shanti was searching her mind to put a face on Kisan; it had been almost a year since she'd seen him. Anjali filled in, "Yes, he's grown up and in college now. See, this is the last picture he sent. He doesn't fight with Priya anymore. Remember how they used to fight when they were little? I was just getting his room ready for him, and *phut!* I made our flat lose its current." Anjali was using Indian idiom more and more. "I'm waiting for the electrician to come—he's so late already."

Shanti smiled patiently. "Here it's Indian standard time. Maybe he'll come later; maybe he'll come tomorrow."

Just then the doorbell rang, and Anjali sprang up to answer. Thank God, a workman was shaking out his large black umbrella. His raincoat was dripping. Despite the protection, the man's hair was rain-plastered to his head—but he flashed a grin and carried a toolbox.

In three hours, the man had fixed everything but the air-conditioning. Well, thought Anjali, we'll have to use the fans tonight. When she had started remodeling, Anjali had wanted to air condition the whole flat until everyone convinced her it would be prohibitive in cost and impact the rest of the electrical supply to their flat, maybe the building. So they had single window units put in the drawing room and two of the bedrooms.

Shanti and Vinod insisted they didn't want one. Vinod said, "Why, *beta*? We have managed so long with fans only. We don't need fancy air conditioning."

Anjali had tried to convince them, "You'll be more comfortable and sleep better when it's hot and humid."

They protested, Vinod saying, "I feel bloody cold when I am in air conditioned rooms. Shanti and I will probably become sick from it." After a while, Anjali gave up. The old couple was dealing with enough changes anyway.

After paying the electrician, Anjali walked into the dining room to examine the large hole the workman had put in the wall. Poor Shanti and Vinod could not have napped much with all the banging he'd done. Now that hole would have to be filled in before the dining room could be painted.

She looked at the large ornate rosewood table which seated twelve; Shanti and Vinod had not used it in years. In the room sat a side cupboard filled with Shanti's old crockery. Anjali looked around again to see where she could put the new Spode sets she had bought before she left Seattle. Yes, she had splurged, but people gave huge parties in India, so she'd bought two services for twelve. They sat in boxes. She would have to get them out of Kisan's room where they'd been temporarily stored. She'd have the boxes moved into the servants' quarters.

Sighing, she walked to her bedroom, changed into a comfortable cool caftan and lay on her bed. She was excited about Kisan's visit, eager to hear his opinion on the changes she had made to the flat which he hadn't seen in several months. Kishore was always lavish with his praise. Shanti and Vinod never interfered with or influenced any of her plans. More and more, the older couple spent their time in their bedroom emerging only for meals and when visitors dropped in to see them. When Kishore, Anjali, Priya and Kisan had their friends over, they stayed discreetly out of sight. Even so, Anjali tried to be always sensitive to their feelings when she made a decorating decision.

The flat was pretty much finished, so she could call Sonali again and get more actively involved in the project for abused women they had worked on together. She lay on her back, hands upturned at her sides and took some deep yogic breaths. Tears started creeping out from under her closed eyelids. Her relaxation had let her guard down.

She turned on her side and hugged a pillow. They had been back from Seattle more than two years now, but she had not entertained at home because the flat was not ready. When Kishore had to host business associates, he took them to the club or to a restaurant. The flat had been turned upside down for a long time, but finally things were falling in place. The dining room needed paint and lights. That was all that was necessary for guests. Soon they could open their doors to company.

Anjali imagined all the praise that would be heaped on her—her sense of color, her artistic taste. Yes, yes, she would like to show off her work of the last two years. She sat up in bed, tears wiped away, now quite excited. She would phone the painter and have him start as soon as possible. The electrician would have to repair the wiring and put in new light fixtures. She would go to Chor Bazaar to find just the right sconces.

Chor Bazaar! Thieves' Market—what a find. When Roopa suggested they shop in Chor Bazaar for two difficult to find side tables, Anjali was skeptical. She preferred shopping in comfortable air-conditioned stores. Finally, she succumbed to Roopa's persistence, and they went to Mutton Street (what a name!) with a sense of adventure. A plethora of antiques, junk, trinkets and trash greeted them. No care was taken to display the goods invitingly—instead everything was haphazard, chaotic and rather like a treasure hunt where you could come up with exactly what you wanted or nothing.

On her first visit, she was nervous, unused to the hard bargaining expected on this colorful street. But there the perfect tables were! She knew to cut any asking price in half. When the owner's voice rose in indignation at her insulting offer, she felt intimidated and walked away. Roopa, at her side, whispered, "Good, Anjali! Now just keep walking."

She was disconcerted by the owner who began speaking even louder and gesturing wildly for her to return. Soon his voice softened. "Come, madam. I will give you *bonni*, special price, because you are my first customer today. For no one else would I give such a price. I am losing money on these beautiful tables. Come, madam, give another two hundred rupees." But she stood firm until he took the money, touched it to his eyes in thanks for the first sale of the day. It would bring him good luck, even though it was a humiliatingly low price, he said. Anjali had felt triumphant, and now Chor Bazaar was the first place she thought of when she wanted sconces for the dining room. What was the name of the store with lamps heaped in a corner? She frowned in an effort to remember. Ah! Taherally's. She would invite Roopa to go along tomorrow.

So she continued to plan her first dinner party. They could easily have thirty or forty people without crowding the flat. She would make sure Kisan and Priya invited a few of their friends as well. Then, abruptly, her imagination applied the brakes. She'd thought of food.

Wonderful as Rama was, the only person who could cook Kisan's favorites, it would be impossible for the now old man to manage such a large affair. Besides, his repertoire was almost exclusively Indian. Anjali wanted to serve exotic dishes like chicken with prunes and olives, a risotto with mushrooms, a tomato bruschetta—such dishes. Dear old Rama, he would be willing and eager to try, but no. Anjali wanted her first party to be splendid—she would look around for a chef trained in cooking western style.

Rama was in his seventies. He must be tired of working. She would approach Kishore when the time was right. That evening, after Kishore had his usual two gin and limes, she talked to him. He was relaxed and comfortable, watching the news on television. Vinod and Shanti were in their room, reading. So Anjali sat next to Kishore on the new couch and started speaking about the party. He was barely paying attention, engrossed in the news. When she went into the description of the menu, she subtly revealed her true reason for the conversation.

She began to ramble on about needing a cook who could make the dishes she wanted so badly to serve—pastas, risottos, souffles. Kishore kept grunting his agreement until, exasperated, she abandoned subtlety and said, "Don't you think Rama should be offered retirement so he can go to his family?"

At that Kishore turned his full amber-eyed attention to her. "What rubbish, Anjali. Rama thinks of us as his family. He's been with us since I was little."

"Yes, that's true. So he must be in his seventies and he's definitely slowing down. I'm thinking of him, Kish. It'll be too hard for him to cook for the kind of parties we'll want to give."

"Look, Anju, he can help your main chef, he can be—what do they call it? Oh, the sous chef." Kishore was smiling at the thought. He knew Rama would never give up his sway of the kitchen.

Anjali continued, "Don't you think he's tired of working, Kish? He's getting so old. You know he's constantly dropping pans, poor man. And then he feels mortified. Look, why don't you ask him if he'd like a generous lump sum and he can finally go and live with his family and never have to work any more."

Now Kishore was frowning. "I don't know, Anju. He's been here forever and…"

"At least you should give him the choice, don't you think? Let him make his own decision rather than you thinking you know what's in his head. He may be waiting for the day when he doesn't have to cook another samosa."

"You may be right. I shouldn't make his decisions. I'll talk to him before your party, okay? Now tell me more about your plans."

And thus Anjali and Kishore inexorably and with no malice continued on their fateful path.

Kisan

H E WAITED IN LINE AT Sahar airport, jiggling his backpack and his laptop into more comfortable positions. It was always like this, every goddamn year. Eighteen to twenty hours of mind-numbing flight followed by this eternal stagnation at Indian immigration—always, always, always in the middle of the night. It was muggy and sticky, and the sickly smell of sweat, hair oil and urine bludgeoned his vulnerable senses.

Stop being a baby, he told himself. Soon, he would pick up his luggage and go through the green channel avoiding the customs inspectors because he had nothing to declare. Then he'd be out of this rancid airport into the comparatively fresh air. Mummy and Daddy's new driver, whose name he couldn't remember, would be at the people-choked entrance holding up a sign reading KISAN, the rain streaking the letters to illegibility. In the air-conditioned car, he could relax.

When he'd gone to Seattle eight years ago—oh, so reluctantly—he'd been excited to come back every summer to see his friends. With each succeeding year, he had less and less in common with most of the boys he'd gone to school with. Except Goutam, Goutam of the camel ride memory. Goutam had gone on to Princeton, so they met during their spring and Christmas vacations in the States, both coming to Mumbai in the summers. They had conspired and coaxed their parents to let them travel to see more of India. They had seen the Taj Mahal and the palaces in Rajasthan last summer—this year they wanted to go to Bangalore and from there to Kabini Lodge in the Banarghatta jungle to see tigers and elephants in the wild.

He wondered how his grandparents were doing. He retained the picture of his grandfather as a bluff, vigorous man with strong opinions, the moral touchstone of the family. How Kisan still loved to listen to his stories, to play chess or Scrabble with him. Each year had diminished both his Amma and Papa. He understood why this was happening with his Amma. In fact, this year he was bracing himself to see a major deterioration in her condition—it had been four years since she'd been diagnosed with Alzheimer's.

In the car, finally speeding along almost deserted roads, Kisan surrendered to the rhythm of the rain, letting it lull him to an almost sleep. They reached Marine Drive, and he watched the waves of the Arabian Sea splash and spray the rocks. Soon they would be at Chowpatty Beach, the happening place every evening, crowded with lovers, families, kids—low cost entertainment for everyone. He would have to lie to Mummy, sneak away and go to the bhel puri stands at this beach. Involuntarily, he salivated as he thought of the spicy puffed rice mixed with tamarind and mint chutneys, onions, green chilis and the unique flavor that was Mumbai served on small, crispy puris. Oh yes, he was going at the first chance—as he had every year. If Mummy knew that he ate street food, she would be aghast, visions of cholera, plague and worse in her mind.

She and Daddy were waiting up to greet him when he arrived home, and after the hugs, he went to his room and crashed. It was three-thirty; with luck he could sleep until eight. It was barely six when he was awakened by the harsh cawing of a large crow perched on his window sill. Ducking his head under a pillow, he cursed Mumbai for having so many birds. Weren't they scared off by the congestion? No, little sparrows, big kites, crows, hawks, even vultures all battled to get any little scrap of food. This particular black cawing creature wouldn't quit no matter how vigorously he tried to shoo it away. Finally, at seven-thirty, granting victory to the stupid crow, he showered and went into the drawing room.

Mummy was waiting to show him the changes she had made, and as he walked around the room with her, he was amazed at what she had done in such a short time. "Well, Mummy, you even beat Indian standard time and the *chalta hai* attitude! This is really fantastic," he said. She glowed.

At breakfast, he basked in the warmth of the smiling faces. Yes, he had missed them, his parents, his grandparents and Priya, who seemed to have grown about six inches in a year. Shanti smiled and smiled and held his hand in her soft one. Vinod used a cane now, but still went for his daily walk.

Kishore looked more serious, his forehead furrowed with permanent lines. Kisan hated to think it, but his Daddy was becoming stodgy and pompous. Mummy still had her effervescence, bubbling with pleasure at his praise for her decorating talent. Acknowledging the generosity of Vinod and Shanti, she told Kisan how easy the older couple had made it for her, saying, "Do you know, Kisan, when I wanted to change the old furniture, Amma said these pieces hold our memories, but you should make your own memories with your own furniture. Isn't that wonderful?"

As Kisan looked around, he thought this is not a dysfunctional family. In the U.S. it seems every family is dysfunctional. It's only a matter of degree. Here in Mumbai, in this flat, they are recognizing each other's needs, granting space, following tradition yet allowing modern ideas. Then he wondered what was hidden here, what secrets he would find if he began digging. In India, people didn't bare their innermost problems; they usually lived with them, or snapped.

The most awe-inspiring example of a dysfunctional family in his experience had come with his reading of *As I Lay Dying* in his junior year of high school. Faulkner's language brought the strange characters of the Bundren family to vivid life. He remembered being entranced by the names: Anse, Cash, Jewel, Darl, Vardaman. There seemed to be no intimacy or love in that family, yet they carried their decomposing dead mother to another county to bury her with her kin, as they said. The lives of the siblings moved in separate planes, never intersecting, never even coming close, but beneath all the unexpressed chaos ran a strong undercurrent of devotion. The Bundren children were bound together by indissoluble family ties that ran deep. He'd wondered about families and their bonds ever since. Simultaneously repulsed and enthralled by Faulkner's story, he was haunted by it still. It was puzzling, a tough read, about a family that he could never learn to like. Ultimately the paper he wrote on the book brought him the only B+ in his school career.

Even *The Great Gatsby*, his favorite book that year, depicted seriously flawed characters: lawbreakers and rich unfeeling brutes living behind elegant facades. When he talked to his teacher at the end of the year, he jokingly said, "You know, Mr. Coughlin, I could never write a great book because my family is not dysfunctional." And Mr. Coughlin laughed with him and then asked, quite seriously, "Have you looked under the surface? Why don't you dig a bit on your next trip—you may be surprised by what you find." Yes, now he was older, more mature, he would dig. After all, he didn't really know what was behind his uncle Dev's and Shilpa's divorce. Hmm, maybe his family was dysfunctional after all, living behind an elegant façade.

His fascination with human complexity and societal customs and rituals had made him take more sociology and psychology courses at Harvard. He was seriously thinking of changing his major and abandoning the math-engineering path it was assumed was his rightful one. This past semester he had done a research paper, a comparative study on the care of the aging in the United States and India. It had left him feeling glad to be Indian, from a country where elders were not marginalized as so many were in the U.S. Now, during his summer visit, he would be more keenly observant. Where better than with his own family and the upper echelon of Mumbai society?

After all the obligatory visits to relatives and friends, Kisan settled into the expected monotony of his summer visit. Sure, there were parties almost every evening, but it was with the same crowd, the same drinking, the same conversation. These young men and women had been his friends at school, and now he had so little in common with them. At one party, he looked around the wealthy, hard-drinking, forced laughter sharing crowd and thought, "Damn! This is a Gatsby party, with Daisy and Tom and Nick all transported to a different country and later century." With that new perspective, he began to look for similarities between his reading and his life, applying what he had been studying to what was around him. But most of all, he wanted to know the story of Dev.

Whenever Dev came for lunch, Shanti monopolized him, and Kisan could not talk to him frankly. So he made a date to meet his uncle at the Willingdon Club one morning. They sat on the verandah watching the rain soak the lawn, Dev sipping beer and Kisan drinking lime juice. Pretty soon, Dev ran out of questions to ask him about his studies at Harvard, so they sat in companionable silence. Kisan finally built up the courage to ask, "Devuncle, I always felt a tension between you and Papa. I know he doesn't approve of your career, but I think his refusal to talk to you is deeper than that. Am I wrong?"

Dev looked over quizzically, one eyebrow raised. Kisan thought the years had not been kind to his uncle—he had a little pot belly, and his dissipation showed in his lack-luster eyes with dark bags under them. His hair was streaked with gray, and he looked older than Kishore.

"You're right, Kisan. I'm sure you saw it all the time you were growing up. I am the black sheep in the family, never good enough for my father."

"Was there anything in particular that got him to the point where he shuns you—I mean, he won't even be in the same room with you. I'm sorry, if you don't want to talk about it, that's fine; it's none of my business."

"No, no. Why not? You're my favorite nephew, why shouldn't you know these things? You know Papa always hated my drumming; he wanted me to have a career like your father. But, you know, Kisan, we have to do what we want to do in life, or what's the point of living, isn't it? My career, or lack of it, was bad enough for Papa, but the final straw—tell me, have you heard the story of Anita from your parents?"

"Who's Anita?" asked Kisan, perking up with excitement. Maybe Mr. Coughlin was right; there were mysteries to be unraveled.

And Dev told the story of his once-in-a-lifetime love of Anita. Oh, she was beautiful, she could sing, she was his for the plucking.

Ordering another beer, Dev continued, "But Papa would have none of it."

"Why not? She sounds perfect for you, nai?" Kisan was eager to hear more about the cruel way his uncle was ripped from the arms of his lover and forced to live a conforming life—the stuff of novels. Maybe his family was dysfunctional after all and would provide fodder for a book.

Dev sighed and nodded. "Yes, she was. But you know what? She was an Anglo-Indian and therefore not worthy to marry into the family."

Kisan felt punched in the stomach. Caste and class prejudice in his family? He thought of his parents and grandparents as the most accepting and liberal of Indians. Sure, when he was in elementary school in Mumbai, along with everyone else, he knew which kid was a Gujarati or a Marwari or whatever, but it never *meant* anything to him. Did it really mean something to his parents? Were they secret bigots? What else would he find out?

"Come on, uncle! This was what? Ten, fifteen years ago. Don't tell me Papa and Amma rejected her because of caste? What about Mummy and Daddy? Surely they sided with you?"

Tears filled Dev's eyes and he ordered another beer, allowing the liquid to coddle his pain. He sipped it slowly and exaggerated, "I was without friends at that time. I was all alone. No one cared. They only cared that I didn't bring shame to the family." He settled back to tell his story, to tell his tragedy to the first sympathetic ear he'd had in years.

Kisan listened as Dev painted a picture of the beloved Vinod as a martinet, unforgivingly brutal when it came to Dev. He was a man driven to crush the two passions Dev had: Anita and music. Kisan's own parents who should have supported this true love had stepped to the sidelines.

Dev said, "I don't want to speak against my brother; after all he is your father. I must tell you I was shocked, bloody shocked I tell you, when he said she would never fit into our family because of her low birth and lack of family connections. He asked how could I bring her to the flat when relatives or friends came over—she had nothing to talk about, nothing in common with anyone. What could I do? I couldn't hurt my father and mother; they were getting old, and I had brought them enough unhappiness. Besides, I knew my father would disown me, and if that happened, I would never even see my Amma again. I finally gathered the strength to break it off. Telling Anita goodbye is the hardest thing I've done. I listened to my sainted mother, the only person who didn't speak against me, who told me that it was my karma and I should accept it. What else could I do?"

"When I was in school, there weren't many Anglo-Indians that I knew of. What's wrong with them?" Kisan asked.

"Nothing wrong with them. They came into being when the British ravished or raped young Indian women and produced children the sahibs wouldn't acknowledge. So they were half-breeds, spurned by Indians and the British alike—their existence shamed both sides in some way. It happens everywhere, *beta*—look at the mulattos in America. They too are the result of interbreeding, aren't they? In America, it was plantation owners and their slaves. In India, it was tea plantation overseers and leaf pluckers, hah! It's the same all over. Anyway, Anita married the son of a rich man and left Mumbai and went to America. So that's my sad story."

Kisan felt a chill as he listened. At the moment, he had no special girlfriend—but would his parents raise hell if he wanted to marry an American? An Asian-American? What about an African-American? He'd never tested those waters, had he? But now he was talking to

Devuncle and learning from him about his father's and grandfather's hidden prejudices. Were they really hypocrites? He couldn't think of that now. He had to keep the conversation going with Dev.

"Then you met Shilpa?"

"Actually, Amma arranged that marriage for me. We were happy for some years, then she got tired of my ways—well, I'm sure you've heard of my dissolute ways." He looked over, and Kisan, looking down at his shoes, nodded. "I really tried to give up the drinking and stuff, but I'm just weak. I don't blame her. God, I miss my little Arunbeta, you know. Have you seen him lately? Isn't he beautiful?"

Kisan nodded again, stayed and talked for a few more minutes, looked at his watch and said that he was expected for lunch at Kalpana. He thanked his uncle for meeting him and left. He'd thought digging for family dirt would be interesting; instead it had left him feeling dizzy, queasy, his unconditional faith in his father and grandfather profoundly shaken. Did they really reject a woman outright because of her caste? These two men were his heroes, his gods, espousing the highest ideals, teaching him iron-clad truths on which he'd built his own values. They proved to have feet of clay—and Kisan's throat felt raw with tears. Dammit! Unaware that he was echoing words that Vinod had said about his own grandfather, Kisan thought *my Papa is now reduced from a hero to a mere human—and so is my Daddy, and I feel adrift and alone.*

After he reached the flat, he couldn't look his parents or his grandfather in the face. More than once he started to ask about Anita, but couldn't. Hadn't his digging brought him enough pain? Was there anything anyone could say that could mitigate this duplicitous behavior? He needed the jungle where everything was unadulterated. Thank goodness the jungle trip was coming up in two days.

Banarghatta provided that solace. Before sunrise and at dusk, Goutam and he were taken by jeep into the depths of the jungle. The bottomless silence cushioned against city noises soothed Kisan. Leaves washed clean in the gentle mist rustled and only natural noises were

205

amplified. How marvelous it was to suddenly come across a herd of elephants—wild females encircling a calf protectively. How noiselessly they'd disappeared into a thicket of trees. How does one lose a herd of elephants, for God's sake, and so quickly, Kisan thought, shaking his head in wonder.

The guests at the lodge ate all their meals by a lake where the guides cooked for them over open fires. And somehow the food tasted better than any from the best restaurants. At night, Goutam and he sat in darkness lit only by a crackling wood fire and watched fireflies dance. Adventurous monkeys came scampering down the trees trying to steal food. Occasionally they heard a rumble, and their guide told them which animal was searching for water or a mate. They met several families who were also enjoying the jungle and envied the one couple who had actually seen two tigers sunning themselves openly in a meadow. Both he and Goutam had a better time than they anticipated and determined to return next year.

Back in Mumbai, Kisan found his mother in a flurry preparing for a big shindig, the first in the newly renovated flat. And Kisan was in time to observe the scene where Rama the cook was the victim of unwitting cruelty intended as kindness.

It was lunchtime at the flat, and Kisan was in his own dream world, wondering what he would call this summer—the summer of my disillusion? Slowly he became aware of the mood change at the table. Kishore was talking to Rama, who was grinning, his eyes bright with the pleasure of expected compliments. Slowly Rama diminished in size. His eyes became lightless, his grin folded into his cheeks, and he visibly shrank. Kisan began to pay attention to the conversation. Kishore was thanking Rama for his many years of devoted service, offering him a pension, suggesting that he return to his village and his family. Kisan felt as if he were watching a scourging. Shanti and Vinod sat silent and ashamed.

After some moments of awkwardness, Vinod spoke up. "You can't send Rama away, Kishore *beta*. He has no family besides us. His one daughter doesn't know him. What will he do?"

Kishore said, genuinely bewildered, "Rama, aren't you tired of working? Wouldn't you like to enjoy your old age with your grandchildren?"

Rama, dumbstruck, could only shake his head. Vinod spoke again. "*Beta*, he doesn't know his grandchildren—only young Kisan here and Priya and Arun. We cannot push him out of the only home he's had all his life. Even if he cannot cook any more, he must be given a room in this flat."

Quiet Shanti spoke up, "Only Rama knows all the dishes that are our favorites—Vinod's, Kisan's, yours. Who else will cook for us? I am sure Anjali, *beti*, you want to have a young cook who knows your kind of cooking, but Vinod and I are used to Rama and he is used to us. He must stay." It was her voice that sealed Rama's fate, and it was agreed that he could stay, whether or not he could cook.

And Kisan looked from the gray old man who had spoiled him with his delicious pakoras and samosas to his grandparents, also gray and shrunken. He crept out of the room, his chest constricted and tight. He threw himself on his bed and wondered: is this what it feels like? Does growing old bring with it a squeezing of the space you had occupied as your right? Dear Rama: he'd happily given his life over to this family, sacrificing his own. Now he had nowhere to go—his grandchildren were strangers to him and would look on him as just another mouth to feed. His reign in the kitchen was toppling; he was being forced out. Poor dear old Rama! Thank goodness Vinod and Shanti saved him.

And Kisan had a gut wrenching insight about his grandparents: the large flat in which they had raised their children, welcomed and cherished their grandchildren, thrown rollicking parties, lived a full life—this flat had dwindled for them into their one bedroom. And the constriction continued at this very moment. Kishore's conversation with Rama was covertly an action affecting them too. It would have removed yet another familiar and comfortable part of their life. With Rama gone, Shanti would have been even more isolated and confused. And Kishore and Anjali were motivated by feelings of caring and kindness—toward Rama and certainly toward Vinod and Shanti. Kisan wished he were ten years old again, when the complexity of human behavior did not interest him, when everything was joyfully accepted at face value.

What a revelation this vacation had been. He needed time to absorb all that he had learned, all that he had understood, and all that had hurt him. As he turned onto his side in the bed, he started counting the days until his flight to Boston.

Vinod

RETURNING FROM HIS WALK IN Kamala Nehru Park, Vinod shook out the raindrops from his big black umbrella and wiped his shoes on the sodden mat. Sometimes he wondered why he did this daily walk in the drizzle or in the heat. It was always one or the other. He sighed as he put the umbrella on the outside porch where wet clothes flapped on the lines. Of course, the blouses and tee shirts would smell musty and dank, but Anjali's dryer couldn't handle all the sweat-imbued clothes that needed to be washed daily.

How have we lived here for so long, he wondered. He and Shanti should have bought a house in Bangalore where the weather was not so debilitating, where there were homes with spacious gardens and flowers. He shook his head; we thought the best thing was to give the flat to Kishore and live with him and Anjali. After all, when one is old, the greatest joy comes from watching grandchildren grow. Priya gave them such pleasure living in the flat, sharing her school stories, her paintings.

Sadly, now that Dev and Shilpa were divorced, they saw less and less of Arun. Vinod knew that Dev came for lunch with Shanti often, but he himself had not spoken to his son since the day after he'd had his heart surgery. As each month and year went by, he knew he should forgive Dev and welcome him back into the family. After all, how much time did he and Shanti have left? He had only two sons, and this separation gave Shanti such pain. Maybe, one day, one day soon

What a shame Kisan came only for his summer holidays. That boy was Vinod's pride. A wonderful young man he had become, so smart and levelheaded. Vinod felt a twinge of unease when he remembered Kisan's visit last year. Something had happened that had suddenly made Kisan distant. Vinod remembered nights of playing chess when he had the expectant feeling that Kisan was on the verge of asking him a question. Vinod could only surmise that the answer would have been so painful that Kisan couldn't even hear it.

It was soon after the boy returned to Boston that year the horror happened in America. He could still hear Kishore's rasping voice yelling, "Papa, Papa, come see this! The TV. Oh my God!" Vinod and Shanti were reading quietly that evening, waiting for dinner, when that shout pierced the flat. They dashed to the drawing room and watched the terrorist attacks on the World Trade Center unfold. He'd felt the same hollowness in his stomach that accompanied each bloody battle that erupted between the Hindus and Muslims in India every few years. But this desecration was beyond anything he'd ever witnessed. Voice quivering, he asked Kishore how far Kisan was from New York. Since two of the flights had departed from Boston, did Kishore fear that Boston may be under attack too? How many more manned weapons did these godless people have?

Even now, he felt rage and despair mingle whenever he thought of all those people who died. After that day, whenever he and Kishore spoke of politics, he heard an underlying strain of suspicion tinge their talks. He realized that they both were beginning to share an increasing antipathy toward not just Pakistan but Muslims. How could this be? Muslims had been not merely tolerated but an accepted part of life in India. Yes, occasionally religious tension led to explosions between Hindus and Muslims, but still. Intellectually, he understood that the Muslims who were his friends, educated and cultured, were as appalled and enraged over the attacks as the rest of the world was. Yet he found himself more and more uncomfortable in their company. Previously friendly arguments and debates with them were now fraught with tension, where a joking word carried a sheathed meaning, or was interpreted with suspicion. And what about Kishore? What about his business dealings? Was mistrust coloring his everyday world as well? Still, despite the large Muslim population in India, there had been no repercussions in Mumbai from the Trade Center attacks.

This antipathy affected family life at Kalpana as well. As long as Vinod could remember, they'd had a Muslim driver. Kishore used a flimsy excuse to dismiss Aziz who'd been with them for some years. And Vinod didn't protest; he did not raise his voice in defense of Aziz as he had for Rama. Walking toward his room, he wondered if he was losing his moral spine.

He saw Shanti shuffling from the drawing room to their bedroom. How snail- paced but relentless her disease was. He knew that almost every day Shanti forgot that her favorite chair had been moved from the drawing room to the bedroom, so still she searched for it, bewilderment fogging her eyes.

Whenever he talked to Shanti, he searched deep into those eyes to find the vibrant woman he had married. She was disappearing inexorably. She forgot the names of her grandchildren, even Kishore's and Anjali's sometimes. Vinod knew it would not be long before she would forget his too. What was becoming clearer in her mind was her childhood. Ah, she spoke vividly about her parents and growing up in a small town near Mumbai. She remembered childlike adventures she shared with her brothers or sister, simple things like shopping or grand festivals like Divali. Even though her parents and her brothers and sister were all dead, she talked of visiting them. Then her face would grow animated, the light would shine in her eyes—until she looked around and a lucid moment wrenched her back to her pitiless now.

He followed her into their bedroom, their sanctuary. With a start he saw she was not in her chair but standing against the balcony wall and letting the rain mist her upturned face. For no reason that he could fathom, he felt acutely and urgently alarmed. Gently, he called her name, and holding her hand, led her in to the bedroom. Shanti looked at him and smiled, but it took her a minute or so to realize it was Vinod, her husband. He walked her to her chair, still holding her hand tenderly. He scrutinized her eyes, dreading that she might have taken yet another step on her regressive journey into her past. No, thank God! Today she had bathed, combed her hair and worn a fresh sari, which was now quite wet. Her eyes were bright, happy to see him. He called for Kamini, the nurse, to help Shanti change into dry clothes.

The smell of incense was strong in the room—she must have recently done her puja. That was one thing she did not forget. For him, the smell of jasmine or patchouli wafting through the house inevitably carried with it the powerful memory of betrayal. Shanti did not understand how she had been betrayed, and for that one thing he was glad that her memory was fading. But he understood. And sometimes, just a little, he rued his decision to deed the flat to Kishore.

Now he let the memory play itself out, painfully and painstakingly—a repeating video tape. It had happened only last year that time when Kisan had become distant. It was that year Anjali had finished decorating the drawing room, painting the walls yellow, orange, all sorts of colors, and buying lamps and new sofas. The flat with all these changes was too different, almost alien for him and Shanti, but what could they say? It was no longer the home they knew, no longer their home really.

That year Anjali planned a big dinner party while Kisan was still with them. The dining room with its large table begged for a fancy dinner party, and Anjali naturally wanted her friends to come, see, and compliment her handiwork.

He was aware but unmindful of Anjali ordering the servants to bring in boxes from the spare room. She was always moving things. This time, when the boxes were opened, she invited Vinod and Shanti to admire the beautiful china set she had brought back from America. Indeed, it was beautiful and Vinod and Shanti praised her taste and told her how lovely it would look on the gleaming rosewood table.

Then Anjali lamented the lack of space to permanently keep the precious china. She had bought enough for twenty-four guests. She looked around the flat as if expecting a room to magically appear. And shockingly it did.

Vinod cringed at the memory of what happened next. Anjali sweetly turned to Shanti and said, "There is this small room which only you use for your puja, Amma." And Shanti looked at her, a half-smile tentative on her face, so anxious to please, so eager to do anything to make Kishore and his family happy. And Shanti did not comprehend what Anjali was asking. Vinod did, but he was sure he misunderstood. Surely not—surely Anjali was not asking Shanti to sacrifice the puja room. She couldn't be.

Anjali went on, "The workmen are still here. I can ask them to build some shelves in your bedroom, and we could move all the idols in there, close to you, Amma. What do you say?"

And Shanti quavered, "You want my puja room? Vinod, please tell…"

But Vinod had cravenly skulked out of the room, bitterness rising in him until he felt sick, afraid of what he might say to Anjali. Had she discussed this with Kishore? Had Kishore agreed as long as she did it when he wasn't home? Vinod had left the room because he couldn't bear to witness this rape of Shanti's innocence. How could Anjali, how could Kishore strip her of all her dignity? He had sat in his chair, guilt, anger and regret roiling inside him. Slowly, Shanti had crawled into their room, ineffably sad. She'd looked at him dry-eyed and said, "I told her she could have it. After all, how long am I going to need it, isn't it?" She had lain down on her bed then with her face to the wall.

From that day, she shrank. She became lethargic and idle. One time Dr. Rajan was paying a social visit, but really checking Shanti's health. Vinod had been on his walk, and when he returned he overheard them talking.

Shanti said, "I am so tired, Raju. What is the point of living like this? Every day I forget more and more. Anjali and Kishore are very good to us—but look! Vinod and I are now living in this one small room. My Dev comes only once in a while. I have no friends. I can't play cards any more. I feel so useless. I want to go, Raju. Every day, during my puja, I pray to Krishna and Rama to take me, take me away. I don't want to be a burden on Kishore. I want to go Raju, I want to go. Please help me? Please?"

And Dr Rajan looked at her compassionately and repeated the standard answer. "Shanti, you know it is in God's hands. He is the one who decides when your time will come. You know I cannot do anything. Besides, you have many good years."

But Shanti was silent. Vinod stood outside the room for a long time, dumbstruck. The conversation didn't shock him. He understood that she felt she had nothing to live for. As Vinod looked into his own life, he thought the only thing he lived for was Shanti. Without her, life had no meaning. If he wanted her life to have meaning, he should give her a reason to live. He resolved to make amends.

He walked into the room cheerfully greeting Dr Rajan and Shanti, and carried on an inconsequential patter ignoring Shanti's obvious distress. In a few minutes, the doctor left, and Vinod, turning to Shanti, said, "I've been thinking that the time has come for me to welcome Dev back into this house. How long can I go on not speaking to my son? What do you say, Shanti?"

"What? What are you saying? Who are you talking about?"

"I said that you should ask Dev to come to dinner so he and I can talk again." He was rewarded by the happiness that slowly spread across her face.

He knew he had done the right thing. Yes, he had been punishing Dev because he could not bear what his son had done with his life. But he was also punishing himself and Kishore, and most of all, Shanti. Time had come for him to swallow his pride. In his remaining years, he needed to take a measure of his life. He had led a good life, a fruitful and productive one. Could he allow it to be stained by a stubborn rigidity that ridiculously demanded he not speak to his own son?

As Shanti shuffled off to tell Anjali the news, to phone Dev and invite him for dinner, and to tell Rama to cook a special meal for Devsahib, Vinod settled down in his worn but comfortable chair. He couldn't help smiling, so pleased was he with his decision. How long did he and Shanti have left? It was time to be succored and nourished by children and grandchildren. He was hurting Shanti, himself, and Kishore. Kishore blamed Dev for causing Vinod's second heart attack and had been cold to his brother. Vinod knew he should help mend that rift as well. The boys would need each other when their parents were gone.

Gradually his smile waned, and he settled himself more comfortably into his chair and rested his head against the back cushion. The sound of Shanti's despairing voice as she begged Dr. Rajan for help to release her from this life was faint in the background of his mind. He thought of what their lives had been reduced to. Shanti had a small balcony on which she tended three or four potted plants—tulsi, marigold, jasmine—flowers she could offer the gods during her puja. One rickety chair was set there, so when the weather was pleasant she could sit outside. They had their bedroom, which now included her idols on two shelves, and her favorite chair by the window.

He could intellectually understand how Kishore and Anjali needed to make the flat in their image. It was logical; they were young and this was their first home in Mumbai. They were not willfully abandoning their parents; they were kind, trying to include the older couple in many of their activities. However, their actions, though understandable, had in fact squeezed Vinod's and Shanti's space, their horizon. And, try as he might, Vinod could not emotionally accept what this constriction had done to Shanti.

He looked over at the shelves with the idols where she had recently finished her puja. The incense stick had almost reached the end of its perfumed life and formed a slender ribbon of gray ash snaking down on to the wooden shelf. He stared at it, gazing at the tiny pinpoint of flame which would soon go out, and his eyes filled.

He looked at the idols that Shanti worshipped. How much faith she had. He wished he could believe as completely as she did, give over control of their lives to an unseen but pervasive great soul, the Atma. Would anything have turned out differently? No, he did not have such blind devotion. He'd lived according to his moral compass—a good life, with charity and compassion.

If there were a God, then he rewarded those who had lived honorable lives with children who would continue the legacy. Kishore reflected Vinod's teachings and virtues. He was and always had been proud of Kishore. Kishore, Kisan and Priya were his and Shanti's rewards for the life they'd led.

Then he finally articulated an idea which was amorphous and cloudy in his mind, but which had haunted him since his falling out with Dev: If God chooses, he punishes us with our *disappointment* in our children. Yes, he was deeply disappointed in Dev, always wondering what had caused his younger son to be so unlike anyone else in the family. But now he thanked God that his castaway son had a mother who loved him and kept him close to her with unstinting devotion. As he thought of the evening dinner with Dev and Kishore, Shanti, Anjali and Priya, he felt a flutter of excitement. The whole family together again under one roof. He sighed as he remembered Shilpa and Arun. One step at a time.

Shanti now had a reason to be happy; she would have her beloved son free to come and go. Maybe Arun would come more often as well. Vinod had begun to repair the damage that had torn their family. He took off his glasses, wiped his eyes and waited for his wife to return to him. The family could be whole again, be one again, scars and all. When Shanti came back into the bedroom, he was glad to see that she looked alert and excited. For a few brief moments, she had taken charge. She had told Anjali about Vinod's sudden forgiveness of Dev, she had discussed with Rama what to cook for Devsahib's visit, and she had called Dev and invited him for dinner that night.

Dev

So finally Papa had relented and asked Amma to invite him for dinner. What would they talk about tonight? It wasn't going to be easy; he was excited and fearful, terrified. He must not screw this up. He hadn't talked to Papa since his heart surgery about four years ago, nor had he seen much of Kishore since he had returned and taken up residence in Kalpana. Dev knew that Kishore blamed him for Papa's heart attack and had resolutely stayed distant. And whither Kishore went, Anjali was sure to follow. She had tried—he gave her that—to keep in touch with him, but he found it bloody painful when he went to have lunch with Amma to see all the changes that Anjali was making to his childhood home. Whenever he went to the flat, he was startled by the colored walls and the new furniture. And he transferred all his resentment of the changes to the person making them.

Amma, sainted woman, would never say anything against Kishore and Anjali, but even she would sometimes whisper, "So what do you think of the new sofas? Don't you think they are too small? I liked the divan we used to have in the drawing room. Remember, *beta*, how many times you fell asleep on it?" Yes, he remembered. His sweet mother, never thinking badly of anyone, especially her Kishore.

He leaned his head against the back of the chair as he thought of how much his mother had aged—her face was still unlined but her eyes looked lost, searching for some direction, looking with decreasing recognition at everything she had lived with her whole life. He knew little about her illness, but he felt anguished by her progressing deterioration every time he saw her.

Dev sat alone in his flat, the one inherited from his father, now absent of Shilpa and Arun. He knew that Shilpa would never come back; she was too bitter about him and considered his drinking a lack of will. If only he had tried harder. She stopped believing him when he said that he was really trying hard and never followed through with actions. He couldn't blame her. He considered himself lucky that he could see Arun a couple of times a week. But it was so unsatisfying, sitting with his son in Shilpa's flat with unseen eyes of servants flickering from heaven knows which corner. He usually played some video games with Arun, let the child roundly beat him, then left. Not much connection this way. In a couple of years it would get better, when he could take the boy out to teach him cricket or tennis. God! He really had screwed up his life. Shilpa was the best thing that had happened to him, and he'd thrown her away.

Now he was destined to grow old and die alone. He was too old already, in his forties, to be the party guy he used to be. He had no interest hooking up with the several young nubile women who found him irresistible still. That flaring of lust in the pit of his stomach and groin had faded months ago. He tired early at raucous parties, especially when he drank—and when he still, occasionally, took drugs.

He slumped in his comfortable easy chair with his feet on the table and called for Jagdeesh, his only live-in servant, to bring him another beer. He sipped it, thinking he'd make the next one a shandy—beer mixed with lime juice that was a legacy of the Brits. His blue silk shirt was open revealing a gold chain glinting through his black chest hair. The hair on his head was more streaked with gray now, but still thick and unruly. His dark eyes no longer sparkled with flirtatiousness. They told the tale of his dissolution, reflecting pain and a naive incomprehension about how he had come to be at this point in his life.

The advent of his impending visit to Kalpana had made him thoughtful, though the beers warped his logic and slowed his thoughts. He remembered his father's long ago birthday party at which he'd first introduced Anita to the family. She'd been beautiful and so worshipful. She'd depended on him—she would not have walked out like Shilpa had. He had been a fool to let Anita go. He'd already forgotten having an identical thought about Shilpa only minutes ago. He confessed to his inner soul that the big difference between Anita and Shilpa was that Anita deferred to him and was submissive. And he'd liked that. Why had he listened to Kishore? Why had he been so afraid of his father's wrath? Maybe he wouldn't be in such a solitary state if he had followed his heart.

His mind drifted to that surprising evening four years ago when he'd picked up the phone and heard Anita's husky voice on the other end. She sounded perky as ever and suggested meeting for dinner. Heart racing, for the first time in his marriage he'd lied to Shilpa and gone to dinner with Anita. He chose an obscure restaurant where none of his friends would go, and he wouldn't be seen. When he got there, she was waiting, lazily stirring a rum and coke. She was as beautiful as he remembered.

As they waited for their orders, he noticed a brittleness about her. There was an edginess around her still gorgeous hazel eyes, and her pouty mouth had developed flinty sharp lines that crept from the edges of her lips down her chin, not quite wrinkles, but precursors of them. He asked about her husband, but she said he was a boring stay-at-home. As the evening progressed, she drank immoderately and became careless with her speech. She began spilling nuggets about her marriage which she said was a sham. The generous Mr. Amarnath, so magnanimous with a flat and a lakh of rupees for her parents, had really offered that as hush money. Oh, he was so wicked, if only she'd known Mr. Amarnath's conniving plan beforehand, things might have been different. With her voice increasing in volume and pitch, she told Dev that her husband Mohan was impotent, had never made love to her. And Dev's heart had surged, selfishly happy that she'd not had sex with her husband. Then, immediately he repented, imagining what it must have been like for her.

"Remember the fun we used to have in bed, Dev? Well, I'd flirt with him—but he'd just say he was tired and turn away. Not even once…" and she started circling the top of her glass with her finger. "What was wrong with him? What was wrong with me?" And Dev thought silently, "Perhaps the bugger is gay,"

Anita had been miserable in America with a cold, uncaring boob for a husband and no one to talk to. In Tennessee, there were not too many Indian people to befriend her. Her dreams of becoming a music star died in Nashville; she could not abide country music or Old Opry that was so pervasive in the land of Elvis. After three suffocating years, she came back to Mumbai with Mohan. And now they were living in the lavish flat of the wealthy Mr. Amarnath.

Dev could see what her life had become: she was trapped. She couldn't get a divorce without jeopardizing her mother's living situation. She feared that maybe Mr. Amarnath would take his flat back. Who knew? She tried to voice these fears to Dev, but she was incoherent with emotion and slurred speech. He blotted out as much as he could of the rest of the evening, filled with revulsion about her and about himself. He wished she had not returned into his life. How on earth could he have thought she was the one for him?

Shaking his head and returning to the now, he looked at his watch: three o'clock. His barber at the Willingdon must be reopening his shop, ready for evening customers. Dev combed his fingers through his untamed mop. It was so long, it was curling around his collar. Papa would hate it. *Achcha*, time for a hair cut. Finishing his shandy in a gulp, he called for Jagdeesh to bring the car around. Jagdeesh was not only his cook and housecleaner but his driver as well. Shoving his wallet into the back pocket of his jeans, he slipped on a pair of sandals and rode to the Willingdon. He would be well-groomed for the reconciliatory dinner. Surely Papa would look at him with forgiveness, maybe even pride, if he knew how Dev had resisted the hypnotic lure of Anita.

Oh so reluctantly, his mind slid back to that night of his dinner with her. He'd walked a very intoxicated Anita out of the restaurant. As they waited for her car, she grabbed his hand and dug her nails into his palm. "Please, Dev, take me somewhere. I don't want to go home. You don't understand what I have to do…"And Dev, remembering Shilpa, knew he never wanted to get embroiled with Anita again. But for one split moment, he was tempted to sweep her into a taxi, take her to a hotel and ravish her.

With her eyes darting frantically, desperately, she squeezed his hand and gasped out her pleas. "It's not Mohan, it's not. I don't care about him. Oh, Dev. Do I have to tell you? It's Mr. Amarnath…"And Dev had pushed her away, repulsed by what she was saying. He put his hands over his ears to shut her out, but she wouldn't stop her flow of words. He stared at her with the same horror he'd felt when as a child he'd once watched a mongoose fight and bloody a cobra. She painted the picture of her father-in-law, a rich, greasy old man who must have deviously contrived to get Anita into his household from the very start. Just as Dev's heart had involuntarily leaped when she told him that she had not ever slept with her husband, his heart was equally repelled by the image of her sexually servicing the father of the impotent husband.

He shuddered now in the air-conditioned car, squirming at the memory and felt guilt wash over him. Whenever she called him, and she did, constantly for weeks after that night, he hung up on her. He was a married man; he did not want to be enmeshed in an affair. She had dug her own grave, and he had tossed the earth over her. He did not dare to think about his part in her fate. One thing she'd said so long ago haunted him still: "My kind of people have to look after ourselves." And look where it had led her.

The car pulled up into the covered car porch at the Willingdon, and Dev got out slamming the door behind him. He strode over to a comfortable chair in the barber shop, told Harish he wanted a haircut, a scalp massage and a shave. He slipped his sandals off and called for a pedicure. Harish warmed some oil for the scalp massage and began kneading it onto Dev's head. The pedicurist brought warm water for his feet and began vigorously rubbing them with pumice and soap. Comforted, he closed his eyes and tried to think of the evening ahead. Excitement and trepidation mingled in him.

Later, he dressed carefully in a dazzling white chudidhar and black silk kurta. He looked in the mirror, wishing his eyes were not so bloodshot. Dark bags made him look like a wrinkled Sharpei, his eyes sunken in the hollow sockets. He massaged under his eyes gently. He even had the beginning of jowls. He stretched his neck and slapped under his chin with the backs of his hands to no avail. Oh, well. He was ready to meet his father and brother. Though he felt like the prodigal son, a story he remembered from his school days, he knew there would be no fatted calf waiting for him. That would always be reserved for Kishore.

As his car neared Kalpana, his heart plummeted to his stomach. He rubbed his clammy hands with a handkerchief. When he rang the bell at the flat, the door was opened by Vinod himself. The old man put his arms around his errant son and said, "*Achcha, beta.* It's good you are home." Hugs from Shanti, Anjali, Kishore and Priya followed, and Dev felt the abysmal void in his soul slowly filling with their love.

Shanti led him to a sofa and sat him down, so happy to see him here with the family. When dinner was served, the awkwardness that had started the evening had evaporated. They sat around the large table talking and laughing comfortably, almost a complete family again. Dev learned about Kishore's new job, Anjali's travails with decorating the flat, Priya's successes and frustrations in school. Dev told them that he took drum playing opportunities at different night clubs now; he was able to demand good money for his engagements, or "gigs" he called them. Shanti and Vinod sat smiling, happy to see Dev back again.

Long after Priya had gone to bed, when Amma and Papa were nodding in their chairs, Dev got up to leave. His unvoiced wish was that he could stay here, in his old room secure in his mother's indulgence. When he went to say goodbye to her, she roused herself and asked him to lunch the next day. Vinod echoed her invitation, saying, "You should come more often, *beta*. I have missed you." Dev's eyes filled as he thought how much he had suppressed his love of his father, substituted it with anger. How violently he had craved Vinod's approval which he thought was reserved only for Kishore. Now Vinod's words "I have missed you" felt like a benediction, a salve for his bruised psyche.

As he drove home, the trepidation and excitement with which he had arrived had changed to elation and sorrow. So many years lost when he could have basked in his father's love. Yes, he would go to lunch tomorrow and many times a week; he had time to make up.

And so he went more and more often to the flat, walking straight to Shanti's and Vinod's room. He always came after her puja so as not to disturb her. If it was not raining, he often found Shanti on the little balcony watering her few plants. Sometimes he found her standing at the railing, transfixed, staring up at the little patch of visible blue or gray sky. What was she searching for? Other times, she'd be looking down at the cars driving into the complex and the bicyclists running errands. She was startled whenever he called her name, bewildered at first, then smiling to see him.

Vinod would be in his favorite chair, reading or doing the *Times of India* crossword puzzle. If he was not busy, he would be looking worriedly at Shanti. He was always happy to see Dev, especially since Dev could make Shanti laugh. The little Lhasa Apso Hari would leap around yipping excitedly, and his boisterousness too tugged Shanti back to her current reality. Sometimes Anjali, if she were home, joined them for lunch; otherwise, it was just the three of them. Vinod and Dev found joy in their rediscovery of each other, and finally they did not expect something that the other couldn't deliver.

Dev was as happy as he'd ever been. Even his tenuous bond with Kishore grew stronger. When Dev visited in the evenings, after the parents had gone to bed, the brothers reminisced, relishing the good memories they had created in their childhood flat. Anjali smiled indulgently, though she bristled whenever they teased her about any of the changes she had made. Or they all talked about the health of their parents—Shanti's Alzheimer's was progressing, but because there were so many people around, she was physically safe and lovingly cared for.

And one Saturday, Vinod opened the door with Arun in his arms. The little boy stretched his arms out to his father and was enfolded in a bear hug. Dev could barely hear Vinod say, "Shilpa knew you were coming here today and thought that this little *beta* would like to see you as well as his grandparents." Priya was home as well, so with Arun as the catalyst, the three generations sat together in the drawing room. Vinod and Shanti were content to give up their afternoon naps so they could watch Dev and his son play on the marble floor with toy cars. Priya brought out coloring pens and encouraged Arun to draw. Dev hoped and prayed that Shilpa would come to pick Arun up. Did this gesture mean that she may forgive him? Was there a chance?

At five o'clock, the bell rang, and Dev rushed to open the door. It was Sandeep, the servant, sent to pick up Arun. After giving the boy a hug and kiss, Dev surrendered him to the servant, then walked dejectedly back to his chair. He saw Vinod looking at him with deep sympathy—complete sympathy, unmixed with any admonition or reproach. Shanti walked over to ruffle his hair and squeeze his hand. Vinod merely said, "Maybe you will see little Arun more often. We are also happy when the little *beta* is here." And Dev was glad that neither of his parents tried to give him false hope that he could return to a better time and have a happy family again. Neither did they tell him that it was all his fault.

One afternoon when Dev saw his mother on the balcony staring up at the sky, he went to her and drew her in to the bedroom and tenderly asked her, "What are you looking at, Amma?"

"I am wondering when Vishnu will call me to him," she replied.

Dev was appalled. "What are you saying, Amma? Don't talk like that. What rubbish you are saying."

And she shook her head at him and said, "*Beta*, I am so tired. Can you understand?"

Dev told Vinod what she had said. Vinod nodded and said nothing.

"Come on, Papa, why don't you say something? Why do you even let her go on the balcony?"

"*Beta*, she has very few pleasures left; her tulsi plant is one. Her puja room is gone; her favorite chair is no longer in the drawing room. She is slowly failing to recognize even her family. Can you understand that she is afraid of losing her mind? She thinks she has nothing to live for; your coming here gives her so much pleasure. You must keep coming, *beta*. She lives through you all. I can only share her memories."

"But doesn't the idea frighten her? Doesn't it frighten you, Papa?" Dev asked. And, yes, he understood. Many times in his darkest hours, when he had been at the nadir, in his drug induced abyss, he too had thought of escaping. But he had been anguished then—alone, so alone. His mind had been warped by drugs and alcohol. His dear mother, who had lived such a good life, her mind was being eroded by an implacable disease. Thank goodness she was not alone; she had her whole family around her—husband, sons, grandchildren—and servants to fulfill her every wish. So Dev asked, "Doesn't the idea frighten her?"

And Vinod looked at him and said, "Sometimes the known is more frightening than the unknown."

"What do you mean?"

"Each of us goes to sleep at night expecting that tomorrow will bring us something new, perhaps something good. What if you *know* that tomorrow will bring you the same or worse terror than today? Then the nights are filled with fear. When we sleep, even if we are in the same room, even in the same bed with someone, we each sleep alone. That is the loneliest time of the day or night. When I look at your Amma, when I say goodnight to her, I can see the fear in her eyes. And I can do nothing to help her through the night. I am very afraid of what tomorrow will bring to her...and to me," he ended in a whisper. He cleared his throat, raised his hand in a blessing and said, "When we know that tomorrow will bring *you, beta,* we can go to sleep a little less afraid."

Dev sat down and put his face into his hands. He sagged under the burden of his father's words. He shook his head tugging at his hair. Why, why had he been so cursed, so arrogant? Why had he pitched so many futile battles against this man and lost precious time with his mother? What a fool! Listening to his father's wisdom now, he vowed inwardly to do all he could to make their lives easier. Slowly, his heart expanded as he realized that with this conversation his father had confided in him. He had been allowed into his father's mind—his soul where his hopes and fears lived. Dev could not imagine a more valuable gift.

Yes, he could understand now why his mother gazed at the heavens looking for release. He would not say anything about it to anyone. He wouldn't contradict her when she mentioned it. He would be like his father—understanding, accepting, and easing the pain however he could.

Slowly, he rose from his chair. He looked into his father's eyes and nodded his understanding. He walked over to his mother and took her hand to lead her into the dining room for lunch. As Dev approached the door to the bedroom, he heard his father get out of his chair; then he felt his father's hand gently come to rest on his shoulder.

Priya

PRIYA WAS HAPPY THAT DEVUNCLE was coming more often for lunch and dinner. She liked Devuncle, and his visits made Amma and Papa happy. She worried constantly about her grandparents. Mummy and Daddy were so busy with their own lives, they were neglecting the old folks. A recent incident made her even more concerned. One morning she saw Amma go into the room where Mummy stored her china and stuff. It used to be Amma's puja room, and Priya realized with a start that Amma still remembered it that way. She peered in to see Amma sitting cross-legged on the floor with her *rudhraksha* beads in her hands. Her eyes were closed and she was chanting, "Hari Rama, Hari Krishna." In front of her were not her revered idols but stacked brown boxes with neatly packed china and vases. From under her closed eye lids, tears were slowly wetting her cheeks. Priya stood paralyzed and afraid, not knowing what to do. Fortunately, the nurse, Sister Kamini, came to take Amma back to her room. Priya told Mummy about it, but Mummy said there was nothing they could do.

Kisan was right—she hated him for being right. Amma was forgetting the family slowly. The other day she'd thought Daddy was her brother. She had called him Vasant and said, "When did you come? How long can you stay?" And the look on Daddy's face! He looked as if someone was twisting a knife in his stomach. Priya had to look away from the raw pain in his eyes. She couldn't imagine what it would feel like if her own mother wouldn't recognize her, wouldn't know her name.

Then there was that time at breakfast. This was the worst of Priya's memories. They had all been sitting around the table; Shanti was smiling and buttering her toast. She'd turned to Anjali and sweetly asked, "Who am I? Can you tell me who I am?" Anjali's eyes had flooded, and Priya had run from the room. She couldn't bear to think her Amma had lost her sense of self. Why, even a baby, when it first begins to talk has a clear feeling of "I". Priya had even written to Kisan about it. He'd emailed her back and said that Alzheimer's patients often suffered such unimaginable losses. So, Priya decided to work out a way to help Amma remember her name.

Every day before going to college, she'd walk cheerfully into Amma's room to spend some time, just talking about friends and stuff. And in the evening, she'd wander in casually again. And she always said, "Hello, Amma, hello Papa. It's Priya come to trouble you again." There, she'd made it easier for Amma to remember her.

As she chose a sea-green print salwar kameez for college, she thought about how glad she was not to be going to America for university. Both Mummy and Daddy kept urging her to look into different schools; they said the opportunities were better there. Yes, it had been hard to leave Seattle after 6th grade. She'd really wanted to go with her friends into the middle school at Lakeside. But then she'd had no choice and she had returned to Mumbai swearing never to forget her sixth grade friends. And for at least two years the wires between Seattle and Mumbai burned up with email and IMs all the time. That first year the phone bills were enormous. Inevitably, lives and interests diverged and the furious communication dwindled to the occasional "how the heck are you these days?"

Priya began to love living in Mumbai, loved taking the bus from the Malabar Hill flat to J.J. School of Art. Kisan, from his lofty perch at Harvard, kept telling Mummy and Daddy that she'd do better at the Rhode Island School of Design. Rhode Island! With temperature barely over freezing half the year. And the population in the whole state didn't equal even half of Mumbai's. She didn't want to be a designer—she wanted to follow her heart and paint and draw what she felt. She and Kisan had had a real screaming match about it last year when Mummy and Daddy had been out.

"You don't know what's good for you, Priya. I'm telling you." Kisan had shouted.

"Stop telling me! Just stop thinking you know what's best for me. You're not me, Kisan. Your head is full of facts and stupid science. You haven't any idea what I feel, so leave me alone."

"Come on, Priya. Rhode Island School of Design is world famous and you'd have an amazing opportunity…" he argued.

Then she'd started crying; she hated to cry in front of Kisan. She'd barely whispered, "Time, that's all I want. I want to spend time with Amma and Papa—and I think that's more precious than any amazing opportunity." Her reply stopped him in his tracks, and he actually shut up. He even looked abashed, especially when she told him that she thought Amma and Papa were terribly lonely. She even said that Mummy and Daddy with their busy social lives didn't pay enough attention to the old folks. Kisan stopped bugging her after that.

She could get into designing later, if she wanted, but it was really exciting to be in Mumbai where new talents were burgeoning. She looked over at a businesswoman on the bus, wearing an Indo-European outfit: smart slacks and well-fitted top and thought, "If I want to, I can design clothes for trendy women and for western markets right here. Wouldn't my friends in Seattle be tickled by that?" In fact, her friends were constantly writing her that many of the fashion trends in the U.S. lately included clothes made in India and of Indian design. She thought of the large new upper middle class breaking out in India, and she wanted to be here, at the creation.

Mummy was happy to have Priya around. Mummy and her friend Sonaliaunty were working with abused women the way they had before the move to Seattle. They'd just recently set up a warehouse kind of place for the women to work so they could earn money and be able to leave their brutish husbands. Now Mummy and Sonaliaunty were doing the hard job of persuading the women to come and work there, to gain some self-confidence. Some who feared for their lives had come and were glad. Priya hadn't broached the subject yet, but she wanted to teach the women some rudimentary painting. She wondered if Mummy and Sonaliaunty would agree. Who knew? Maybe they'd start a new Maharastrian art rage!

As she saw the old building which housed the Art College, she gathered her bags. It had been founded in 1857 by a Parsi, Sir Jamshedji Jeejeebhoy. Imagine being the first baronet from India during the British Raj! Anyway, he'd donated money to start an art school, an engineering school, and now there was an architecture school as well. It was really hard to get in, with very few spaces. Priya had been lucky to qualify. Everyone at the college was supremely talented, and she loved the atmosphere in the old building.

As she left after classes, she looked out onto an angry downpour. She thought of calling home and asking the driver to bring the car, but chose instead to ride the bus home in the pelting rain. Her head was filled with colors and swirls that she'd played with during the day. She ran home from the bus stop, winding the dupatta around her head as an impossible shield. She rang the bell to the flat, and when Kamini opened the door, she squished into her room to change out of her sopping clothes into blue jeans and a saffron colored t-shirt with a black rangoli design. Drying her hair with a towel, she went into the kitchen and coaxed old Rama to make some nice fresh pakoras for tea.

When they were ready, she carried a plate of steaming pakoras, and the smoke wisped upwards towards her face framed with her dark hair, curly and damp from the rain; she wore no make-up, and her shiny skin added luster to her large brown eyes. She raised a pakora to her lips and took a delicate nibble—and the gesture was so graceful, so unpracticed, she looked like a model for one of her own paintings. Priya was nineteen, careless of her own beauty.

She carried the plate into Amma's and Papa's room with her usual greeting, "Here is Priya come to trouble you again. Look what I brought you for tea…" But Amma was on the balcony getting soaked in the rain. Papa was with her, trying to pull her into the room. And he was shouting, "No, no, Shanti. You must come inside. Come, come with me. Yes, yes, come, come. We'll talk about it tomorrow. Ah, See! Little Priya is here. We mustn't frighten her, no?"

And Priya stood transfixed in the doorway, dread churning her insides. She wished Kisan were here to talk to. She wished Mummy and Daddy were home more. She wished she knew what to do.

She slowly walked to the balcony and helped Papa bring Amma into the room. Kamini, who was getting tea from the kitchen, came running in and took over drying the old lady and changing her clothes. And all the time, sweet and gentle Shanti kept repeating louder and louder,

"Let me go! Let me go! Let me go!"

And Priya, who had never heard her grandmother raise her voice, was frightened, uncomprehending. Did Amma want to be on the balcony? Where did she want to go so badly? She did not dare ask Papa whose shoulders were shaking—he must be cold from the rain. And he was wiping his face, wet from the rain, she thought. When Kamini brought Shanti back, dry and sobbing, he too changed into a dry drawstring pajama and kurta. Then he came and sat by Amma and stroked her hair and hands, soothing her, calming her, saying, "No, not today. It's raining, see? Tomorrow, you can go and I'll go with you. Yes, you'll see. We'll go together."

That night when she mentioned the incident at dinner, both Mummy and Daddy said that part of Amma's illness was her strong desire to return to her childhood home. Daddy said, "Have you noticed how much she talks of her brothers, her home. She wants to be taken there. It's all part of this wretched Alzheimer's—I wish there was something we could do." And he pushed away his half-eaten meal and sat back with a sigh, his lips tight.

Mummy looked over at Priya with a warning in her eyes: Don't talk about this anymore, it said. It upsets Daddy too much. Priya wondered whom she could talk to about her fears.

Before she went to bed, she peeked into her grandparents' bedroom. Only the night light cast a dim glow. Papa was sleeping on his side. Sister Kamini was lying in the other bed, cradling Amma and humming a soft lullaby. Amma seemed quiet and peaceful, perhaps asleep. And that sweet scene of her grandmother embraced and soothed to sleep appeased Priya, and she tiptoed to her own room.

So Priya swallowed her fears, but that night and for many nights, she was haunted by the sound of a desperate voice begging, "Let me go, let me go."

And the news spread, grabbed people by the throat, constricted their hearts.

And people asked, shocked, incredulous, *Who?*

And then they asked, *When?* because people like to fix things in time even when time is irrelevant.

And then they asked, *How?* because people like to have details to imagine, even if the details are horrific and make them wish they had not asked.

And then they asked, *Why?* The universal question which no one could answer.

And some said, *"It was their fate."*

And others said, *"yes, it was their karma."*

And they trembled inwardly at the mystery of life.

And they fearfully thought of their own karma.

But the family never ever saw their subtle hand in this karma which now had become their own.

(Three years later)

Anjali

Anjali had one errand to run before she picked up Sonali to go to "Gayatri", the shelter they had opened where women were now working on sewing machines, making bags, cholis and salwar kameez outfits. In operation for nearly two and a half years, Gayatri had had one successful exhibition and sale which raised not only the self-esteem of the women but money for them. It was gratifying to see how eager and happy they were.

Anjali had Shankar drop her off at the entrance of the Bombay Store and told him to park close by; she wouldn't be long. She needed to buy a wedding gift for one of Kisan's friends. "Send something really ethnic," he'd said. She browsed the departments, wandering with an eye for ethnic.

She neared the area with the candles and soaps. And there it was: the faintest hint of patchouli floating on invisible smoke from an unseen incense stick.

The intangible aroma hit Anjali so powerfully, she felt dizzy and had to find a chair. She sat, pale and shaking, fending off concerned sales clerks. She knew she had to get home before she was plunged into a maelstrom of memories.

After some time, she wiped her face and hands with a handkerchief and hoped she could leave the store without fainting. She knew she looked ashen and sick; she was drawing solicitous glances and offers of tea from store personnel. She called Shankar on her cell phone and asked him to pick her up at the front door. He asked, surprised, "Madam is finished so soon? *Achcha,* I'm coming!" Poor Shankar, now he wouldn't even have time to get his cup of tea and gossip with his fellow drivers; she'd been in the store a mere fifteen minutes. She couldn't bear to be in a place where that aroma could hit her again. Never before had a scent wrenched her into the past with such a powerful pull. As she waited for the car outside the store, she called Sonali and cancelled their appointment, promising to explain another day.

In the car, she sat stiff and rigid. Smiling Shankar asked if he could take her to Sonali's; she could just shake her head. She did not allow herself to think of the patchouli, of incense sticks, of pujas—and certainly not the memory the patchouli had brought back to her. She could not weep in front of Shankar—she wanted to get home, to close the door to her room and in solitude allow the feelings to wash over her.

Finally, they arrived at the flat. She hurriedly told Shankar she wouldn't need the car for the next two days, and ran for the lift. Shankar and the watchman looked at her with concern in their eyes: Madam was not well?

In her bedroom, she threw her handbag on the floor and kicked off her slippers. On the bed, she curled up drawing her knees close to her chest and rocked. It had been over three years since Amma and Papa …She thought she had reached the stage of acceptance, of resignation. Would it never come? She closed her eyes tight, but she couldn't stop the voices, the colors, the smells of that day from buffeting her.

It was old Rama who'd called, sobbing that Amma and Sahib were gone, *gone.* When she and Kishore reached the flat, they found a house full of wailing neighbors, servants beating their breasts, strangers and passersby on the street gathering to watch the tragedy unfold. All Kishore and she wanted to do was to make everyone go away and grieve in isolation. How could they make any sense of the unthinkable?

Their anger at his parents had been monumental. How could Amma and Papa have done this to them? Hadn't Kishore and she done everything to provide for their comfort? And poor Kisan, home on vacation, had heard the screams and run out. When Kishore and she found him in his room, he was catatonic, arms clasped around himself, shaking uncontrollably.

Anjali clung to her pillow and rocked, just as she had three years ago. She felt herself falling into the same deep pit of despair from which she had crawled out with painstaking effort. Guilt whipped her inside. Shanti and Vinod had been the kindest of parents to her—she who hardly knew her own. And what had she done in return? She had turned their house into a shrine to her own taste, in her own image. Because Shanti's chair didn't "go" with Anjali's new look, it had been moved to Shanti's bedroom—Anjali blissfully unaware of the pain behind Shanti's eyes.

Why had she been so blind? She'd stolen Shanti's puja room. Because she herself was not religious, she'd never understood the importance of Shanti's daily puja. Now, on her bed, she cringed as she remembered moving the idols to two shelves in their bedroom. For what? For space to store china in soulless brown boxes. She had wrenched the heart of this flat from its moorings for *things*. She deserved the worst anguish— she felt responsible for Amma's and Papa's unhappiness and ultimate death. Her total commitment to the abused women of Mumbai was her penance. Maybe Shanti would forgive her.

She turned over in bed and reached into a drawer of her night stand. She smoothed a well-worn piece of paper and re-read the letter Vinod had left.

Vinod had written: *Dear Kishore, Anjali and Dev, We have chosen to leave this life and go on to the next. Do not blame yourselves for our decision. You have given us great joy and pride and always tried to do everything for us. It is time for us to go. Shanti feels her life has no meaning, and without her, I know mine does not. We bless the children Kisan, Priya and Arun. Love them and guide them well. We give you all our blessings too. Take care of each other. Papa and Amma.*

She slowly rose from her bed, went into the bathroom and splashed cold water on her swollen eyes. She did not glance at herself in the mirror. Purposefully she went towards Shanti's and Vinod's bedroom. In three years, she had not changed a single thing in it. When she had overnight guests, she had the beds made, fresh towels put out, but she never touched the furniture.

Now Anjali tiptoed over and sat in Shanti's favorite chair. She looked at the view of the rain-streaked building next door to which she had condemned Shanti and shuddered. She turned to the shelves where the idols still stood. She recalled the tinkling bell and the fragrant incense that were part of the daily ritual. In the past three years, she had not allowed the burning of incense in the flat; the memory it carried of Shanti was too painful. That's why the patchouli in the Bombay Store had been so unexpected and raw.

One old incense stick lay forlorn in front of the idols. Slowly, warily, Anjali picked it up and sniffed. An almost imperceptible aroma—it still carried an aroma. Holding the stick, she cautiously went on to the balcony. She could smell the ocean, Amma's dear Arabian Sea. She stood looking down at the hard, unforgiving cement below and wondered at Amma's and Papa's courage.

Had they been afraid? Had they wondered what lay ahead? Had life become so unbearable for them? It was not Anjali's place to question why they had chosen to end their lives by jumping off this balcony. They had lived a wonderful life together. *That* was their legacy—their life, not their death. Their life must be remembered.

And there, on the balcony, the very center of the anguish, the guilt, and the sorrow, holding the incense stick, Anjali knew she must cling tight to all the memories they had bequeathed to her. She would remember Shanti's nonsense songs for the children, her gentle touch, her devotion to her gods and her family. She would remember Vinod's wisdom and his moral strength.

She walked in from the balcony closing the door behind her. Before she left the room, she tenderly laid the incense stick in its place in front of the idols.

Kishore

Kishore hoped that Anjali wouldn't be awakened by his leaving the bed at three in the morning. He swung his legs over the side and stood up gingerly. His bare feet were silent on the marble floor, but he could not subdue his thumping heartbeat which seemed to fill the room. He walked out of the bedroom and into the drawing room straight to the cupboard where he kept the liquor. He needed a shot—he would open the precious bottle of Glenfiddich his friend Ron had brought him from England.

He sat down with a glass of the amber Scotch, sipping it slowly. He thought—he had hoped, prayed—the nightmares were over. For several weeks his sleep had been undisturbed, but tonight the dream was particularly vivid. How much of it could he recall? He closed his eyes and remembered sloshing through knee-deep water, trying to reach Priya who was in some kind of peril and was calling him. When he finally reached her after fighting the strong current, Priya had turned into Shanti, a young Shanti, the mother from his boyhood, her black hair cut softly around her face, dark eyes shining with love. When he reached out to help her, she slipped through his fingers.

He'd been haunted by dreams of Shanti and Vinod since their terrible death. After each dream, he would waken and recall Rama's distraught voice babbling incoherently, remember the rush home from his office, the noise and confusion at Kalpana, Kisan in a traumatized state, Priya inconsolable. All these memories would rush to him in a tangled overload of sensory images, and he would relive the impact of the horror. Kishore had wanted to hurt himself, slash himself, pound his head against a wall until it bled, but he had to be the calm one organizing others, trying to soothe. He drank the last drop from the glass, and poured himself another. He couldn't sleep now. He rubbed his blood tinged eyes and watched a pattern of red concentric circles form then fade.

Was it a blessing to see Shanti and Vinod in his dreams? Was it his way of holding on to them? Now three years later, it was still difficult for him to accept their self-inflicted deaths.

When Dev's friend Deepak had overdosed years ago, Amma had consoled Dev with the words, "It is his karma." And Kishore tried to draw comfort from that philosophy. But how could such a grisly end be the fate of two such good people? He wished he'd inherited the faith of his mother; she took such comfort in her daily puja. Her gods provided the answers to most of life's mysteries—at least, for her, enough to live in serene acceptance.

Kishore thought he was more like Vinod for whom the answers came in facts, figures and science. Kishore had agonized for these past years, had wrestled with the critical question: why had they done it? And the answer still eluded him, would always elude him. Certainly Vinod's last letter provided no real comfort. Their lives had not been miserable; they had not been abandoned and alone; they lived with their family who loved and cherished them. Where had Kishore been blind? He knew he was too wrapped up in his career and work, but that was the way Vinod had been. He shook his head, still searching.

Yes, he and Anjali had changed the flat, but Shanti and Vinod seemed to encourage it. Resting his head against the back of the sofa, he looked around at the sage green and melon walls. The furniture was not Amma's and Papa's; he remembered moving Shanti's chair into their bedroom. He squirmed as he thought of Anjali moving the puja room. And without warning, guilt and remorse flowed over him. What had he and Anjali done? They had driven his parents into a small room, crushing their souls. Added to that was Amma's irrevocable disease. Taken in total, they must have felt that their tomorrows would always be arid and eventless.

Kishore sat with his elbows on his knees and his face sunk in his hands. He wanted a physical pain to distract him from his inner agony. He slapped the heel of his hand against his forehead. He pulled his graying hair. It wasn't enough. Nothing soothed him.

And so he sat, drinking alone in the dark, a successful and brilliant businessman. When the liquor buzz started to calm his pain, he got up and staggered to bed, hoping to catch an hour or so of stupefied sleep. He turned his back to Anjali and arranged his body far away from hers. Really, it was her fault; why did she have to change the flat so radically? He remembered the time she had persuaded him to have Shanti's chair moved. How could she have done that to Shanti?

And then Kishore turned the accusatory spotlight on to himself. He worked long hours. Was he ever at home to talk politics or cricket or anything with Vinod? No! Anjali usually had some function they needed to attend or some party at the flat. And Amma and Papa always ate early so they would be out of the way. They said that. They felt they were in the way, so they had removed themselves permanently.

His eyes were burning. He rubbed them again, and they were dry and prickly. He needed to sleep and be ready for the meeting of the board of directors in the morning. He tried to make himself comfortable; then he thought of how the sympathy and understanding of his bosses and co-workers had faded so quickly. It could be translated as "What's done is done. Let's get on with what we have to do now." Of course, they had rallied around him and his family soon after, and he had taken a week's leave. But when he got back to the office, it was just another Monday.

He began to doze off, but startled himself awake because Vinod was smiling at the edge of his consciousness. He was so present, with his balding head, the dark intelligent eyes and his glasses dangling on a chain. Why couldn't Kishore welcome these visits and listen to what Vinod had to say? He willed himself to sleep again.

As his breathing evened, his mother appeared to him. Shanti was making a lunch for Kishore, packing a sandwich in plastic wrap and putting it in a brown paper bag. (Never in his life had she made him sandwiches for lunch—that was Rama's job.) Then she smiled at him and cupped his face in her hand. He heard a shout, and Vinod was playing ball with a six-year old Kisan, kicking the ball until it flew into a bedroom. They chased it, and both disappeared over the balcony, and Kishore raced after them, reaching the hip high wall, then falling, falling, falling…landing with a hard jerk on his bed.

He was sweating. He must have screamed or groaned. Anjali made a sleepy, snuffling sound, turned and reached an arm over his waist to soothe him. He shook her off, sat up and let the tears come.

Anjali sat up too and asked him, "What's wrong, Kish? Did you have a bad dream again?"

She looked at him and saw malevolence in his eyes and the tight downward curl of his lip. She gasped and lay down again, face averted.

In a drunken tirade, he blamed her for her insensitivity to his parents, for her selfishness and desire to change their world, and for her social pretensions which required him to be at parties so many nights. Thus lifting the burden off his shoulders, he took his pillow into Kisan's room and slept on his son's bed.

Dev

DEV WASN'T TOO SURPRISED TO get a call from Anjali asking him to dinner. Ever since he had been a welcome visitor during Shanti's and Vinod's final months, Anjali often invited him to spend evenings with them at the flat. What had surprised him was the call from Kishore asking him over. Kishore was happy enough to see him, but he'd never before called with an invitation.

Dev dressed himself for tennis; now Arun was old enough to wield a racket, Dev took him onto the club courts and tossed him some balls as often as he could. Arun accepted the circumstances of his mother and father living apart because divorced couples were becoming more and more commonplace. Dev had also accepted living alone. When he became lonely, and it was not that frequent, he always found some young woman or divorcee willing to spend time with him, make love to him and indulge him. He hadn't lost that seductive power. He wondered if he would ever feel like marrying any of the women he'd enjoyed. No, he was content living the life of a bachelor responsible only occasionally for his son.

The happiest he'd been in recent times was when he'd visited Shanti and Vinod, when he'd been greeted with a smile, and when his father finally accepted him for who he was. Their death had left a gaping void in his heart, but he, more than anyone, understood why they had taken that last terrible step.

Perhaps he understood because his life was and had always been so chaotic, not orderly and controlled like Kishore's. He had confronted grief and sorrow and loss many times over in his years. When Anita had left to marry that rich man's son, he'd been inconsolable and accusatory, blaming his father for his rigidity and intolerance. He'd felt the same emptiness when Shilpa left, taking Arun with her. Then he could blame only himself.

He sat down in his favorite chair and put on his Nikes, tying the laces carelessly. He thumped the strings of his racket against his hand, then slipped on a wristband, not because he needed it but because the white contrasted nicely with his brown skin. After playing for a while, Arun would go off with the ayah for a swimming lesson Shilpa had arranged. Then Dev would pick up a few sets with some of the other players, preferably mixed doubles. A young woman—her name was Sushila?—had been partnering him recently, and he liked her moves.

As he waited for his son to arrive, he saw himself, dark and dashing at twenty, playing a few hard sets with his friend Deepak. He closed his eyes and leaned back in his chair remembering the good times he and Deepak used to have. The parties, the booze and the drugs yielded both highs and lows. What reckless daredevils they had been. And the murky fog in which their minds danced had lured Deepak to suicide.

That evening when he found Deepak would forever be etched in his mind because it was the first tragedy he had met face to face. Vinod said Deepak had chosen to love drugs more than family. Shanti had rendered a gentler verdict, saying it was Deepak's karma. Most of all, his mind played Vinod's words from that evening repetitively, "When I go, I wouldn't want to be alone, Shanti; I want to be holding your hand." Well, they'd had their wish—together at the end, holding hands.

How could he even dare to compare his panting and lusting after Anita or even his serene love of Shilpa to Vinod's and Shanti's? In all his years, he'd never ever heard either one of them utter the words, "I love you." When he'd been a teenager and falling in love several times a month, he'd thought Vinod ignored and neglected Shanti. In his later years, he marveled at the strength of their devotion to each other. And in their last few months, when he and Vinod were not adversarial, he was in awe of Vinod's dedication to Shanti and the way he helped her to preserve her dignity.

How deeply the old man understood the anguish his wife was suffering. That afternoon he'd told Dev, "Sometimes the known is more frightening than the unknown," and he'd gone on to explain Shanti's increasing isolation from everyone around her. Soon, she would feel completely separated and so alone. "No one should know such utter loneliness," he'd said.

So while Dev was grief-stricken when the tragedy happened, he was not surprised. A love as strong as theirs demanded that they be together always. When he got the call telling him to come quickly to the flat, he knew. And for the first time ever, he was the one who comforted Kishore, soothed Anjali. He was the one who was able to talk to Kisan and Priya. He understood—he had been to the brink himself more than once.

The doorbell ended his reverie, signaling the arrival of an excited Arun, and Dev took his adored son to play tennis.

That evening, he felt apprehensive about the dinner with Anjali and Kishore. The call from Kishore was strange—something was wrong. When he got to the flat, he found Anjali nervous and strained. She was dressed in a gray salwar kameez, and it sapped the color from her skin; he saw worry lines around her eyes he'd not noticed before; even her hair was not as carefully careless as usual. She had it tied back in a pony tail and wisps had broken free making her look almost unkempt. Dev had never seen her like this.

He finally settled her down with a gin and tonic and poured himself a Scotch; Kishore had finally opened the divinely smooth Glenfiddich, thank God. He sat back in his chair placing his left ankle on his right knee. He told her about Arun's brilliant shots on the tennis court, and how the boy was growing. He did not get the expected response from her. After a few perfunctory inquiries about Kisan and Priya, both in the States now, Dev looked straight into Anjali's eyes and asked, "Tell me what's wrong, Anjali."

"Nothing. Why should you think something's wrong? Because I asked you to dinner, huh?"

Dev smiled. "No, no. But I can see you're upset. And for the first time, Kishore also called me for dinner. Something must be wrong."

"Oh, God, I feel ashamed even to say this. Dev, Kish blames me for Amma's and Papa's deaths."

"What utter rubbish. If he'd paid attention…" he stopped as they heard the key in the front door, and soon Kishore was with them. Dark circles under his eyes couldn't be hidden by his wire rimmed glasses. The frequent tightness of his expression had left deep lines both above and below his lips. Kishore looked more miserable than Anjali. But he wobbled a smile at his brother and said,

"*Achcha,* you're here. Pour me a nice big glass of Scotch on ice, okay? I'm going to change out of this wretched suit."

When he went in to shower and change, Anjali told Dev about the confrontation that early morning. She was almost weeping when she said, "He thinks if I hadn't painted the rooms and changed the furniture, if I hadn't moved Amma's puja room, they might still be with us." Her hazel eyes were large and luminous as she looked to Dev for absolution. Dev silently believed that Anjali had taken drastic steps to remodel the flat, but that was not important now. And surely Kishore had gone along with all the alterations. He needed to convince Kishore and her that while Amma and Papa might have been uncomfortable, they had accepted the next generation's radical changes.

He walked over to the Scotch bottle and poured himself another and one for Kishore. He wanted to give Anjali time to compose herself because she was on the verge of breaking down. Soon Kishore emerged from the bedroom looking fresher and livelier.

He began inconsequential chatter with Dev—cricket scores, politics, music—anything but what was uppermost in their consciousness. Finally, Dev said, "*Bhai,* we need to talk about Amma and Papa."

Kishore tightened his lips and looked at Anjali as if she had betrayed him. She looked studiously at her nails, avoiding her husband's glare.

Dev plowed on, "We all feel an enormous sense of guilt—I know I do. How I let Papa down; all my life I disappointed him. How many nights I agonized over my behavior and the effect it had on them. You, Kishore, were always the son who did everything right. You even moved back here from Seattle, just to look after them. I know you, Anjali, and you too, Kishore, feel guilty about remodeling the flat and changing the furniture, the puja room and all the things you did to make this your flat."

He continued with a sigh, "You know I was lucky. Somehow Papa forgave me, and I came over often to spend a lot of time with them during their last months. Of course you were working, Kishore, so you couldn't be here for those lunches, but you knew what was happening. Amma was deteriorating. She didn't recognize us often; she had fewer friends, no parties, no card games—less and less to live for. When I came over, so many times I would find her on the balcony, looking for relief from one of her gods. Papa told me that she feared going to sleep, and she was terrified of waking up. She was always afraid of what the morning would bring. None of us can even imagine what she was suffering."

Kishore and Anjali sat silent and still, hoping that Dev's words would offer solace. Dev continued, "We know how devoted they were to each other. They thought each other's thoughts. I think at some point, Papa recognized that her condition meant that life for his Shanti held no dignity, no meaning any more. Once he determined that, he must have decided that he had no life without her. So I think he made her a promise—that they would be together on this final journey. It's quite amazing, nai?" Dev looked through his tears at Kishore and Anjali, now sitting with clasped hands on the sofa.

"It's been more than three years. We should let them go free without tying them here with our need for forgiveness. They deserve their peace. Amma would say it was their karma, written a long time ago. Remember them for their goodness. Let us go toward our own karma now."

Priya

SHE PUSHED HER WHEELED OVERNIGHT bag in front of her at the Mumbai Chattrapathi Shivaji International airport, crushed in the throngs of passengers that arrived each early morning. She had never been away from home before, and this was the first time she was returning to Mumbai after being gone two years. Alone. In the U.S. She hadn't slept at all on the twenty-three hour flight, kept awake by crying infants, the constant interruptions by the stewardesses, the extreme discomfort of the pinched space that the seat allowed. Now she was finally in the airport, and she remembered Kisan's complaint about arriving in Mumbai. "The humidity slaps you in the face" he'd said. "You get into line and smell the sweat, the pee from the disgusting bathrooms and the hair oil." She'd always felt he complained too much—but grudgingly she admitted he was right.

She got out her John Grisham paperback and started to read, fanning herself with her passport case. Finally, it was her turn to have her passport stamped, tell the bored, perspiring customs inspector that she had nothing to declare and go out onto the street.

Of course she was beset by taxi drivers and hotelwallas all wanting to give her a ride to town. She spotted faithful Shankar with a big grin on his face waving his white Nehru cap at her. Pushing his way through the crowd, he was by her side taking her bags and jabbering while he steered her expertly to the car and blessed, blessed air conditioning. Exhausted as she was, she listened to old Shankar—poor man, he had happily given up a night's sleep to pick her up. She was so pleased; she could understand him. She hadn't forgotten her Hindi.

She leaned back and relaxed finally. All too soon, her tummy began to rumble with worry. She had been gone more than two years. What would it be like to be home? What would the flat be like without Amma and Papa? And how would Mummy and Daddy be?

The damp sea air with its mustiness brought Mumbai back to her. Priya shuddered with sudden cold as she remembered the horrible day Amma and Papa had left them. She had been in college, of course, and since she had turned her phone off, no one could call to warn her. She'd arrived home to find bedlam—Kisan in his room, mute and trembling, Mummy and Daddy weeping and blaming themselves, Rama and the other servants loudest in their breast beating and keening. She remembered her quiet rage and the sense of betrayal. She had chosen to stay in Mumbai primarily to be near her grandparents, and they had abandoned her without warning. And she had wept in solitude in her room.

Devuncle had been the first one to speak to her. He'd come into her room and held her as she cried. He didn't try to stop her tears, just rocked her gently until she had cried herself out. He was more of a comfort than Daddy or Mummy that day. He was calm, resigned to an expected tragedy. He told her how unhappy Amma was with her family and friends fading and disappearing from the reaches of her mind. Priya remembered asking, "Why did Papa have to go too?" And Devuncle's answer had been so full of love, "Without her, he had no life. He didn't want her to go on this final journey alone. He'd always protected her and been by her side, hadn't he, *beti?*" Yes, Devuncle had been everyone's support and strength. No one expected it from him, but in this time of despair, he had found redemption.

The flat in Mumbai had been plunged into such despondency. Daddy and Mummy just couldn't shake it off. When Priya tried to talk to them about it, they told her not to worry, to concentrate on her college. She'd turned to Kisan who was back in Boston, and they instant messaged each other often. This tragedy brought them closer and Priya began to tentatively seek his advice. Kisan suggested that Daddy and Mummy seemed stuck in their guilt and depression, and Priya should think of leaving, striking out on her own. It had been several months since the suicide, and it appeared that Mummy and Daddy were still deep in the doldrums. But Priya could not think of leaving Mummy and Daddy; they needed her!

Then one day, Devuncle joined Kisan, telling her that she needed to get away. Kisan had urged her to apply to his revered Rhode Island School of Design, but she didn't want to be in Rhode Island, in the cold, cold, cold of winter. Instead, she had applied for and received a scholarship to Otis College of Art and Design in Los Angeles. L.A.had proved to be just fine.

Riding home on the eerie almost empty streets of early morning Mumbai, she hoped Mummy and Daddy would be surprised and pleased with her gift. But she wouldn't show it to them first. No, she'd planned it very carefully.

In Los Angeles, she'd been homesick often. Although everyone she met was friendly, she felt lonely in a city dependent on cars. She spent many weekend evenings alone in her small studio apartment thinking of life in Kalpana where there were always people in the flat and the chatter of voices. Friends were always dropping in. All those afternoon teas with her grandparents became precious memories, often recalled.

To her dismay, she found herself beginning to forget the fine details and contours of Amma's and Papa's faces—their expressions, the smiles which lit up their eyes. How could this happen? They had been pivotal all her life; they had molded her. Their legacy was in her bones, in her sinews. How often she heard their voices saying something silly, or something profound. But of them, of their physical being, she had only a photograph in which they were serious and unsmiling. And her mental photograph had altered from a vibrant color print to a black and white, now fading to sepia.

And so she began. In those lonely evenings, she lovingly painted her Amma and her Papa. On her canvas, they were smiling, happy. Vinod, in his customary sparkling white pajama and kurta, had his spectacles hanging on a chain so she could paint his dark brown eyes crinkled at the edges with his smile. Shanti was clad in a turquoise sari, and she held some brilliant orange marigolds; she looked alive and radiant. The essence of them glowed in their eyes. They stood by a window; behind them was the gray Arabian Sea.

And thus, in her loneliness, in her pain, through the magic of her fingers and the love in her heart, she brought them to life

The morning after her arrival, when Daddy had gone to work and Mummy had gone to shower, she had taken the portrait and carried it to Vinod's and Shanti's room. Slowly she opened the door, her heart aching knowing the emptiness she would find. She whispered, "Hello, Amma, hello Papa. It's Priya come to worry you." The silence that met her was absolute.

A few sun rays filtered through the grimy glass panes, and dust motes danced in the light. Everything looked the same. Amma's faded chair was facing the streaked wall, and her idols still sat on the shelves. Priya looked over to the bed where she had seen Amma being cradled and lulled to sleep by Kamini. She walked over and ran her hand over the thin bedspread. She picked up Papa's glasses, still on their chain, on a table next to his reading chair. Gently she blew the dust off and put them back.

She tiptoed around the room she hadn't entered since she last had tea with them, oh, over three years ago. She took the portrait and placed it on a table, leaning it against a wall. The blues and golds in the painting warmed the room.

"There! Now you are not only a photograph."

And they smiled at her.

Kisan

THE IMAGE FLOATS INTO HIS head, unbidden and unwelcome. He sees them on the hard gray cement, legs splayed, necks at an impossible angle. And blood. And then the screaming starts—the servants from all the flats, the neighbors, the passersby. To stop the horror, he focuses on one thing. Papa's left hand nestles her right, protectively.

When it did happen all those years ago, Kisan was home on holiday, reading quietly; then he heard the sickening thuds and the screaming. He rushed down and when he saw her green sari and his grey pants, he could not comprehend the reality of what was before him. It was as if his true self wafted above and watched the scene of a young man who could not—would not—absorb the grotesquerie of his grandparents lying on the bloody cement.

He turned and fled into the building, took the lift to the fourth floor and stumbled into the refuge of his room. He sat on his bed and started shaking. He hugged his shoulders, but couldn't stop the trembling. Not even when the sobs came, deep and guttural. He sobbed until he felt eviscerated. He lay back, weak. Rage washed over him. He thought, how could they do this to us? Yes, they were getting old, and Amma's memory was failing. But they lived with a family who loved them. They didn't have to take such an irreversible step. Kisan held on to that anger for a long time, but eventually it faded and an accepting serenity replaced it. Amma would have said it was their karma—and one must accept that.

Now when Kisan visits Mumbai on vacations, he always goes into their room. It is still the way they left it, as if waiting for their return. He sits in Papa's chair and rests his arms on the threadbare part of the upholstery. He strokes the fabric where Papa's hands or arms had rested. He puts his head against the spot darkened by Papa's hair. He closes his eyes and feels Vinod's presence fill him. Soon Kisan can smell his skin, he is so close. Papa lowers his glasses and lets them hang on the chain around his neck so he can look into Kisan's eyes. He raises his right hand to emphasize a point. He explains the complexities of life with lucidity. His goodness and wisdom will always be at Kisan's core.

Kisan looks over at the corner where Amma kept her idols. Her prayer bell gently tinkles while she murmurs and chants. When she lights the small wick in the brass aarti, acrid smoke wafts towards his chair. He can't help but smile when she precisely holds a match to the incense sticks releasing the sweet smell of patchouli.

He closes his eyes to hear her sing again the nonsense rhymes of childhood. He fills himself with her warm voice which read him stories every night. He remembers her soft hands smoothing his unruly curls, and her lips whispering kisses into his hair when she thought he was asleep. Her hands smell faintly of sandalwood soap and lime.

So when Kisan sits in their room and feels them so close to him, he believes he is the luckiest man alive to have known his grandparents— these grandparents—and to have had them be the essence of his life, of him. And he thinks…

They spent every waking day together for fifty-five years. They chose to continue to be together as they adventured into the unknown. They shared a love so rich, one that we "young ones", as he called us, will probably never begin to fathom. They never spoke of it—they just lived their love. Their choice was not wrong; we cannot and must not judge it to be wrong. They held each other's hand so they would not be alone when they left and when they arrived.

My Amma. My Papa.